Fractured Frazzled Folk Fables and Fairy Farces

Fractured Frazzled Folk Fables and Fairy Farces

By

Jay Dubya

Published by
Jay Dubya
Hammonton, NJ 08037
2833_8

ISBN 978-1-58909-241-9

Other Books by Jay Dubya

Adult Fiction

Black Leather and Blue Denim, A '50s Novel
The Great Teen Fruit War, A 1960' Novel
Ron Coyote, Man of La Mangia
Frat' Brats, A '60s Novel
Pieces of Eight
Pieces of Eight, Part II
Pieces of Eight, Part III
Pieces of Eight, Part IV
The Wholly Book of Genesis
The Wholly Book of Exodus
The Wholly Book of Doo-Doo-Rot-on-Me
Thirteen Sick Tasteless Classics
Thirteen Sick Tasteless Classics, Part II
Thirteen Sick Tasteless Classics, Part III
Thirteen Sick Tasteless Classics, Part IV
Thirteen Sick Tasteless Classics, Part V
So Ya' Wanna' Be A Teacher!
Mauled Maimed Mangled Mutilated Mythology
Fractured Frazzled Folk Fables & Fairy Farces
FFFF & FF, Part II
Nine New Novellas
Nine New Novellas, Part II
Nine New Novellas, Part III
Nine New Novellas, Part IV
One Baker's Dozen
Two Baker's Dozen
RAM: Random Articles and Manuscripts
Time Travel Tales
Modern Mythology
UFO: Utterly Fantastic Occurrences

Bee 17, Part II, Short Stories
Bee 17, Part III, Short Stories
Bee 17, Part IV, Short Stories
Bee 17, Part V, Short Stories
Bee 17, Part VI, Short Stories

Young Adult Fantasy Novels and Stories

Pot of Gold
Enchanta
Space Bugs, Earth Invasion
The Eighteen Story Gingerbread House

Contents

Description

In *Fractured Frazzled Folk Fables and Fairy Farces,* Author Jay Dubya goes right to work retelling Aesop's Fables into "A Sap's Fables." Adult renditions of "The Town Mouse and the Country Mouse," "The Boy Who Cried Wolf," "The Wind and the Sun," "A Wolf in Sheep's Clothing," "The Lion and the Mouse," "The Crow and the Pitcher", and "The Rabbit and the Turtle" are all cleverly portrayed. Other famous fables rewritten into adult accounts are "The Fox and the Crow" "The Goose That Laid the Golden Egg," and "The Grasshopper and the Ants".

Folk and Fairy Tales from England, France, Germany and Russia are also imaginatively assaulted and converted into adult-oriented stories. Jay Dubya thoroughly corrupts children's favorites "The Three Little Piglet Brothers," "The Flashing Elves," "The Golden Goose's Goosing Curse," "The Notorious Sleeping Beauty" and "Petite Red Riding Hood".

Other classic stories that are not saved from degeneration are "Jack's Magnificent Beanstalk," "Hansel and Gretel Dumkoff," "Little Ebony Sambo," "Rapunzel's Draping Hair" and "Tom Thumb's History." Finally, the author completely corrupts into adult parody rewrites "Peter W. and the Wolf," "The Rumpelstiltskin No-Spin Zone," "Beauty and the Beastly Beast" and "Flakey Snow White and the Seven Midgdwarfs".

Fractured Frazzled Folk Fables and Fairy Farces is Jay Dubya's twenty-first e-book. This humorous adult satirical work is definitely not written for or to be read by children.

"A SAP'S FABLES"

"The Town Mouse and the Country Mouse"

A gay Country Mouse was quite elated that his shitty city cousin (the more sophisticated Town Mouse) had accepted *his* invitation to visit the rural rodent for dinner out in the boondocks. The mentally challenged gay Country Mouse gave his straight city cousin all of the best food the host could steal, for mice are stupid imbeciles and can't produce any food of their own and must be dependent on other creatures for survival. And so, the straight, shitty, city mouse ate dried beans because he had constipation and also crusty bread crusts, lice, rice and rancid peas so that the urban critter could pee more on top of a cornered, smaller food rival when a creature such as a cockroach or a spider pissed him off.

The more worldly Town Mouse pretended that he was enjoying tasting the tasteless food that had been cheaply provided by his moronic, tasteless cousin, so the rodent sampled tidbits here and tidbits there while wishing that he were back home eating more aristocratic entrees. Then the shitty, city mouse had something relevant to relate to his distant gay relative after consuming *his* pathetic dinner.

"How can you eat this garbage all the damned time? Are you trying to achieve malnutrition? I already have bad indigestion. Why don't you visit me in the shitty city for a decent meal?" the obnoxious visitor asked his slightly retarded Country Mouse cousin. "Once you eat the scrumptious city foods I savor, you'll never give a rat's ass about country cuisine again. I guess that simple country mice like yourself know little beyond rice and lice, to be concise."

The Country Mouse apologized for offering a lousy lice and rice dinner and agreed to accompany his streetwise, straight, shitty city cousin to Leatherhead, a London suburb where the inhabitants' skulls look and feel exactly like used rugby balls. The two, knuckle-headed turd brains arrived at their destination late at night for the grand feast that had been awaiting them.

"You are tired in addition to being fucked up!" the shitty City Mouse observed and described to his naïve cousin. "Rest here while I find some delicious city food for you to simply sample. I hope you don't die before you violently choke to death!"

So, the Town Mouse obtained and soon delivered such wonderful edibles as nuts, cake, dates, fruit and cat droppings to his appreciative Country Cousin.

"This food is quite excellent, especially the pleasant-smelling animal litter!" The Country Mouse gleefully yelled. "I should've worn my *dun*garees and my Texas shit-kickers! Maybe I can move to the shitty city and write a witty ditty about kitty's titties when I finally get down to the nitty-gritty."

Then the imbecilic Country Mouse heard a loud screech and noticed an enormous black and white creature scampering into the room. The Country Mouse leaped from his table and smashed against a chair's leg, leaving his skinny ass and tiny balls lying behind in his wild-dash frenzy. The visitor madly skittered in dizzying circles until the scared numbskull found a safe sanctuary in which to hide.

The intimidated Country Mouse stood trembling as he contemplated his narrow escape from annihilation. 'I'd rather have lousy common food in the country than enjoy eating dates, nuts, fruit and cat shit while being confronted with unbearable danger here in the Greater Metropolitan London area,' the frightened visitor thought. 'Oh shit! The big black and white cat has found my skinny ass and tiny balls in the middle of the room and is kicking my privates all over the goddamned place! I really need the services of a fantastically good plastic surgeon right now! I'd rather have my balls broken in the peaceful country than abused and eaten in the shitty city!'

"The Boy Who Cried Wolf"

An idiotic Shepherd Boy used to entertain himself and aggravate his adult companions by yelling, "Wolf attack! Wolf attack!" simply to stimulate the villagers to run toward him with their rakes, clubs, golf clubs, pitchforks, table forks and scythes. After the all-too-moral townspeople would show-up to render their' assistance, the stupid asshole would loudly laugh in their faces hollering, "I was only clowning around! When's the next damned circus coming to town?"

"You shouldn't joke when it comes to serious matters like wild attacking wolves, young man!" a villager holding a nine iron and a baloney sand wedge admonished.

"I always wear two pair of pants in case I get a hole in one!" the Shepherd Boy smartly answered the critic.

"Stop crying wolf!" a second fellow brandishing a long knife insisted. "Someday you'll regret this stupid shit you're always pretending and then shouting it to us hardworking, concerned villagers! Next time Asshole, dial 911! Without the damned area code!"

"I refuse to stop playing my silly wolf prank just because I like seeing you hypocritical Methodists, Presbyterians, Episcopalians and

Lutherans get your bowels in an uproar," the naughty Shepherd Boy mockingly replied. "Stop acting like a dumb bunch of neurotic village vigilantes!"

"Someday you'll regret those very words your loose lips have ignorantly articulated!" a fellow wielding a pitchfork screamed like a maniac as the incensed villager angrily threw his weapon at the ducking boy and then watched in horror as the prongs penetrated the village undertaker's chest.

One day a lost wolf really did show-up in the boy's sheep herd, and the callow youth yelped, "Wolf! Wolf!"

But the villagers went-on with their daily chores and ignored the boy's urgent pleas for assistance. The wolf cheerfully killed seven of the sheep, and when the prankster shepherd boy valiantly approached the predator with the pitchfork that he had removed from the undertaker's chest, the wolf easily slaughtered the obnoxious teenager and then wolfed him down, too.

'Shepherd boys taste much better than morbid undertakers do!' the satisfied wolf thought with a smile upon his furry face. 'Liars are never believed, so that's why I generally prey and feed on immature shepherd boys who persist in fooling around all the friggin' time! I'm still a trifle hungry! Oh well, here's the damned remainder of village undertaker for dessert!'

"The Wind and the Sun"

Once upon a time, when everything could express thoughts including people without tongues, including animals, rocks, and also pre-humans with rocks in their heads, the Sun and the Wind got into a big argument as to which one was stronger. In today's world of solar and wind energy, this type of disagreement would be a no brainer, but in ancient times before man had developed science and basic logic, such ridiculous tales were quite popular.

The Sun and the Wind eventually agreed to have an experiment and put the matter to a peculiar, prehistoric litmus test. "There's an old idle jerk-off down there on earth," observed and stated the Sun to the Wind. "Let's see who first can make the wrinkled, old curmudgeon take his dirty old coat off."

The Wind figured it would try first and give the old man a good blow-job, something that the primitive codger hadn't had in decades. The Wind blew and blew, despite the fact that Mr. Sun was boisterously criticizing its endeavors by yelling, "Mr. Wind, You' suck!" over and over again. The harder the wind blew, the colder the atmosphere became, and the old man wound-up buttoning-up his trench-coat to protect his wrinkled old ass and his already shriveled balls and corresponding pecker.

Then after the stubborn Wind was finally out of breath, the determined Sun volunteered to implement its strategy. When naughty Mr. Sol smiled (because the competing sky object was achieving a hot erection), the contest participant suddenly began glowing and giving-off massive amounts of heat. The old man felt blood circulating in his chest, arms, face, legs and penis, and soon sweat was cascading-down the ancient geezer's face along with his back.

'Shit! This sudden warmth is fantastic! I honestly haven't been this hot since I was a young stud working as a bouncer in a bisexual whorehouse, many moons ago!' the old geezer reckoned.

The energized man was so warm that the dumb-shit sat on a huge rock and threw his cloak to the ground, and the heat recipient was so hot that the nitwit worked his erection for thirty full minutes until he popped a huge load and happily died seconds later.

"A Wolf in Sheep's Clothing"

A hungry Wolf (nobody ever feels sorry for a poor hungry Wolf) disguised himself in a cheap sheep costume and joined a flock of stupid sheep that deserved to die because they didn't know how to do anything but graze in a pasture and then voluntarily submit to being slaughtered. The clever Wolf killed and munched on many lambs and when he ate their mouths, he had lamb chops.

The shepherd was too busy admiring himself in a pond reflection to ever notice the clandestine activities of the nefarious Wolf. The cunning predator used humor to entice each of the targeted sheep. Once it told a sheep during a previous attack, "Mary had a little lamb, but when it was discovered that little Mary was having triplets, the doctors were really fuckin' amazed!" The victimized lambs became so amused listening to the Wolf's absurd rhetoric that they died laughing, so the sagacious Wolf didn't even have to exert himself to earn a decent meal.

The shepherd was feeling wild and woolly, and as a result, the crazed numbskull decided to take one lamb from his diminishing flock of sheep for his own next meal. The ignoramus butchered his largest lamb with a sharp machete, and without realizing exactly what he had done, had killed the disguised, greedy Wolf by mistake.

"This is the best lamb meat I've ever eaten!" the shepherd admitted to himself while sitting alone at his campfire. "I'll bet that not even a rambunctious Wolf tastes as good as this furry lamb does. Oh well, mares eat oats and I eat lambs, and little lambs eat ivy, a kid will eat ivy too, wouldn't you! Now don't all of you fucked-up assholes reading this story wish that you were kids again?" the not-too-bright herdsman indulgently laughed.

"The Lion and the Mouse"

One day a not-too-intelligent Mouse ran right across a sleeping Lion's paw and accidentally woke-up the king of beasts. The Lion was furious at being aroused from its deep slumber. The savage predator grabbed the tiny mouse and was about to rip it to shreds when the little rodent screamed-out, "Mr. Lion, I didn't mean to disturb you! If you let me go, I shall be grateful and will attempt to return your benign favor some fine day!"

"Absolute Bullshit!" yelled the Lion. "What could a little pipsqueak rodent like you possibly do for me? You're even too small to rub my ass with! Ha, ha, ha! Oh well, I'll let you go for now because I don't want to hear Mr. Gorilla and Mrs. Hippo tell me that I'm a jungle bully for intentionally picking on you, little Mouse! I don't like when other area creatures accuse me of bullying!"

Seven days later, the Mouse's keen ears detected a Lion roaring in the distance. The lazy King of the Jungle had been caught in a hunter's well-camouflaged trap. The wily Mouse inspected the Lion's dilemma and heard its cries for assistance, but the arrogant rodent refused to render its help and then slowly walked away.

"Oh. little Mouse; please gnaw away the ropes of the snare so that I may escape," the afflicted Lion bellowed in vain. "Please honor your word when you promised that you would return your favor for me not eating you whole a week ago today!"

"Sucker!" the miniscule, scrawny Mouse yelled as loudly as he could. "You should've found yourself a more honest Mouse that keeps its promises and not have believed an undependable rogue such as myself who perpetually fibs and prevaricates! Now Mr. Lion," the devious Mouse continued its unique narrative, "please enjoy yourself at your next destination, whether it be the zoo, at the circus, in a museum, or as the main course on the hunter's dinner table!" the Mouse exclaimed with a wicked laughing voice.

"The Crow and the Pitcher"

A Crow was very thirsty and desperately needed to drink water. The birdbrain finally spotted some of the desired liquid at the bottom of a vacated pitcher that had been set-down near a well. 'How can I get that delicious water to my beak?' the Crow wondered. 'I have no hands with which to raise the pitcher to my snout! If only that pitcher were a beaker, then I could easily indulge in my bleak beak fantasy!' the blackbird imagined.

Finally, the alert Crow's vivid mental operations produced a viable plan. 'I can drop tiny stones into the pitcher one at a time, and then the water will gradually rise up to the top so that I'll be able to satisfy my thirst and drink!' the in-need bird theorized. 'The more pebbles I drop into the pitcher, the more water I'll be able to lap out of that sucker! Little by little I'll accomplish the trick, which I'll have brilliantly turned into an achievable task!'

The Crow didn't realize it, but the village drunk had left the almost empty pitcher at the well and that it originally had been filled with gin, which is transparent and looks just like water. When the Crow's pebble addition scheme had brought the liquid rising-up near the jug's mouth, after sampling his quest, the weak-brained creature thought, 'This is the best well water I've ever had the pleasure of tasting! I'm going to savor every ounce of this wonderful, delicious agua! This well water tastes really well!'

Soon the Crow became quite intoxicated and then too inebriated to even remember how to fly. The afflicted blackbird tottered and tripped all around the pitcher, and then its thin legs came to the edge of the well where the imbecile accidentally fell into the shallow pit and promptly drowned. Oh well, all's well that ends well! Now the blackbird has nothing to crow about!

"The Fox and the Crow"

A crafty old Fox once witnessed a Crow taking-off with a piece of cheese in its beak and determined that *he* was going to confiscate the delectable food morsel. When the Crow landed to consume its coveted find, the Fox accosted the preoccupied bird and facetiously greeted, "Good morning Mr. Crow. You're really a beautiful bird sporting your magnificent black shining feathers that appear absolutely dazzling in the sunlight," the scheming Fox flattered.

"Get the fuck outa' here and stop harassing my ass!" the Crow crowed. "Why don't you go bother an eagle or a falcon for heaven's sake? Can't you see that I'm very busy right now? And foxes are supposed to be smart critters, right!"

"Well then, my fine feathered friend," the shrewd Fox proceeded, "it's too damned bad your voice is rather terrible despite your physical beauty. If you had a singing voice to rival your splendid feathers, then indeed you dear Crow would be the absolute Queen of Aves."

The sensitive Crow became rather petulant upon hearing what it considered to be a direct insult. And so, to show its intense pride, the zany Crow began crowing incessantly to convince the Fox that she indeed possessed a singing voice to match her alluring black feathers. The cheese obviously had dropped from her beak so that the preoccupied singer could amply serenade her most recent critic.

The alert Fox reached out its paw and avariciously grabbed the dropped piece of cheese. "Let me give you a bit of sage advice!" the sly Fox declared. "Don't ever trust flatterers, even if they are very charming foxes."

"And let me give you a bit of advice in return!" the livid Crow yelled. "This is how I get rid of annoying, nuisance, nosy foxes. That cheese you've just swallowed has been tainted with arsenic and your ass is about to die in thirty seconds."

The Fox immediately stuck its paw down its throat to induce vomiting while the malicious and very dangerous Crow laughed its feathery ass off!

"The Rabbit and the Turtle"

A haughty Hare was bragging to a group of other forest animals about how swiftly he could sprint when an unimpressed Turtle overheard the rabbit's arrogant boasts. "I'll race you and will definitely win!" the Tortoise challenged. "You'll never live this embarrassment down!"

"Fine with me!" answered the overconfident jackrabbit. "I'm so fast that I'm *hare* today and gone tomorrow! Ha, ha, ha!"

"Okay Idiot King," replied the Tortoise. "But I insist that Mr. Fox be the contest's judge. I need to have a shrewd eyewitness to determine that you didn't cheat."

"I never cheat in a race," the haughty Hare stated, "and I only cheat on my wife! That's the whole damned truth, and you heard it straight from my harelip."

The Fox agreed to be the event's deciding official, and the two contestants lined-up at the starting position. After the count of three, the fleet-footed Hare took-off and clearly was defeating its opponent by a wide margin. Knowing that he was far ahead, the quick dasher, feeling certain that he would easily be the victor, laid-down on the turf to take a brief nap.

An hour later, the very slow Tortoise came upon the sleeping rabbit and thought, "You dumb fuckin' asshole! Life's not a sprint; it's a friggin' marathon! The same damn thing applies to this long-distance race we're involved in!"

When the sleeping Hare finally awoke from its extended slumber, the rabbit rushed forward at top speed, but when the Finish Line eventually came into sight, the Turtle was just in the process of crossing its intended goal amidst the cheers of thrilled animal spectators that had the foresight to wager the smart money on mental intelligence instead of betting on sheer natural ability.

"Oh shit!" the Hare complained to the patient, triumphant Turtle. "I had underestimated your determination!"

"It's a good thing we took off in Sweden," the Turtle gasped-out in raw exhaustion. "Otherwise, I never could've made it so easily to the *Finnish* Line."

"The Goose That Laid the Golden Eggs"

Once upon a time in the Land Where Stupid Things Happen, a Man owned a Goose that had at every golden opportunity produced a Golden Egg every day. The Man dared not put the special Goose in a cage with any Gander that would lay any Goose it took a gander at. The Man was afraid of getting his Golden Goose that laid the Golden Eggs getting laid by any Gander that would goose and then lay any old Gilded Goose.

'And what the hell would the young chicks look like?' the Man curiously thought. 'Would they be Golden Chicks or what? I can't take that friggin' chance although I must confess, I could use another Goose or two that lays these wonderful, precious Golden Eggs! Maybe I'll take the time to screw the Goose myself and find out what the fuck happens!'

The Man was slowly-but-surely becoming rich selling the Golden Eggs a dozen at a time to the Commanding General at nearby Fort Knox. But the stupid jerk-off knew little about *Biology*, having flunked the course seven times in high school. Being greedy, the owner sliced open the Goose's stomach seeking to acquire all of his accumulated treasure at once. Then the avaricious fellow could blow town, move to Mexico, eat tacos and adroitly avoid heavy *IRS* scrutiny.

'This damned dead Goose on the inside looks just like any other damned dead Goose does!' the low-educated Man bitterly realized. 'I'll have to give the foul fowl to my wife, and then we'll consume the bird for dinner. When my wife finds out about what I had done to curtail my income, then my doomed Goose will really be cooked!'

"The Grasshopper and the Ants"

On a beautiful, sunny, winter morning somewhere on the damned planet, several dozen Ants (a few of them were also switch-hitting uncles) carried their February supply of food out of their colony's anthill so that the edibles could dry. A hungry Grasshopper (that looked a little like a weedy toilet) came by to admire and desire the food on display.

Since the industrious Ants paid no special attention to the starving Grasshopper, he initiated a conversation with the ambitious, tiny, busy insects. "Could you please give me something nutritious to eat?" the Grasshopper pleaded. "I'm starving!"

"Why the hell were you partying all last summer when you should've been storing food away for the winter?" the head gay Ant asked. "Learn to prepare for the future, you fucked-up parasite!"

"Now I truly regret confessing to you that I had neglected to do so," the somewhat remorseful Grasshopper answered. "In July and August, I was too preoccupied singing, dancing and getting laid."

"Well then," said the Ants in unison, because they all out of sheer instinct thought the same ideas and spoke the exact same words simultaneously, "we strongly advise that you live the remainder of this winter on singing, dancing and getting laid. Learn from us Ants that no one has the privilege to play all the time since work should always precede frivolity!"

So, the disappointed Grasshopper became excessively pissed-off, killed all of the sanctimonious Ants and ravenously ate them for breakfast, even though he was a Grasshopper and not a Raven. Then the still-famished diner entered the anthill commune, found some grub in the maternity ward and gulped-down nursery insects for dessert. 'That all tasted super!' the satisfied Grasshopper imagined. 'Tomorrow I'll find another colony of nasty, egotistical, holier-than-thou Ants and acquire my next rewarding meal just like I've feasted on this fine winter morning.'

"The Lark and Its Offspring"

A Mother Lark was tending her nest of fledglings in a ripe grain outfield, which was located right next to Duke Snider, Mickey Mantle and Willie Mays in the farm's centerfield. One day, she was drinking her nest' tea when all of a sudden her little offspring became quite excited and very animated.

"I heard the Farmer tell someone that it was time to notify the neighbors to help him harvest the grain," the tiniest of the birdbrains communicated to its mother. "Please Mother; take us away from being nestled in our nests before our nothing-to-brag-about domicile is completely obliterated."

"Don't sweat the small stuff!" the Mother Lark answered as happy as a lark. "If the retarded Farmer is relying on his lazy neighbors, the world will probably end before the goofballs ever start their labor! But since you little birdbrains are still in the learning phase of your young, delinquent lives, listen carefully to whatever the mentally challenged Farmer says to anyone; even when the nincompoop talks to himself. Ya' stupid, dumbass, little birdbrains understand *that* scenario?"

The next day while the Mother Lark was out prostituting and bartering sexual favors for food, the Farmer exclaimed to his Wife in the dell, "Damn it! Why can't you be as promiscuous as that damned Mother Lark so that I could get a fresh piece of ass in town while you're out screwing around! Anyway," the disgusted grower continued his prattle, "this grain field needs cutting as soon as possible. I'll contact our apathetic Relatives to come and assist me in my futile agricultural endeavor."

"Fuck-off!" the Farmer's aggravated Wife vociferously articulated with disdain. "You're a lousy bullshitter besides being a constipated turd shitter!"

When the horny, kinky Mother Lark returned from being again impregnated, the exuberant young birds reported the Farmer's latest conversation to their sex-addicted Mom, who was not too impressed with their need to show alarm.

"Look you neurotic, little hemorrhoid heads," she imperatively replied. "I know for a fact that the Farmer's Relatives are too busy harvesting their own grain and pumping the poop out of each other's wives, so they'll only come and assist if the Farmer's prudish Wife starts putting-out for anybody, including her frustrated fit-to-be-tied, impotent husband. But be sure to pay attention and reveal to me whatever you hear so that I may find it funny, and then laugh my tiny tits and ass off!"

The following morning, while the Mother Lark was out again whoring around under the announced pretense of gathering food for her obnoxious offspring, the Farmer said to his illegitimate Son by an extramarital affair, "Listen you Son of a Bitch. I can't prolong the essential harvest any longer. We'll hire a crew from town tonight, and tomorrow we'll get the whole crop hauled out of the field. It doesn't pay to go against the grain, if ya' know what the hell I mean!"

When the Mother Lark returned to her nest and heard the story from her young chirping Meadow Larks, the bird-lady related the following instruction to her pesky Children: "It is now time for us to get the hell outa' here! When humans determine that they must take action on their own rather than depend on lazy and irresponsible Neighbors and Relatives, it can be accurately ascertained that the lackadaisical imbeciles finally mean business. Let's leave this rotten nest before the crazy field plunderers destroy our home and then savagely kill our asses either by accident or on purpose!"

"The Miller, His Son, and the Other Jackass"

In prehistoric times, a happy-go-lucky Miller and his facetious Son were one day escorting a jackass to sell to some anonymous, gullible village idiot at the local market. Several young whippersnappers without whips were making fun of the Miller and his Boy for both walking while one of the two could have been riding on top of the decrepit ass.

"Look at the two pathetic dunces!" one Paleolithic juvenile delinquent boomed to his equally idle companions. "The dumb about-to-die jackass is smarter than both of their retarded brains put together!"

"Yeah," a hooligan associate promptly agreed. "You can always tell when it's Miller (and Son) time around here."

The father listened carefully to the insolent sarcasm, so the weaver directed his son to hop-up onto the jackass's back because "Two jackasses are obviously better than one!"

Then an old man met his Miller acquaintance outside a dilapidated country inn and several minutes later said to the innocent boy, "You foolish good-for-nothing parasite; get your fat ass off that ass and let your fatigued Father enjoy some ass for a change."

The humiliated Son's face turned blush red with guilt and shame, so the lad climbed off the beast of burden and begged his Father to ride into the village so that no other village idiots could criticize their morning excursion.

Soon the itinerant pair and their ancient jackass encountered another village codger who neurotically complained, "How utterly selfish you are old man to ride while forcing your young son to suffer walking and getting sore feet all the way to yonder village!"

The Miller demonstrated his mortification by allowing his Son to ride with him atop the listless 'who gives a shit' jackass's back'. An old lady approached the two at the primitive village's municipal borderline. "You two lazy shitheads ought to be ashamed of yourself'!" the bitch adamantly squawked. "You're encumbering that beast with an intolerable passenger overload. You two dolts should be carrying the poor jackass on your excursion, so assholes, swallow your pride and get your dumpy asses in gear!"

The obedient Miller and his more belligerent Son dismounted the ass, bound its frail legs onto a suitable pole and proceeded to carry the very confused animal upside-down into the village marketplace. When the odd trio entered the center of the deteriorated hamlet, the two moronic humans had made such an extraordinary sight because other more intelligent bumpkins and their sons were attached to long poles and were being carried around the town's center square by jackasses having very low *IQs*.

The abundant village heckling and the accompanying haranguing predictably annoyed and perplexed the Miller's unsophisticated jackass so much that the disgruntled animal kicked himself free from its tethering, rolled-down a steep embankment, tumbled into the nearby river and drowned in an apparent suicide.

The irate Miller was so livid and so outraged that the village visitor lifted the long pole that had been used to convey the jackass and swiftly beat the shit out of everybody that dared mock him in the village square. On the trek back to his dumpy abode, the Miller had some sagacious words for his sometimes-derelict teenage Son: "We've lost the jackass because we tried to please everyone and eventually wound-up pleasing no one!" the upset Miller regretfully admitted. "That's why I thrashed the feces out of all of our garrulous critics, stole their asses and then sold them for this handsome profit represented in this large bag of gold. Come on Son," the Miller implored. "Let's find the nearest brothel and I'll show you the fuckin' time of your life!"

"Belling the Cat"

Once in medieval times happening *amid evil* that was occurring in the world, an aggressive and egotistical Cat was busting a Mice's family's balls really good. The Mice clan therefore organized and held an emergency meeting to counteract the existential threat imposed on them by the ornery antagonist.

During the rodents' urgent executive council session, a Young Mouse arose from obscurity and proposed that a bell be put around the vicious Cat's neck so that the Mice could all hear the furry animal approaching from afar. The smart fellow's suggestion elicited tremendous acknowledgment and great applause originating from the other appreciative rodents in the assembly.

When the audience's clapping finally ceased, an Old Mouse rose to render his startling opinion. "The young Mouse's idea is all right in principle," the elderly vermin began, "but who among us has the balls to dare hang the bell around the Cat's furry neck?"

After a pregnant moment of absolute silence, the wise Old Mouse proceeded with orating his clever analysis. "It is often much easier to suggest a plan than to carry it out," the aged codger observed and revealed. "And it is my erudite conclusion that it takes a lion's balls to hang bells around that big Cat's neck. Since we all have tiny Mice testicles, none of us are sufficiently qualified or capable of enacting the brazen Young Mouse's plan. That's why we should convince a naïve, virgin female mouse to enact the Young Mouse's plan!"

"The Dog, the Fox and the Stream"

A delighted Dog was carrying a piece of tender meat in his mouth when the canine came to a narrow bridge that crossed a stream. The curious-but-suspicious canine glanced-down into the clear water and perceived his shadow. 'Holy shit!' the pooch thought. 'It's another dog in the water with a much bigger piece of meat in its mouth than the one I now have!'

The inexperienced mutt stuck its neck under the bridge's side and lurched for the tantalizing chuck of porterhouse. In doing so, the foolish cretin dropped his own meat bonanza into the stream and consequently was without any meal because of his excessive greed. The saddened pot-licker left the vicinity after learning a very important moral lesson.

Soon a hungry fox rambling by stopped at the bridge and noticed the dog's cut of porterhouse resting in twelve-foot-deep clear water. After contemplating "the spectacular mirage" for a full hour, the Fox scampered away and concluded, 'I didn't want or need to eat that goddamned hallucination anyway!' So, the fortunate fish swimming in the creek enjoyed the most wonderful feast of their aquatic lives.

"MYTHS, LEGENDS AND FOLKTALES"

"The Three Little Piglets"

Once upon a nursery rhyme, there were three little arrogant, corpulent piglets that lived in a tiny house with their pissed-off mother, who was pissed-off because all three of her lazy pork belly sons lacked basic motivation and ambition. Her wise strategy was to evict them out of the house so that the mother hog could enjoy some well-earned peace of mind and on the side, some well-deserved piece of ass.

"I want you three worthless, freeloading dolts out of my house immediately," the adult pig screamed rather emphatically. "I'm sick and tired of making your beds, cooking for you three imbeciles, washing your dirty clothes and slaving away as a prostitute just because you three parasitic punks think the damned world owes you a living!" the mother pork-belly rankled. "I'm fed-up with being your domestic servant and your personal valet. Now get the hell out of here you good-for-nothing swine before I make a phone call and sell your friggin' asses to the local butcher!"

And so, the three listless, lethargic idiots left home without any money or accumulated savings to build their separate homes because the triplet piglets despised one another and intensely hated living with each other for twenty-one long years in their hooker mother's modest stone dwelling.

The first little fat stubborn piglet, who lived in a complete self-destruct mode, decided to build his new house out of straw. Since the first piglet was rather conceited and out of touch with everyday reality, the ingrate was quite proud of his lackluster accomplishment after his weak house had been crudely constructed of the very flimsy and ridiculously weak material. Even the damned door was fabricated out of smelly straw, which was held together with a lot of horseshit, elephant dung and cow manure.

One day a hungry wolf, who was also the Local Building Inspector, came by to see if the newly constructed straw house had been built to meet area code. But the devious. obstinate little piglet refused to let Mr. Wolf inside to inspect the new property. The frustrated Building Inspector therefore screamed into the smelly straw house from the front steps.

"Let me in so that I may check your plumbing, toilets, sinks, bathtub, shower, carpentry work and flimsy electricity," the Building Inspector formally requested. "According to my accurate records, you never applied for a damned Building Permit, and you don't possess a damned Certificate of Occupancy. Learn to respect the goddamned safety code rules and regulations that have been diligently established by the Pig City Council for your own freakin' protection."

The first little piglet, whose name was Pig Headed Pig because he never listened to anyone from his all-too-patient, prostitute mother to the Local Building Inspector, ignored Mr. Wolf's demands and simply stayed in his tiny, stinking straw abode with his chubby knees trembling and clattering against one another.

"I will not open my straw door and let you in to write-up a hundred meaningless citations and violations," the ornery Mr. Pig Head Pig replied. "Go ahead and bother and annoy some other area asshole more compliant homeowners."

"You don't even have a bill of sale proving that you own this property and stating that you've legally purchased this land from someone else," the aggravated Wolf complained. "My office has no such bill of sale copy verifying that you own this damned land your straw house with its thatched roof is situated upon. You just simply tried to make a hay house while the sun shines. How could you be such a stupid, pigheaded, dunce-like asshole?"

"I'm not going to let you in because I don't want to hear any more of your bureaucratic, government bullshit!" Mr. Pig Head Pig yelled. "Go bother my two shithead brothers, or someone else, and leave me the hell alone!"

"You don't even have an outhouse when you've indirectly admitted that you have no toilet or necessary sanitary facilities!" livid Mr. Wolf criticized. "You've really pissed me off so much Mr. Pig Head Pig that I feel compelled to take the law into my own hands."

Now if Mr. Wolf the Building Inspector were a trifle smarter, the Pig City Building Inspector would have set fire to the straw house and then have a roasted piglet for breakfast. Instead, Mr. Wolf took a very deep breath, and the hog molester huffed and he puffed, and he blew down the straw house in what amounted to a fantastic blowjob. The little piglet sprinted his obese ass over to the second pork-belly's domicile while the local weather bureau reported that a mild tornado causing minor damage in the vicinity had occurred.

Mr. Pig Head Pig had dashed to his bother Mr. Pigsty Pig's pigsty, which had recently been constructed out of balsam wood. Although the frail house was a bit sturdier and better made than the flimsy straw house, it still had not been constructed up to local building ordinance standards. Soon the perplexed, out-of-breath Building Inspector arrived on Mr. Pigsty Pig's illegal property.

"This is the local Building Inspector speaking," Mr. Wolf hollered after violently knocking on the thin, wooden door. "I need to check your plumbing, toilets, sinks, bathtub, shower, carpentry work and flimsy electricity," the city official bellowed. "According to my accurate records, you never formally applied for a damned Building Permit, and you don't possess a damned Certificate of Occupancy, either. Learn to respect the goddamned safety code rules and regulations that had been diligently established for your own freakin' necessary protection."

Mr. Pigsty Pig ignored Mr. Wolf's verbal demands and simply stayed inside his tiny wooden house with his chubby knees trembling and clattering against one another.

Although Mr. Pigsty Pig was much sloppier in appearance than his two slovenly brothers were, the porky resident was just as lazy and just as stubborn as they happened to be. "I will not open my wooden door and let you inside to write-up a hundred meaningless, fucked-up citations and violations," the ornery Mr. Pigsty Pig replied. "Go bother and annoy some other asshole homeowners."

"You don't even have a bill of sale proving that you own this property and have legally purchased this land from someone else," the irate Building Inspector vehemently complained. "My office has no bill of sale copy verifying that you own this damned land your poorly constructed wooden house is situated upon. You just simply tried to make a wimpy wooden house while the sun shines. How could you be such a stupid, pigheaded, overweight, obese asshole?"

"I'm not going to let you inside my residence because I don't want to hear any more of your inane, ridiculous, bureaucratic government bullshit!" Mr. Pigsty Pig yelled through his balsam wood front door. "Go bother my fat-assed brother Mr. Hogshead Pig and leave me and Mr. Pig Head Pig alone!"

"You don't even have a necessary outhouse when you've indirectly admitted that you have no bona fide toilet or essential sanitary facilities!" about-to-go-ballistic Mr. Wolf criticized. "You have really pissed me off so much Mr. Pigsty Pig that I presently feel compelled to take the law into my own hands."

Now if Mr. Wolf the Building Inspector were a trifle smarter, the hungry rogue would have set fire to the wooden house and then would have two roasted piglets to consume for breakfast. Instead, Mr. Wolf took a very deep breath, and the impulsive jerk-off huffed and he puffed, and the predator eventually blew-down the aforementioned wooden house. The two little piglets sprinted their obese asses over to the third pork-belly's house while the local weather bureau reported a second mild tornado causing minor damage in the general vicinity.

The third little piglet triplet was Mr. Hogshead Pig, whose weird-looking forehead was shaped like a large storage barrel. Mr. Hogshead Pig was a bit more intelligent than his moronic brothers Mr. Pig Head Pig and Mr. Pigsty Pig were. After the two frightened brothers had raced to the brick house that Mr. Hogshead Pig had shrewdly erected, Mr. Wolf, all out of breath, appeared at the front door and wrapped his already sore knuckles.

"Let me in so that I may formally check your plumbing, toilets, sinks, bathtub, shower, carpentry work and flimsy electricity," the Building Inspector requested. "According to my accurate records, you never applied for a damned Building Permit and you don't possess a damned Certificate of Occupancy for this brick house. Learn to respect the goddamned safety code rules and regulations that have been diligently established for your own freakin' protection."

Mr. Hogshead Pig, like his stubborn brothers Mr. Pig Head Pig and Mr. Pigsty Pig, completely ignored Mr. Wolf's boisterous demands and simply stayed inside his tiny brick abode with his chubby knees trembling and clattering against each another.

"I will not open the door to my brick house and let you in simply to write-up a hundred meaningless, fucked-up citations and violations," the ornery Mr. Hogshead Pig replied in a similar manner as his hardheaded, disobedient, indolent brothers had done. "Go and bother and annoy some other innocent, ass-sucking homeowners."

"You don't even have a formal bill of sale copy verifying that you own this pathetic property and stating that you've legally purchased the land from someone else," the agitated Wolf indicted. "My office has no bill of sale authorizing that you legitimately own this damned land upon which your brick house is situated. You basically tried to make a brick house when the sun shines, and for all I know, you and your two slippery brothers hiding inside might also be into moonshine besides sunshine. How could you Mr. Hogshead Pig be such a stupid, pigheaded, ingrate asshole?"

"I'm not going to let you into my brick dwelling because I don't want to hear any more of your absurd, bureaucratic, government bullshit!" Mr. Hogshead Pig yelled back. "Go bother some other innocent homeowners and leave me the hell alone!"

"You don't even have a suitable outhouse when you have indirectly admitted that you possess no toilet or other sanitary facilities!" Mr. Wolf vociferously criticized. "You have really pissed me off so much that I presently feel compelled to take the law into my own hands."

Now if Mr. Wolf, the incensed Building Inspector, was a trifle smarter, the carnivore would have used dynamite to explode the brick house into ten thousand fragments, and then would have had delicious bacon, ham, pork chops and baby back ribs for breakfast. Instead the angry Mr. Wolf took a very deep breath, and the asshole huffed and he puffed but was totally unsuccessful at blowing-down the sturdy brick house. The local weather bureau reported a blustery tornado in the Pig City vicinity, which turned-out to be nothing more than an area blowhard releasing some stale wind from his powerful lungs.

Mr. Wolf became so pissed-off and so livid at his embarrassing failure to destroy the brick house while imitating a cyclone that the notorious meat-eater clambered-up onto Mr. Hogshead Pig's roof, climbed-down the brick chimney, and directly fell into a steaming cauldron of water that the pleasure-loving owner had originally planned to use for a hot tub. The outsmarted wolf severely scalded his ass along with his other personals while thrashing-around inside the steaming cauldron, and the bad luck Building Inspector had to be immediately transported by ambulance to the local Pig City Hospital's emergency Triage Burn Center. In the Triage Sector, the defeated Building Inspector was professionally treated for suffering from first, second and dangerous third degree burns along with emphysema and high blood pressure symptoms.

The lazy but now-happy piglet triplets lived merrily ever after in Mr. Hogshead Pig's tornado proof, "Building Inspector proof" brick house, which had been admirably constructed and built as well as any brick shithouse in the entire damned Pig City Metropolitan Area.

"The Flashing Elves"

Once upon a whim in the lazy somnolent village of Bustercherrie in the land of Bustdarebawls, there lived a poor shoemaker named William with his wife Meredith. Times were extremely harsh for Willy Shoemaker and his wife, the former Meredith Rottsi. In fact, William Shoemaker was so impoverished that he was on a starvation diet and just owned enough leather to make one more pair of shoes.

"Perhaps I shouldn't gamble, drink, smoke, philander and buy pornography all the damned time!" Mr. William Shoemaker admitted to Meredith. "Being old is much worse than getting old!"

"Your bad luck better change for the better soon or else I'm outa' here for good; I'll be going back to live with my wealthy parents and having to put up with their verbal bullshit!" the wife sarcastically replied. "They always said that you dear husband were a non-entity with aspirations of amounting to absolutely nothing," the wife critically chided. "Now let's have some lousy sex before we go to bed because I don't like having lousy sex in bed!"

So, after the dejected shoemaker and his sex-starved wife had another lousy sixty-nine session, Meredith retired for the evening and her husband returned to his cruddy workbench and cut-out the pattern for his next and maybe last set of woman's work shoes. Then after sentimentally completing his mundane enterprise, William hobbled into the home's only bedroom. And after committing his soul to the Devil for the hope of personal gain, the totally fatigued pauper went right to sleep without even passing through drowsiness.

In the morning after again praying for earthly reward and eternal damnation, William "Willy" Shoemaker entered his humble shop only to discover that the leather for the pair of lady's shoes he had laboriously cut-out had already been magically manufactured into a finished product on the worktable. William was so astonished and his mind was so addled that he couldn't even think crooked. The shoemaker lifted the splendid shoes up to his eyes to examine them more closely. 'To hell with heaven!' the impoverished tradesman marveled and thought. 'I'm going to pray to hell every night and every single morning if this is what the fuck's gonna' happen! These shoes are so well stitched that they appear as if a master-craftsman had painstakingly fabricated the pair. In fact,' William further imagined, 'they're stitched much better than my damned appendix and double hernia scars! That doctor who performed the operation was a real shoemaker who had turned chief hospital surgeon!'

That same morning a wealthy gentleman came into the modest shop, scrutinized the newly produced shoes and declared that he wanted to purchase them at any cost. William was quite thrilled at the good news, for now the old codger would have sufficient funds to purchase leather for two pairs of ladies' dress shoes and then have enough money left over to buy a bottle of wine, a used condom and a loaf of bread to boot.

"Are these shoes for your wife or daughter?" William innocently asked the ecstatic wealthy customer. "They're very expensive, you should know."

"Mind your own damned business," the stranger caustically answered. "But if you really have to know the truth, you nosy bastard, they're being ordered for me to wear. I'm the proud new stripper and lap dancer at the local gay and lesbian inn."

After again having lousy unorthodox sex with Meredith, William cut-out the material for two new pairs of women's shoes, prayed to Satan for eternal damnation and then retired for the evening. The next morning, the inspired shoemaker again pledged his soul to hell and then cautiously entered his humble workshop.

Two additional pairs of women's shoes had remarkably been manufactured and were waiting for William's scrutiny on the aforementioned worktable. The shoemaker was positively thrilled to death, although still quite ill-prepared to die and go to hell. Later that morning, two customers came into the formerly unpopular shoe shop and merrily bought the two new pairs of women's footgear.

"And they weren't even couch dancers at the local gay inn," William euphorically disclosed to Meredith. "By the end of the month, if production keeps doubling daily, I'll own the biggest shoe factory in all of Bustercherrie and also in all of Bustdarebawls."

"You're saving more soles than the freakin' Pope or the freakin' Devil is!" Meredith commented and indulgently laughed. "There's no business like *shoe* business! Ha, ha, ha! Now let's go have some bad upside-down oral sex!"

One evening three days before *Christmas,* the local citizens were all out at the village gay and lesbian inn getting drunk and celebrating the Winter Solstice, simply because none of the homos' and lesbians in the gay community (here a gay hamlet) were too religious or "morally insane". William had spent the entire previous day assiduously cutting-out the patterns for sixty-four pairs of women's shoes, and his multiple venereal disease wife was so excited at the prospect of not having to return home to her strict arrogant "I told you so!" rich parents that she industriously assisted William in his dedicated endeavor.

"Meredith, what do you say we sit-up tonight and observe who is performing this wonderful workshop service for us?" William cleverly suggested. "After he or they complete his or their wonderful task, we and the stupid heels doing the labor, whoever the hell they may be, could have a wild orgy to celebrate *with a bang* the upcoming Winter Solstice!"

"Yes William, that type of variety could really spice-up our sex life," Meredith promptly agreed. "We could have a fantastic orgy, and I could wear your new jock strap and you could wear my newly acquired pink bra, corset and matching fish-smelling panties."

"You must confess," William articulated to his exuberant wife, "this nightly doubling of shoes at exponential proportions is rather extraordinary. By *New Year's Day,* we'll be the wealthiest people in all of Bustercherrie and by the *Epiphany,* we'll be the richest couple in all of Bustdarebawls! At last dear wife, I'll have enough money to pay for a goddamned circumcision!"

"You're absolutely correct," Meredith concurred, "and wonderful things like this never happened to Mama and Papa Rottsi! My greedy parents never enjoyed such phenomenal magical occurrences! Soon we'll be able to thumb our noses at the meager inheritance the demented shitheads have planned for me!"

That evening the couple shrewdly set a rusty lantern burning in the far corner of the workshop and then furtively hid in a closet so that they could observe the benign intruder or persons performing the fabulous craftsmanship. At midnight, William and Meredith saw two little, naked, dwarfs enter the shop, each benefactor having an exceptionally long, limp hose hanging out of his clothes reaching all the way down to his knees. The short, half-naked, stocky, cocky visitors quickly organized the various tools and materials that William had conveniently left at the workbench to their own fancy, and then the dwarfs industriously went about their business without conversing or even looking at one another. And in a mere three hours, the two nude trespassers with the impressive sexual apparatus jointly and hastily *flashed* out of the premises.

"Did you see their fabulous tools?" the wife marveled after she and her husband felt gay for a moment and came out of the closet.

"No, I didn't!" William Shoemaker remarked. "They didn't use my little tool to make the damned shoes, that's for damned sure! But I must believe you that the two dwarfs did have tremendous donkey-like fadorkenbenders, though!"

The following morning, the shoemaker's wife explained to her lethargic husband, "Those little men with the big, long, limp dicks have made us the richest people in Bustercherrie," Meredith Rottsi related, "and we ought to show them our gratitude. They must be very cold running around this part of Europe all half-naked in the beginning of winter. I'll make them little pants, shirts, waistcoats and huge jock straps, and since you always say that I'm a 'nitwit', I'll even knit them both a pair of green stockings."

"I hope these damned fat elves, or whatever the hell they are, don't switch allegiances and start working for jolly old St. Nicholas in *his* workshop!" the husband warned. "But I'll cooperate and make each of the little fellows a pair of shoes to do clubbing at either the local popular gay and lesbian inn or at the local straight tavern, which has only three nightly patrons!"

By dusk, all of the clothes, underwear and shoes had been made for the two short half-naked men, and William worried if he and his spouse's gratefulness might backfire-on or jinx their recent good luck skein. When midnight arrived, the two zany dwarfs (having the sexual equipment of giants) entered the workshop as usual, faithfully performed their much-appreciated service, and then enthusiastically donned the garments and shoes that had been laid aside for them. Next, the effervescent dwarfs hopped over tables and jumped all about and did cartwheels all over the damned place to express their general excitement and jubilation at finally having decent clothes to wear. Then one zany dwarf said to the other:

> "What spruced-up dandy boys are we,
> No longer poor cobblers, we will be.
> Now that we've got clothes and underwear,
> Let's get our fat asses the fuck out of here!"

And then the diminutive-but-chunky talented dwarfs sped-out of the shoe-shop as if both had suddenly been afflicted with severe diarrhea or feeling a desperate need to rush to either the local gay inn or to the local straight tavern.

The exuberant dwarfs were never again seen in Bustercherrie, but reports in the form of honest gossip from other villages in Bustdarebawls maintain that two highly skilled dwarfs clad in the finest of green clothing hang out at gay and lesbian inns in those other highly respected gay and lesbian communities, and the well-to-do handsomely clad little men revel in eating "corn on the cobbler" at various area taverns.

And as for William and Meredith Shoemaker, the remarkable couple now own the biggest chain of gay and lesbian whorehouses in all of Bustdarebawls, and they are currently attracting investors' attention by issuing an *IPO* to float the current prototype for the first straight-sex brothel in the entire land.

"The Golden Goose's Goosing Curse"

In medieval times amid evil that was quite plenteous, a not-too-bright man named Dunderhead Dumbling had three non-dependable, erratic sons, the youngest one being Dumbdick Dumbling, who was mocked and ridiculed by the entire household, the entire village, and even by the entire very vocal gay and lesbian community. Times were not good for the mentally challenged Dumbling family.

One fine spring morning, the eldest son named Duncehead Dumbling ventured-out into the forest with his axe to cut-down a tree for firewood, but the total fool was mostly motivated because he wanted to irritate and piss-off certain local bisexual environmentalists. Duncehead's overprotective, nutcase mother, Mrs. Dimwit Dumbling, provided the junior amateur lumberjack with a pasty that had covered her right nipple and a bottle of dry wine to gulp-down for lunch, if mentally challenged Duncehead would ever remember that he should eat and drink something before returning home from his rather irrelevant endeavor.

Deep inside the forest, a little old man who happened to be sitting on a stump solicited and tried *stumping* Duncehead by saying, "Give me a piece of meat from your plate and several ounces of rich wine from your bottle because I'm thirsty and hungry and need some nutrition and energy to fuckin' stay alive so that basically, I could piss and shit some more!"

But the oldest Dumbling son wasn't called Duncehead for nothing. "Old Man; you asked me for a portion of my mother's tasty pasty and for a draught from my wine bottle?" the irate fellow bellowed. "Forget it, you wimpy, impetuous jerk-off! I gave plenty to charity at the office!" he fibbed.

And so, Duncehead went about his ordinary business of chopping his axe into a tree and completely ignored the tiny beggar's annoying presence. On the thirteenth unlucky chop, the eldest Dumbling son lost his grip while attempting to impress the little onlooker with his dexterity, and Duncehead quickly made a gash in his right leg when his axe swing missed the tree trunk. So, the oldest son, bleeding badly, returned home with his head crestfallen and bleeding to death; the trekker fully aware that the magical little imp's mischief and *his* own arrogance had caused him abundant agony and embarrassment.

After seeing his brother arrive home in great distress, the second son named Dipshit Dumbling stepped-out on the family shack's front porch and decided that he would finish the job that Duncehead could not complete. The brash youth was generously given a pasty that had covered Mrs. Dimwit Dumbling's left nipple and also a bottle of dry red wine to imbibe. When Dipshit meandered-down the same trail as Duncehead had earlier ambled, he too encountered the little forest rascal that had effectively hexed his borderline-retarded older brother.

"Could you spare some meat and wine for this hungry old man?" the forest spellbinder politely asked the axe bearer. "I need some food and drink to fuckin' stay alive so that I could piss and shit, which incidentally I really take great pleasure in doing!"

But Dipshit Dumbling considered himself to be far cleverer than his former school grades had suggested when the ignoramus had dropped out of kindergarten as a teenager after failing *that* particular grade level seven consecutive times. Dipshit's rather dismal academic performance had branded him "the dolt" of the hamlet, an ignoble position existing just below village idiot.

"Go away old fart!" the rowdy, pugnacious, dastardly knucklehead imperatively yelled. "The more food and drink you consume, the less will be there for me to enjoy! Get the fuck outa' my already mediocre life, you old fucked-up forest runt!"

And when Dipshit Dumbling smashed his axe into the sturdy oak tree for the thirteenth unlucky time, the cretin was so exhausted endeavoring to impress the little imp that the second idiotic son's sharp blade missed its mark, and the stupid Dipshit accidentally cut his tiny balls right off of his abdomen. "Now look at what the fuck I've done!" the young blockhead shrieked.

Upon learning of Dipshit's moronic blundering, the youngest son Dumbdick Dumbling asked his non-genius father if he could prove his value to the family by going-out into the forest and gathering fuel for the stove and fireplace. But ambitious Dunderhead Dumbling had his reservations, even though the simpleton lived nowhere near a hotel, an airport or close to savage Indian tribes.

"Your two harebrained, mentally lame brothers have both lamed themselves," the father patiently explained to Dumbdick. "And now I recommend that you had better stay put inside the shanty because you know even less about chopping-down tall trees than either Duncehead and Dipshit knew."

But young Dumbdick was very enthusiastic and determined and repeatedly bothered and pestered the old patriarch so incessantly that finally the elder consented and told his youngest son to "Grab a fuckin' axe off the wall and get the fuck outa' here!"

Since the youth's portly mother had only two sagging, flabby tits, Mrs. Dimwit Dumbling could not give Dumbdick a third pasty, so she prepared a small pastry and a decanter of sour beer for the half-wit to take into the forest.

A half-hour into his arduous excursion (while looking for the perfect tree to destroy), young Dumbdick was confronted by the same little rogue that had efficiently jinxed Duncehead and Dipshit.

"Give me some food and some of your drink," the little asshole implored, "for I'm quite hungry and thirsty and need to eat, shit and piss in order to keep on fuckin' living."

"Little Jerk-off," Dumbdick disdainfully chided. "I have only a limited supply of food and beverage, but I shall gladly share them with you. So, let's party-on miniature dude before I change my goddamned fickle mind and wildly beat the shit out of you!"

So, the two new acquaintances sat on the forest ground and gleefully ate and drank, but Dumbdick knew that something quite peculiar was being employed when his pastry tasted like delicious roast beef and his cheap beer had the wonderful flavor of rare, premium, delicious, red imported wine.

"Since you apparently possess a benevolent heart kind stranger," the little forest rogue declared, "I shall send a positive blessing on you instead of utilizing my usual cruel curse. Cut-down yonder elm tree and search underneath for some roots that will yield root beer," the little critter instructed. "In addition to the foul-tasting inferior root beer, your search will also discover something quite special that'll make you the envy of your entire family and perhaps into one of the richest men in all the world."

Dumbdick went about his tree-felling activity and skillfully chopped-down the half-dead, termite-infested elm tree, confiscated the lousy-flavored root beer and much to his surprise, the youngest Dumbling discovered inside a hollow a goofy golden goose that suddenly shrieked, "Polly wants a quacker! Polly wants a quacker?"

Dumbdick Dumbling was so thrilled with his latest fowl acquisition that the goofball forgot all about the disgusting tasting root beer and soon anxiously gathered-up the golden goose. The merry finder paraded out of the forest and paced a half a mile to a local roadside inn that featured cheap hookers and kinky couch dancers, the brothel's extravagant participation expense being way out-of-character for the normally parsimonious idiot.

"Why didn't you just go home with your golden goose instead of coming in here to torment me with your frivolous nonsense?" the inn's landlord curiously asked Dumbdick.

"Because there aren't any good whores or couch dancers at my home," the youngest Dumbling honestly admitted, "and neither

Duncehead nor Dipshit have the balls to do male prostitution, even though my bisexual mother once did striptease dancing at *this* very popular bordello wearing nothing except pasties covering her gargantuan nipples! And if I may add, now those particular exploits have made Mom a family legend."

"Yes, I remember the bitch, er, excuse me, your ugly mother very well!" the landlord reluctantly and begrudgingly acknowledged. "Now Dumbdick, please amuse my three lovely horny daughters, and I promise that the whores will in turn entertain you with their abundant femininities!"

When each of the three innkeeper's daughters entered Dumbdick's rented fleabag room, each amateur hooker forgot all about dull, monotonous, straight, gay and perverted, kinky sex, and instead, all three promiscuous whores simultaneously shared the sudden desire to avariciously fondle the beautifully feathered golden goose.

"I must pluck a feather from its tail and rub it against my bushy crotch!" the oldest daughter (a brunette) with the hairiest cookie of the three young harlots delightfully screamed. But then the voluptuous blonde daughter approached the golden fowl and desired a feather to tickle her personals with also, and upon reaching-in to beat her older sister to a golden feather, the blonde bitch's hands automatically stuck to her sister's ass and hips and her fingers would not come off.

And then likewise, the third exuberant buxom sister wanting a golden feather to rub against her red-haired bush. After entering the room and reaching for a golden goose feather to pluck, the horny red-head experienced having her fingers latch onto the second daughter's ass and hips, with the three young sluts inadvertently forming an awkward human chain.

"What the fuck is going on here?" Dumbdick boisterously protested to the three young hookers' during their wild frenzy. "How am I expected to get a hard on and pump you three bitches when you're all more concerned about my quacking golden bird than you are about the limp bird hanging between my friggin' legs?"

The next morning, Dumbdick Dumbling left his rented fleabag room early and carried-off his highly coveted golden goose with the three screaming bitches following behind still attached to either the bird or to a sister's ass and hip. So, wherever Dumbdick Dumbling walked or visited, the three shrieking, naked broads had to follow. Like bizarre lunatics, the encumbered trio had to keep pace with the neurotic idiot's constantly changing speeds.

An appalled parson, needing a convert to recruit into his congregation, accosted Dumbdick in the center of an oat field. "Are the four of you not ashamed of yourselves cavorting around this grain field deliberately sowing your wild oats!" the preacher admonished. "Is this what you call model behavior for the younger generation to emulate?" But then the sanctimonious minister noticed that the three well-endowed females were stark naked and that the trio sported soft, curvaceous bodies. Almost immediately, a large, bulge appeared sticking-out of the preacher's black pants just below the bellybutton.

The shocked parson was so flustered and so aroused (for the first time in nearly three decadent decades) that the reverend instinctively latched onto the red-haired girl's ass and hip and journeyed-off, eagerly joining the wild Saturnalian version of "Follow-the-Leader".

Now the four zany, dedicated disciples rushing after Dumbdick and his golden goose pranced by the parish clerk, who was the parson's principal employee. The clerk had gout in both his swollen big toes and also in his dick, and the bookkeeper suffered from diabetes, foot calluses, planter warts and bunions on both his tender feet. But regardless of the prudish man's physical ailments, the clerk, seeing the gorgeous, naked girls, grabbed onto the parson's ass and hip and volunteered to be a part of the great mobile travesty. The six preposterous idiots (in a line) made their way down the lane and into the crowded center of the remote village.

"Your Reverend," the clerk yelled, "your congregation is stunned at the wild spectacle they're now witnessing, and I must remind you that there's an important Christening that's scheduled to take place in the church this afternoon and that *you'll* be officiating over the blessed ceremony!"

"Who gives a shit about those trivial events?" the blithe-spirited minister yelled over his shoulder in absolute delight. "How many times in our lives do you and I get a marvelous chance to dance with three horny, naked bimbos? Now I want *you* dear clerk to please give me an accurate answer?"

And next the five revelers following the demented Dumbdick Dumbling (it is common knowledge that most fools follow total idiots) and his golden goose passed by three masons, and the avid cement and stone workers were so excited at seeing the three attractive naked bitches scampering around that the first worker grabbed onto the clerk's ass and hips, and next the remaining two men followed suit to then supplement the weird, fast-moving procession meander through the village.

Now Dumbdick veered-off of the main road, and in three hours of crazy frolicking and rollicking across foreign countryside roads, the loony entourage reached the boundary to a neighboring kingdom. The all-too-peculiar parade entered the city where the King had his capital, and the woebegone monarch had only one obstinate daughter that never laughed once in her whole damned sheltered life.

The moody Princess insisted to her frustrated-but-tolerant father that nothing could ever make her laugh, let alone break a smile upon her lips (the ones around her mouth). And the King had just the day before made an official, imperial proclamation that anyone (assuming the person was a non-gay male) that could make his unhappy daughter giggle and laugh should automatically marry her within a week and become the newly appointed royal Prince of the land.

And much to everyone's sudden alarm and humiliation, the moronic Dumbdick Dumbling sprinted up the polished stone steps into the splendid palace carrying his precious golden goose, his route immediately followed by *his* chain of human fools. As soon as the Princess seated on her golden throne observed the crazy spectacle rapidly advancing toward her, she lost her gloomy disposition and let-out an indulgent laugh that nearly shook the sconces off the golden walls and the crystal chandeliers from the jeweled ceiling.

"Look father!" the excited Princess hollered to the very shocked and astounded King. "That silly golden goose has all of those super insane asylum idiots stumbling all over creation, frenetically goosing one another like a bunch of retarded perverts! It's such a fucked-up travesty that I can't stop splitting my gut laughing and farting!"

"You're indeed laughing and farting quite loudly, my dear," the King ecstatically observed and yelled, "so this ongoing hilarious scenario simply means that the asshole fool carrying the golden goose must, according to my royal edict, become your imperial husband and be the next Prince of this fucked-up land!"

And believe it or not, that's precisely how Dumbdick Dumbling became a famous Prince, how the pastor became the kingdom's official archbishop, how the three masons built a colossal Masonic Hall for the clergy, how the straight-laced clerk became the land's regal administrator, and how the three young whores became the King's personal harem. And as to what ever became of the remarkable golden goose, to this day its fate still remains a great mystery that nobody with any scruples gives a royal dump about.

"The Notorious Sleeping Beauty"

Once upon a millennium, an old King and Queen passionately loved each other, but complete happiness had always eluded the royal freaks because their marriage had never produced any children. The King had a dreadfully low sperm count, and the Queen's ovaries produced but one egg in her entire lifetime, and that one egg had a shell so thick that not even a hundred million sperms using a catapult could ever puncture through the damned hard cell wall. And besides that very extraordinary, infertile phenomenon, the Queen was a terrible bitch since every day of every month from age thirteen right through age fifty she was having one continuous bloody period the whole bloody time. Not even the King's most well-manufactured ultra-thick band aids could stop the stench, prolonged bleeding.

"Oh well, I guess we have to go with the flow," the Queen confided to her depressed husband. 'Not even Moses could part my Red Sea!"

"Okay Florence, from now on I'll call you Flo'," the King imaginatively volleyed.

One bleak *April Fool's Day,* a slender moonbeam had penetrated the King's stained-glass bedroom window and also the Queen's vagina, so miraculously, the next morning (forget about this nine-month crap) her Highness gave birth to a beautiful daughter. The King and the Queen were so joyful that the pair screwed each other all night long for the first time in four decadent decades.

Alas (at last) the King and Queen sent-out invitations to Fairy Women all over their kingdom because the worthless royals didn't want to be condemned for being biased against lesbians or dykes, or clan dykes or Klondikes.

"Hey, we sent the Christening invitations out without any messengers to deliver them," the Queen informed her forgetful husband.

"Maybe I should make a decree for the establishment of a bona fide postal service," the King affirmatively stated. "But for now, we'll have to send-out the invitations by means of courier."

Dark valleys and rolling hills abounded in that map-less remote kingdom, and it required several weeks of intensive preparation for all of the planned festivities to finally commence. But a few of the clueless couriers deliberately got lost, and the disoriented assholes staggering around China and Japan never came back to the castle to report their missions (or their intermissions) being completed.

Soon the clopping of horses' hoofs could be heard all day and all night long over the drawbridge spanning the alligator-filled moat and then the cadence continued into the colossal 'white castle', which often doubled as a hamburger stand for hungry knights and jesters from *jesteryear*.

The arriving Fairy Women journeyed from afar to participate in the gala occasion because basically, the old hag bitches had nothing better to do. Each faggot lady brought a special rare gift to present to the newborn Princess, who was destined by fate to own luxurious hotels and fantastic ocean liners in many tropical lands, especially in the Caribbean.

A full week later, the last of the Fairy Women (who was a hoary lesbian whore) rode across the lowered drawbridge and into the castle on a white ass that had numerous bells jangling so loudly that they jangled everybody's nerves. The last mole-faced Fairy Woman, however, possessed incredible potent witch's abilities in the arcane black arts, which of course the wench kept secret all to herself.

The very Potent Bitchy Witch confidently entered the castle's main hall, dismounted from her white ass and discovered the infant Princess fast asleep and being attended to by the royal family's 'head nurse', who frequently serviced the King's erection when the constipated Queen was out in the garden taking a prolonged crap in the tall weeds. Much to the King and Queen's shock, the old Fairy Witch gazed-down at the innocent sleeping infant and instantly articulated an ominous pronouncement:

"Plan as you may, but the day will come,
When spinning with spindle, she'll prick her thumb.
Then in dreamless sleep she shall slumber on,
Until a hundred years have come and gone.
Be glad that I have given this curse,
For I originally planned for the spell to be worse,
So, forget all your worries, your pain and your cares,
Your precious Princess will sleep a hundred years!"

Then the formidable old bitch Witch wrapped her mantle tightly around her shoulders, hopped her exposed pale butt onto her white ass, vigorously yanked the reins and rode the obedient animal out of the colossal hall. The jangling of the bells on the ass's reins, saddle and bridle all jangled everyone's nerves even greater than before as the old Fairy Woman crossed the rickety drawbridge in reverse fashion and soon disappeared into the night's gloom.

"Why didn't you invite the old Fairy Woman to the Christening feast?" the King angrily chastised his wife. "If you had remembered to do so, then the hideous hag would not have pronounced this horrible curse upon our royal daughter. How could you have been so damned irresponsibly negligent?"

"If our daughter lives for a hundred years in suspended animation," the Queen pessimistically stated, "then she'll wake-up being an old wretched spinster even without ever again having the pleasure of using a spinning wheel and a spindle."

"And the old Fairy Woman didn't even tell us if our daughter would awake as an old woman or as a young girl after her century-long slumber," the King realized and added. "May the old Hag's smelly asshole shrivel-up and then experience immediate atrophy."

The extremely concerned King and Queen were really pissed-off as a result of the old Fairy Women's disconcerting hex. "Can't we get the court magician to say some elaborate words like 'curse be gone' or 'hex-a-gone'?" the Queen (who was also known as Mrs. King) asked her fully bewildered spouse.

"This entire scenario is really fucked-up!" the Monarch moaned and sulked. "Now we gotta' watch our bratty kid day and night when we could be out carousing around the gay and lesbian community looking for some fascinating carnal pleasure. Truthfully, I could be gratifying my ego by committing sodomy while making a royal pain in the ass out of myself. What an absolute bummer this friggin' hex is!"

"We should've had the foresight to invite the old Fairy Woman to the Christening party," the Queen remorsefully returned. "Now we must pay the price for *our* grievous omission. I'm so damned upset that I can't even shit a dingleberry!"

"Who'd want to invite that grotesque-looking, ancient Bitch anywhere!" the Queen's regal husband yelled and maintained. "She's ten times uglier than all of history's mortal sins put together!"

The Emperor sent his loyal royal messengers throughout his troubled land, the dispatched couriers instructing the public that every spindle should be destroyed or brought to the castle to be systematically demolished. Some spindles were burned to ash', others were splintered by axes while still others were deviously infested by termite colonies at the King's imperial command. But most of the couriers that had been sent-out got lost or escaped to lands that were more citizen-friendly than the King's deplorable domain, while still the remainder of more industrious messengers simply became priests, monks, pedophiles or entrepreneurial male prostitutes.

"After all of the spindles have been confiscated and incinerated," the merciless King proclaimed, "anyone caught hiding a wooden wheel will have their penis severed or their tits slashed-off and then suffer being decapitated before eventually bleeding to death!"

"Say Husband," the Queen unconstructively interrupted. "We could now make a fortune selling spinning wheels out of some unknown artificial material that would take the place of wood."

"Please keep the remainder of your brilliant ideas to yourself!" the King loudly opined and criticized. "A poisonous mushroom has a higher damned *IQ* than your pea brain has!"

Several decades passed, and one winter evening the royal couple conversed about what had transpired after their hexed daughter's Christening. The adorable, accursed Princess had now grown into a beautiful maiden, who had to wear seven heavy iron chastity belts with rusty locks so that no yeoman or pauper could ever pork or finger-fish masturbate her. But the young heiress was never told why she was being overprotected or why her pubic area was being "chastised." And furthermore, the very gorgeous, curvaceous, naïve Princess knew nothing about the nasty old Fairy Woman and her "very abominable spindle curse."

"What goes up, must come down," mentioned the Queen to her peeved husband. "Spinning wheel turnin' around!"

"Shut the fuck up!" the irritated King balked. "It's bad enough I have to give my blood, sweat and tears grieving over something as dumb as a catastrophe resulting from a cheap spinning wheel! I've neglected my kingdom for twenty-one years now over that shitty-assed fear my mind possesses!"

"And believe it or not," interrupted the acutely alert Queen," the people are much better-off without your insane edicts screwing-up their overtaxed, poverty-stricken lives even more than they already are! The serfs see this spinning wheel bullshit as a definite blessing; that is, from *their* perspective. Some of the more fortunate peasants living near the sea have even accumulated enough savings to buy surfboards and frog flippers."

The afflicted Princess had the privilege of wandering all over the huge white castle and eating as many greasy hamburgers and miniature sliders as she wanted. Despite her propensity for suffering acute indigestion, the future queen was allowed to peep through the castle's wet wall cracks but always had to keep her hands off of her own juicy slit and clit. But one particular castle tower was strictly off limits for the adventurous Princess. She often wondered if the keys to her seven chastity belts had been cunningly concealed inside what was described as "the secret room".

One *April Fool's* evening, the Princess furtively looked behind a draped wall tapestry and discovered the portal to a passageway she had never before observed. Looking around to make sure that no nosy castle voyeurs were scrutinizing her stealthy activity, the Princess slowly turned the access key in the squeaky lock. The castle explorer successfully opened the ancient door and then bounded up the steps as fast as she could, hoping that another seven keys (or one master skeleton one) could be found in the remote turret chamber that would unfasten her cumbersome chastity belts. Right before arriving at her ultimate destination, the fair maiden looked through a wall slit and her pupils perceived a thin moonbeam along with a few early evening stars twinkling in the dark night sky.

'Shit! I'll bet this remote tower will be a wonderful place for me to secretly masturbate!' the Princess thought. "Now all I gotta' do is find the magic key or keys that will remove these seven burdensome chastity belts. My crotch really itches badly, but according to my father's severe mandate, I can only have my servants remove the heavy chastity belts with their entrusted keys every morning and evening when I take showers, dumps and leaks. That's the only damned times I can piss or take a crap!' the melancholy Princess sadly meditated. 'Even when I have to go badly or when my bowels have the damned diarrhea, I still have to hold it until early morning or early evening arrives! Damn it! Why couldn't I have been born a friggin' horny peasant girl with a hundred big-dick boyfriends?'

At the top of the winding staircase, another door prevented the curious visitor from entering into the lone, mysterious upper room. Near the shaded, gloomy portal, the curious Princess peeked through a slight crack in the poorly constructed castle wall and beheld an elderly Hag dressed in lamb's wool, her attire symbolizing that the nefarious Fairy Bitch had returned to ingeniously trick her junior majesty by pulling the wool over *her* innocent eyes.

Upon closer inspection, the royal trespasser noticed that the persistent old Hag was not actively taking a shit into an "in-house" hopper as the observer originally had suspected. Instead, the wicked Witch was using her slender fingers to rotate a spinning wheel while "changing the *composition of flax*", which was never a haunting melody written by either Mozart or Beethoven. The old Hag then beckoned the Fair Maiden in a sinister-but-enticing voice:

"If ya' wanna' witness an old bag spin,
Then lift the latch, and enter in!
But if ya' wanna' leave this weird atmosphere,
Then get the fuck outa' here!"

Naturally the courageous and daring Princess yielded to temptation and lifted the latch, which she had deftly learned to do when she had been an innocent girl enrolled as a kindergartner in the King's "early childhood latchkey program". The shadowy chamber's interior was dank and cold, and as the Young Lady cautiously approached the Old Hag, *she* heard other peculiar utterances being articulated:

"With finger and thumb I whirl my twine,
Making it weave so smooth and fine,
But if ya' wanna' give it a try,
You'll see how time will fly."

The Old Hag spun her flax (before ordinary people had flax machines) with such agility that the Princess envied the elderly wretch's wonderful dexterity despite the old Bitch's quite apparent advanced arthritis, osteoporosis and rheumatism. Then the Old Bag stopped spinning and soon pressed her bony, cold index finger against the stunned Princess's chest, which incidentally was not covered by any chastity belt or bra filled with enormous falsies.

"Your cold hand feels like a dying bird's claw!" the Princess gasped. "Please touch me again. No one has ever touched my tits before, whether the person might have been straight or gay or tri-sexual! Please continue molesting me!"

"Take this spinning wheel away and secretly practice with it!" the old Witch suggested without exposing her shaded, hooded face to her avid listener. "If you don't follow my instruction, my Pretty, you'll end-up being a decrepit, horny spinster just like me. Ha, ha, ha!"

The intrepid Princess quickly possessed the tempting spindle from the old Hag's hands and tucked it under her gown to camouflage its existence. Then the comely, young lady left the off-limits turret room, descended the spiral staircase in a jiffy and thought on the way down to the castle's mezzanine level, 'This entire palace is a goddamned 'no spin zone'! I better be careful about this spindle or else things could rapidly spin out of control.'

Meanwhile, the paranoid King and Queen were searching every nook and cranny of the immense castle looking for their beloved naughty daughter. When the regal rummagers finally entered their daughter's room a second time, both royal pain-in-the-asses sighed with relief upon locating their child, but then the cantankerous royal pain-in-the-ass father mildly reprimanded his aberrant offspring for violating the established and clearly defined palace rules.

"Where the hell have you been daughter?" the King admonished with an accusative interrogative. "Whatever you do, I advise that you don't talk to strangers or discuss your private sex life with strangers that happen to be pimps!"

"Yes darling, where have you been?" the Queen injected in a more sympathetic tone of voice than the one employed by her sex-starved husband. "You really had us both worried half to death."

"But certainly Mother," the Princess answered, "I'm old enough to take care of myself without either you or Pop spying on my whereabouts all freakin' day long. After all my dear, snooping, spying parents, I've passed the puberty plateau. I do have hair on my cookie and besides that particular maturation, sometimes my responsive silver-coin-size nipples become erect when I get aroused. I'm old enough to take care of myself, aren't I?"

"Yes, my dear," the King politely concurred with a sinister smile upon his countenance, "but are you wise enough to take care of yourself when temptation beckons your baser instincts? Forget your silver-coin-size nipples that look quite tantalizing through your sheer garments. Can you take care of yourself by using wisdom? That's the billion-gold-coin question."

And then the very astute Queen suavely queried her cherished Daughter. "My dear, what are you hiding with your hand tucked inside your gown's creases? If it's a hand grenade, don't pull the fuckin' pin whatever you do! If it's a marijuana joint, let me have it to light-up and smoke."

The Princess gave a mock laugh and disclosed to her elders that her concealed object was "a personal secret," but under pressure, the daughter nervously promised her parents that the item wasn't a cucumber, a carrot or a dildo.

"Maybe it is a flower," the sneaky Princess continued under duress, "or maybe I'm holding a token as a lucky charm waiting for a handsome prince charming or gallant knight to come to this God-forsaken castle and expertly deflower me. Maybe it's a pin for my hair or one to use to stick into your fat asses," the Princess screamed at her parents like a maniac. "Or maybe it's neither of those sharp objects but a very graphic nudist colony magazine instead. But I guarantee you two adult dolts that later this night, I shall show both of you pathetic retards exactly what the mystery device happens to be."

And so, putting credence in the Princess's promise, the King and the Queen were for the moment satisfied with their daughter's unusual honesty, which was principally based on conniving and also founded on a most cunning explanation. "Oh, precious Daughter," the King emotionally remarked, "you're so happy and so gay. Maybe in a year or so we'll all take a leisurely vacation cruise to the Isle of Lesbos in the royal yacht!"

After the royal parents finally retired to the *masturbation bedroom,* their great apprehensions about their daughter's veracity began haunting their psyches.

"Tomorrow morning we'll tell our stellar Daughter about the old Hag's disappointing hex after *her* Christening over two decadent decades ago," the King recommended to his spouse. "Our child is now old enough to drink hard whiskey, to smoke marijuana, to experiment with cocaine and to reason on her own."

"She wouldn't dare do anything rash, even if her sensitive skin became severely irritated!" the Queen commented. "Once she knows all about the frightening spindle prophecy, or should I say spindle warning, I'm certain that our only Princess will never yield to randomly experimenting with a spinning wheel, even if she had a silly name like Vanna Whitehead, Sarah Yeahvo or Vera Beach."

But when the King and the Queen were clandestinely discussing their strategy concerning spinning wheels, in the throne room the Princess surreptitiously uncovered and then gazed at the simple spindle that she had swindled from the old Hag. 'Shit! One end is as sharp as a needle!' the evaluator immediately determined. "In fact, it *is* a prickly needle indeed. Oh, how I wish it were a nice, firm, long, thick male prick instead of a sharp, short, spindle needle!'

And as the Princess awkwardly fumbled with the common, small machine, a screech of an owl was discerned at her bedroom window. The sudden distraction caused the Princess's hand to slip on the wheel, and then the sharp needle cut deep into her tender right thumb's skin.

The Fairy Woman's diabolical black magic instantly began taking effect as the first drop of blood surfaced and soon appeared at the end of the Maiden's bruised thumb. 'If I was an 'iron maiden' instead of a human one,' the Princess regretfully thought, 'then I wouldn't have to worry about such a stupid thing as my thumb's skin bleeding and the finger throbbing with pain.'

Soon the victimized Princess felt quite lousy and drowsy, and she slowly closed her attractive, blue eyes. The royal daughter plopped down upon her comfortable mattress and then fell fast asleep while completely enjoying her 'beauty rest'.

An ominous drowsiness rapidly enveloped the entire castle, and at that incredible moment, the sleepy atmosphere kept all of the inhabitants spellbound. The Chief Treasurer ceased counting his gold and silver coins and put his head down on his table; the Royal Astronomer forgot about the heavenly bodies he had been intensely scrutinizing in a girlie magazine; and the Main Butler fell asleep while peeking through a keyhole observing the Queen's six, kinky-minded attendants naked in a pile of horny lusting bodies.

Every person and every living creature in the entire castle from the ants in the walls to the bees in the garden had amazingly entered into a heavy slumber; even the frivolous and dictatorial, petulant King who was halfway through taking a royal shit on *his* most important royal throne. Loud and repugnant snoring was going on everywhere throughout the extensive aristocratic dwelling, but none of the participants was able to hear a single sound, especially the palace's Chief Deaf Mute.

Time glided by as if the elusive phantom had been wearing ice skates, and as the calendar years advanced forward one by one, still the disgusting snoring (which no one that was snoring heard) kept occurring. Even when hard snot balls formed in everyone's swollen nostrils, the vulgar snoring droned on and on throughout the very rapidly deteriorating and now in-need-of-repair castle.

The fair Princess remained young and stunning in appearance (even though no one sleeping and snoring could see her) during the beauty's extended sleep, and everyone in the castle (that was also slumbering) hadn't aged (almost a century later), and each person looked exactly as he, she or it had when the palace's residents had been affected by the nefarious Witch's diabolical spell.

But every spring and summer, the outside weeds grew taller, the briars and brambles in the garden became wilder and larger, and the now vulnerable terraces and walls were eventually covered and laden with moss, algae, fungi, slime and rat turds. And then ninety-nine fierce winters later on another momentous *April Fool's Day,* a lost Prince from a neighboring land viewed the distant castle turrets and ramparts covered in environmental growth and believed that his senses were indeed deceiving him.

'What a fucked-up castle in need of maintenance even if the abominable structure originally was a real bastion of royal lunacy!' the Prince rationally reckoned. 'When I was but a gullible little shit head, my abusive nurse told me about a Fairy Woman's spell in a distant land while *she* was busy nursing me, and I was busy sucking away on *her* hard, luscious, delicious nipples.'

And so, the handsome lost Prince (who had misplaced his compass and his moral compass, too) who never studied a map nor knew how to read one, rode his white steed down a steep hill with his rascally hound dogs barking close behind. Soon, the wandering visitor approached the thick, unkempt hedges and thickets that surrounded the dilapidated white castle that looked so bad that it couldn't now even sell hot dogs or even raunchy dog food sandwiches. The fatigued Prince was rather valiant and was not discouraged by the disarrayed quagmire and by the immense entanglements his disconsolate-looking, bloodshot eyes were witnessing.

'Don't they have any freakin' landscapers, gardeners or lawn maintenance services in this foreign, fucked-up land?' he imagined. 'There isn't one damned access route through this dense growth that is gradually isolating that ramshackle castle from the rest of the world. A tree might grow in Brooklyn, but a fuckin' out-of-control jungle is quite prevalent sprouting-up right here.'

Then the depressed Prince estimated that it would require ten thousand lumberjacks, ten billion ants and ten trillion termites to finally clear-away the excessive vegetation. So instead of starting a raging inferno to deforest the area, the shit-for-brains idiot removed his hunting knife and began hacking away, pretending all the time that each vine was a ruthless monster or a wild ferocious beast attacking his aristocratic testicles.

So, the lunatic Prince slashed, and he severed, and he sliced with his minuscule hunting knife, imagining all the while that the small object was a lethal machete and that his soft, delicate hands were soon bleeding right through his cheap gloves he had gotten as an incentive bonus for opening a bank savings account in *his* neighboring land. By midnight, the obsessed Prince had managed to carve a hole halfway through the dense growth, which was nearly as dense as his thick cerebrum. And so, the wayward fellow therefore decided to camp for the night, making a fire out of twigs, leaves, bark, his own pubic hairs along with the least interesting pages from a tarnished porno' magazine the traveler had kept safely tucked under his saddle.

Then after eating a turnip and taking a half-hour leak, the journeyman Prince was too weak to work his stick and sustain a regular boner, so the jerk-off dozed-off to sleep dreaming of his next hard on. And so, by accident, the night spring wind blew the campfire flames in the direction of the castle, and the raging inferno incinerated and cut through the last fifty feet of surrounding vegetation as if an outstanding miracle had actually transpired.

When the Prince finally awoke, he realized, 'It's a good thing that this queer land doesn't have any forest rangers or my ass would be in jail by now!' And then another monumental thought arose inside his rather diminutive mind. 'This damned enigmatic kingdom doesn't even have any people, straight, gay, bisexual or otherwise. How fucked-up can you get? This strange territory isn't even on a map in any *Atlas* or geography book in any library I've ever been in!'

And as the new arrival slouched-down and crawled through the portal into what formerly was the palace's main garden, the inquisitive Prince could not detect any signs of insects, birds, gorillas, rhinos' or space aliens. The inquisitive intruder next gingerly crawled through the dense underbrush and then stood and carefully walked over the decaying drawbridge, which the former residents had scribbled graffiti symbols all over its beams because it naturally was a drawbridge.

And at the decaying castle's sole entrance, the Prince came across several of the land's sentinels frozen in time and petrified like stone statues standing outside *their* paint-faded guardhouse. The uniformed sleeping soldiers erect on their feet stationed above the muddy moat, and the guards were pissing motionless urine into the water onto two stationary alligators below, but the still sentries, their whizzes and the open-mouthed alligators had all been immobilized in suspended animation as if time itself' had been paralyzed.

The apprehensive Prince reluctantly entered the dark, dismal castle, and after exploring around several passages and corridors, the visitor came to the Princess's bedroom door, which was *ajar* in addition to being a door. Ivy vines and ferns were now abundantly growing inside the bedchamber, making it appear as if the room had been built without a floor right inside the middle of a tropical jungle.

The Prince instinctively looked-down upon the bed and beheld the beautiful royal maiden resting, and his first instinct was to grab her breasts and incessantly fondle them, and his second impulse was to tear her clothes off and pump the poop out of the sleeping beauty until she finally revived to mutually enjoy tremendous dual orgasms. But then the newcomer observed the spindle still gripped by the girl's ten thin fingers, so the nincompoop thought, 'If that thing starts spinning around while I'm screwing this pretty chick, it's liable to castrate me and do more than a basic circumcision to my erect pecker. Perhaps another more discreet approach to get my throbbing glory into her dainty pink panties sometime in the near future would be a more feasible consideration.'

And so, the anxious Prince (who really needed to get laid to help clear-away his repulsive facial acne) bent over and smooched the sleeping Princess on the lips while reasoning, 'Now why can't these be her other lips, the ones situated between her firm legs!' the horny interloper thought. 'That would be one time I wouldn't mind having a *hair* lip! Ha, ha, ha!'

Then the Prince lifted his hunting horn up to his parched mouth and gave the inanimate object the best blowjob it had ever had. The loud blast awoke the Princess, her parents and everyone else in the enchanted castle. 'Oh fuck! How dumb can I be!' the Prince immediately considered. 'Now I won't have any damned privacy while I'm pumpin' this terrific-looking Babe silly!'

The Princess lost her grip on the accursed spindle, and the item dropped to the ground (for there was no more floor in the room because of the dense vegetation that had wormed its way through the cement and stone masonry). The almost comatose Princess opened her eyes (but not her legs), and then she smiled at her courageous rescuer. And it was plainly evident that the Prince blowing his horn had awakened the Princess from her century-long sleep, and it was not a sloppy, messy kiss as is often erroneously believed.

The King and the Queen each had awoken from their century-long siestas, and instead of worrying about their precious Daughter, the ingrates frantically tore off each other's clothes, and the motivated Monarch hopped upon his mistress and successfully laid several miles of pipe with his very aroused personal equipment.

And then all of the other humans in the castle awoke from their sleeps, latched onto the nearest person and engaged in a wild un-orchestrated orgy with moaning and groaning echoing off of every wall, tree and vine all over the damned premises. Straights were screwing straights and also indiscriminately sodomizing gays, so it really was indistinguishable what a person's sexual orientation or disorientation was at that particular time, for perverted sex was happening all over the freakin' palace, and even in the castle's countless trees, and also on the trees numerous branches.

And even the dumb animals forgot about their own species and then began screwing one another. Dogs were hitting-on cats', birds were penetrating frogs, horses were humping away on sea gulls, donkeys were porking pigs, and sheep and bulls were crazily screwing chipmunks and porcupines.

After the remarkable seven-day orgy finally ended, the appointed wedding date had been set. And when the triumphant virgin Prince in quest (and in need of) his first piece of ass carried the Princess into a well-furnished, recently constructed bedchamber, his mouth went agape and his penis shrank to a centimeter when the asshole observed that the beautiful, vivacious maiden had somehow transformed into the wretched old Fairy Hag with a face full of hideous moles, cysts and accompanying warts.

'Oh well!' thought the Prince. 'I'll just close my damned eyes and get this show on the road. An ugly, bad piece of ass is better than no piece of ass at all!'

And the beautiful Princess became the next ugly Old Fairy Woman Hag that would hang around the kingdom waiting for the next unfortunate Princess to be appropriately Christened inside the expansive royal castle.

"Petite Red Riding Hood"

A pretty petite girl who was pretty petite once lived in a remote, nameless village somewhere in southern France. The village was so remote that most Frenchmen didn't have the remotest idea where the hell it was. The child's mother was a racketeer, her father a major gangster, her grandfathers were notorious mobsters and the remainder of the little girl's relatives were common, ordinary, everyday, small-time vitriolic criminals.

The young girl's maternal grandmother was eighty-nine years old and pregnant for the thirty-fifth time. To pass some of the time away, the elderly village prostitute made a red hood for her favorite granddaughter to wear for the purpose of symbolizing to the village idiots that the child was to be left alone because she came from a disreputable family of "hoods". The young French child eventually became known to all local residents living in the isolated village (that appeared on no map) as "Petite Red Riding Hood".

One fine day, the child's mother was busy baking a cake and got a half-baked idea herself. "I just took-out a new insurance policy on you, so go into the forest Petite Red Riding Hood and see how your mentally deranged grandmother is doing," the mercurial-minded mother suggested. "Since I'm baking a cake in the oven, I figured that your horny grandmother probably is carrying child number thirty-six in *her oven* right now! My promiscuous Mommy just could never keep her damned legs closed for ten friggin' seconds!" Red Riding Hood's Mom declared. "Please take this cake and this jar of newly churned butter to her in case your maternal grandmother is again experiencing morning sickness. This food will certainly make her vomit all over the damned place before she can make it to her scummy outhouse *barf-room*, ha, ha, ha."

Petite Red Riding Hood departed her mother's modest home and headed in the direction of the next nearest village where her miserable maternal grandmother resided, since the old Scum Bag had been ostracized from her former village for spreading venereal disease throughout the male population, which naturally, the idiotic men ingeniously transmitted gonorrhea, herpes and syphilis to their unsuspecting wives and mistresses.

The prancing child had to pass through a small dense forest, and if she lived in *this* more dangerous and distrustful day and age, her mother would surely be arrested and convicted for child abuse and child abandonment, or perhaps reckless endangerment, or some other nonsensical, bureaucratic horse crap like that. But in those less sophisticated and simple olden days, when no one gave two flying intercourses about their obnoxious kids, parents and adults could more easily and more readily get away with common everyday child abuse.

Soon Petite Red Riding Hood encountered the conniving Mr. Wolf while sauntering along the dark forest trail. The malevolent stranger desired to mug, molest, sodomize, screw and then devour the beautiful young girl, who was willing to accede to all of *his* sinister and dishonorable intentions except the being consumed part. Since woodcutters were in the area committing a slew of ecological catastrophes (before there were any environmental laws or no-nonsense environmentalists around to protect Mother Nature), the Wolf decided to use guile rather than force to lure the not-so-innocent child (who usually preferred administering the abnormal molesting to victimized adults) into a 'compromising situation'.

"What way are you going little child?" the clever Wolf inquired to create the pretense of genuine conversation.

"Are you a Dumb Ass or what?" the precocious girl snapped back. "Can't you see that I'm walking north in *this* particular direction from the village I call Dikkywhet toward the village of Pussychu! I mean, go to the library in Paris and read a damned phony map and learn basic false geography!"

"And who might you be visiting in Pussychu?" the cunning Wolf anxiously asked while licking his lips. "The butcher, the baker, the candlestick manufacturer, or maybe the dildo distributor? They're all accomplished cunt-lappers over in Pussychu, you know!"

"I'm going to visit my whoring grandmother and deliver a cake and some butter that my mother has prepared for *her* to eat," the little girl with the red hood confidently answered. "Got any more moronic dumb ass questions to ask?"

'Shit, this girl's whoring grandmother once gave me 'the clap'!' the devious Wolf remembered as the rogue symbolically clapped his hands. "Is your grandmother's last name by any chance Hood?"

"Yes," Petite Red Riding Hood replied in a perturbed-sounding voice. "I wish I had a damned horse or pony to ride. I don't even have a friggin' hobbyhorse to ride as a hobby!" the precocious child complained. "Why the hell they call me Riding Hood is really a very big fuckin' mystery to me!"

"Are you related to the infamous bandit Robin Hood?" the Wolf wondered and asked. "And don't try hoodwinking me with an imaginative, fallacious answer my prevaricating Child."

"No Asshole; I told you that my peculiar name is Petite Red Riding Hood," the little girl indignantly yelled. "Robin Hood lives in England and this is France, you fucked up dimwit! Now get the hell out of my way or I'll kick the living shit out of you!"

"One final thing," the unscrupulous Wolf responded with a wicked smile upon his countenance. "Exactly where does this Old Lady Hood live right now?"

"On the opposite side of the mill that's visible down there in the valley," the petulant child aptly stated. "She commits her sex-for-money schemes in any of the four rooms in her red *cottage* when she's not making cheese or farting around cutting the *cheese*. Sex to Grandma is a sort of cottage industry!"

'I'll take the shortcut to this child's grandmother's house in Pussychu,' the conniving Wolf thought. 'Then perhaps I can kill and eat the both of them, Little Red and the kinky old lady. I have a score to settle with the Hood family. Shit! My hairy balls and furry dick won't stop itching!'

After reflecting like a mirror in the bright morning sunlight, the Wolf coyly announced to the wandering child, "I'll meet you again at your grandmother's place. Then maybe we can do a little three-way sex interaction. I have quite an ample appetite when it comes to all kinds of carnal pleasure!"

"See ya' later shit head!" Petite Red Riding Hood defiantly volleyed. "And be careful not to step on any forest land mines I've randomly planted along the way in past jaunts to Pussychu!"

The hungry Wolf scampered as fast as his agile legs could carry him to the aforementioned red house opposite the defunct mill in Pussychu. 'Maybe I can enjoy some satisfying cottage cheese before I enact my dastardly deed in the cottage, or shall I say dastardly misdeed! Ha, ha, ha,' the starving carnivore thought. Soon, the almost famished predator arrived at the small red cottage situated near the dilapidated Pussychu mill, and then the scoundrel loudly knocked three times on the front door.

"Who is there?" the old whore inside asked. "I charge a reasonable fee of three silver coins for the first half hour and three golden doubloons every thirty minutes thereafter for my highly skilled services."

"It is your loving granddaughter Petite Red Riding Hood," the sly Wolf falsely returned in a falsetto voice that was almost the temperamental girl's duplicate. "I've very considerately brought you a freshly baked cake and a jar of rancid butter that my mother has especially made for you." Then the wily Wolf ruminated, 'This is all very good and rationally planned! I've left little 'margarine for error.'

The promiscuous, sex-addicted grandmother then called-out from inside her abode, "Petite Red, pull the bobbin so that the door latch will start bobbin' upward. And I want you to hurry-up and get the hell outa' here after you present me with your fucked-up, worthless goodies! I have a wealthy paying client arriving to service in forty-five short minutes. The transvestite wants the damned works, and frankly, I don't even have the energy to get down on my friggin' arthritic knees!"

The surreptitious Wolf quickly pulled the bobbin and flung open the rickety door. The vile trespasser then entered the house, and without any hesitation or delay, ate-up the old harlot in less than three minutes because the sordid scavenger had been without food for three whole days. The cunning animal next wiped the blood dripping from his mouth onto the kitchen's red tablecloth so that the scarlet coloration blended-in nicely with the crimson-tinted fabric. The still-hungry creature next rushed to the filthy bed, hopped inside and laid in waiting while anticipating the arrival of the inimitable-but-unpredictable Petite Red Riding Hood.

Soon a "Tap, tap, tap" could be heard at the front door. 'The naïve little Bitch must think this flophouse is a goddamned *tap*room!' the Wolf mused. 'Assholes like her deserve to be consumed!'

"Who is there?" the Wolf inquired. "Are you a lesbian or a homo'?"

"Petite Red Riding Hood," the garrulous girl answered from outside.

'Oh well; Petite Red's demise is virtually inevitable so *Taps* is a rather appropriate tune to contemplate.' Then the deceptive Wolf's mind was momentarily addled, so the child-hunter adroitly disguised his raspy voice to fill the void and again asked, "Who is there?"

"Grandmother, are you a retard on what?" the rambunctious girl protested. "I've already told you that I'm Petite Red Riding Hood. I've brought you a cake and a jar of Mom's un-patented butter to butter you up. Get with the damned program and stop acting like a forgetful acid head, will ya'!"

The uncouth Wolf then recalled what the old prostitute Grandmother now being digested in his stomach had previously uttered to him, so the crafty carnivore creatively mimicked *her* familiar entreaty. "Little Red, just pull the bobbin and the latch will rise. Then open the door and come to my bedside so that I may admire every ounce of you."

When the slippery Wolf observed the blonde-haired girl enter the dingy-looking home, the villain very slyly hid his furry body (hairy balls and all) under the bedspread where the old dead Grandmother used to spread her legs to earn silver and gold coins, but what she had done with her legs was indeed another kind of 'bed spread.'

"Please set the cake in the cupboard because I have no cake board in which to put it," the Wolf furtively demanded. "And then Petite Red; come immediately and directly to my bed so that I may fondle and ravish your supple body with unbridled affection, you sweet, little demented child!"

After putting the cake inside the cupboard and setting the sticky butter jar upon the kitchen table, Petite Red Riding Hood removed all of her clothes and undergarments and anxiously hopped into the sack to participate in a little impromptu day action.

"Grandmother!" the bratty kid gasped in alarm. "What long furry arms you have!"

"All the better to hug and molest you with my dear!" the Wolf intelligently replied.

"And Grandmother, what long hairy legs you've got!" the perceptive girl advertently shouted. "I can't wait to go through puberty so that I can get hair around my furless crack and maybe even get pregnant and contribute more white trash to the local population."

"All the better to make you feel warm and fuzzy!" the very keen-witted Wolf exclaimed.

"And Grandmother, what big hairy ears you have!" Petite Red Riding Hood observed and yelled.

"All the better to hear your stupid bullshit, you obnoxious little delectable child," the hungry predator proclaimed as the lustful killer contemplated his next delicious dinner.

"And Grandmother, what large beady eyes you have!" the observant girl marveled and uttered.

"All the better to see and crave your pure chaste body with, my dear," the malicious, sick-minded, abominable Wolf relevantly and covetously explained.

"And Grandmother, what enormous teeth you possess!" the prospective victim enunciated.

"All the better to munch on your tiny tits and pristine slit garden with!" the Wolf promised. "I can't wait to plant a massive cucumber right in the center of your hairless love garden!"

"And Grandmother, what a hairy long dick you have!" the child discovered and shrieked. "Did you have some sort of a perverted sex operation at the Pussychu medical welfare clinic, or what?"

"All the better to pump your cute little well dry with my dear!" the ravenous Wolf impulsively replied.

"You must really think that I'm a stupid shit jumping into this bed with a degenerate lunatic Wolf like you!" Petite Red Riding Hood sagaciously reprimanded. "You'll get your deserved compensation for being a sleazy scumbag right now!"

And after delivering *that* most appropriate threat, Petite Red Riding Hood leaped out of her grandmother's raunchy bed, turned the mattress over and then methodically punched and pummeled the confused Wolf into submission and finally, into utter unconsciousness. Then the young heroine (who was not on heroin) tore-off the animal's four appendages and head, smeared her mother's foul-smelling butter over the five dismembered parts, placed the arms, four legs and torso into the kitchen oven, cooked the furry animal to a crisp and then enjoyed a most sumptuous feast, not realizing for a minute that she was actually also cannibalizing her prostitute Grandmother still being digested in the Wolf's alimentary canal.

"I'll take this roasted Wolf's head to the village taxidermist and have it mounted on my bedroom wall as a splendid souvenir of this most wonderful adventure," Petite Red Riding Hood announced to her dull image in the cracked kitchen mirror. "That ignorant Wolf had no idea that I'm a certified black belt in karate and a master in judo and also in dissection. I got a damned A+ in my biology class cutting-up amphibians and marsupials! I not only know how to kick ass! I also know exactly how to savagely mutilate and then rip the buttocks off a recently butchered carcass!"

"Jack's Magnificent Beanstalk"

Once upon a stupid time, when moronic people abounded and frolicked around upon the pristine earth just like they do today, a poverty-stricken widow abandoned by her husband had a donkey-brained son named Jack and a fairly decent cow appropriately called Milky White. Each and every morning, Jack brought and sold milk at the marketplace, which then he and his invalid mother used the compensation to purchase food, porno' magazines, sexual aid devices like vibrators and penis enlargers along with other basic sundry, everyday necessities.

But one gloomy, gray morning Milky White got pissed-off at being his owners' exploited property and produced no milk, which to Jack and his mother was not any *utter*ly ridiculous matter. The perplexed, avaricious mother and her numbskull son were in an absolute quandary and considered how they might mutually solve their sudden unexpected dilemma.

"What shall we do Jack?" the distraught mom implored her doltish son. "Jack my boy, stop jumping over that friggin' candlestick and listen-up for a second! What the hell should we do, son? It looks like no more nudie flashcards for you and no more spectacular breast implantations for me!"

"Don't get overly depressed Mother," Jack confidently suggested. "I'll read the want ads posted in the town square and get a job in a brothel or in a nightclub that feature acrobatic couch dancers. I've been practicing on our shoddy sofa, and I believe I'm ready to try some davenport dancing for faggot clientele at the local gay bar!"

"Jack, you're underage and must still attend elementary school," the distressed mother chastised while giving her silly son a much-needed reality check. "We have no alternative other than to sell Milky White and use the money to start an adult bookstore or some other business enterprise of that profitable nature. Porn' is definitely the best way to go if we gotta' start from scratch!"

"All right, you've convinced me mother," the easily influenced son cooperatively acceded. "I'll take Milky White to the main marketplace and see what kind of offers I can receive from one of the merchants before you even know that our cow has *passed your eyes.*"

Jack went-out to the dilapidated barn and grabbed the cow's halter-top, which had always been too small to fit as a makeshift bra around Milky White's gigantic udders. The lad hadn't yet reached the village marketplace when a peculiar-looking fellow having a long, curled nose and no visible teeth accosted the naïve boy escorting his non-functioning, on-strike milk dispenser.

"Good morning Jack!" the bizarre stranger began. "Where are ya' headin' with your fancy albino cow?"

Jack had forgotten to ask how the weird-looking fellow knew his name, not realizing that the stranger was indeed his estranged father. "I'm heading toward the marketplace to sell Milky White for cash on the barrelhead," the lazy, callow teenager honestly explained. "Mom needs the dough to start an adult porno' shop, even though the village has twenty-seven similar businesses already servicing a population of eighty-nine horny, sex-starved residents. When your house is a money pit, you need a cash cow, ya' know!"

"You seem to be most competent at selling cows," the seemingly newcomer to Jack's life flattered. "But young man, I'm curious if ya' know how many beans make the number five."

"Ha, ha, ha; that's an old schoolyard riddle," Jack laughed as if the adolescent had feathers tickling under his armpits. "Even my retarded father that I've never known would comprehend the answer to *that* simple ditty. Two in each hand and one additional bean in the mouth! What an absurd, asinine question you've asked!"

"You're quite a remarkable mathematician, and ya' might someday give Isaac Newton some serious competition," the goofy-looking man laughed as the street hustler reached deep into his pants' pocket and retrieved several ugly, irregular-shaped beans. "Now since you're so intelligent at computing arithmetic answers," the garrulous, scruffy-looking gentleman continued his drivel, "I'll make a difficult sacrifice and barter these five miraculous beans for possession of old Milky White there. It's all over the village square that your cow's value has significantly declined because she no longer is producing milk, just like your mother's tiny tits aren't either."

"Do ya' actually think that I'm some kind of mentally deficient jackass?" the insulted boy defensively challenged. "You can shove those ridiculous beans up your ass and then mistake them for small hemorrhoids."

"Ah my lad, but in your haste to judgment you've not truly recognized the potency of these fantastic magical beans," the conman suavely maintained. "If ya' take them home and conscientiously plant them right now, when you wake up tomorrow morning, they'll have sprouted and grown all the way up to the beautiful blue sky."

"You're more-full of feces than the overflowing village cesspool ever was!" Jack loudly replied. "How do I know that you're not a disreputable con-artist like my derelict deadbeat old man was, trying to take advantage of my lack of experience at the art of cow trading?"

"Well Jack, my boy," the gullible kid's irresponsible father role-playing as an honest deal-making cow-trader declared, "if the beans don't grow vines up to the clouds, then I pledge that you'll get your cow back dead and butchered by noon tomorrow. What do ya' have to say about my very interestin' proposal? Good bargains are hard to come by these days."

"Okay, I've always enjoyed being a born loser and a living sucker!" the boy confessed. "Folks say that's exactly how my disingenuous father was often victimized. I guess that being hosed is embedded in my family genes on both sides."

Jack returned home before twilight and reluctantly told his mother about his preposterous negotiation with the total stranger, who in *his* recollection was a stranger, stranger than fiction.

"You should've gotten at least fifteen pounds for that two-thousand-pound heifer," the lad's mother appropriately criticized. "Now, because of your general ignorance, my wonderful adult porno' bookstore won't be worth a hill of beans let alone a mere handful of silly seeds. When it comes to gross stupidity," the mother caustically admonished, "your gullible nature outrivals that of your deadbeat father, whom you never knew or never want to be introduced to."

"If I sow the beans right now, which I must do to follow the salesman's specific instructions," the dipshit son insisted, "they'll grow right up to the sky overnight, and then we could have a big public attraction right here in our backyard. We could even charge admission and sell insurance to anyone who dares climb the glorious beanstalk up into the stratosphere. We'll also probably have to buy a big safety net to put around the beanstalk's base."

"How could you be so futilely fucked-up?" the mother boisterously screamed. "Why must I be so blessed by having an absolute dingbat for a son? Milky White was the best milk provider in the entire county, and her beef would've been worth a small fortune. We should've moved to London and sold her to a Beefeater at London Tower."

"But mother, the man said he would quarter our cow and give us the meat if the seeds didn't grow into a magnificent beanstalk," the mentally deficient son ineffectually argued. "What's your beef?"

"Where's the beef! That's my beef!" the irate mother ranted. "Take that and that you dumb little asshole!" the livid matriarch screamed as she smacked Jack's face silly while indulging in self-satisfying child abuse. And then the disgruntled mom disgustedly threw the solid beans out the window, which thank goodness was open at the time. "And now get your wise ass up to bed and no supper for you, you pitiful, pathetic son of a worthless, good-for-nothing bastard!"

So, Jack dejectedly climbed the squeaky steps up to his pauper's bedroom, and throughout his steep ascent wishing that he were a prince possessing a really big pecker. 'I'm so upset I can't even get a miniature hard-on to slap and smack around to relieve my accumulated tension!' the juvenile idiot regretted. 'I'm more disappointed for my mother's sake because I had been conned into doing an extremely foolish deal. I hope that freakin' seed hawker gets piss in his bloodstream if those magic seeds turn-out to be duds after all.' And then the young punk dozed-off to sleep without ever achieving a satisfactory erection to smack around, fondle and wildly manipulate.

When the foolish kid woke-up the next morning, Jack's bedroom had a rather different appearance. Sunlight was now gleaming inside part of his sleeping area, but dark shadows were prevalent everywhere else. And so, Jack dressed and next sauntered-over to his window, which any normal intelligent, curious boy would have done in the opposite order. The immature dreamer gazed outside the shabby shanty and observed a tremendous beanstalk that had risen all the way from the ground up to the magnificent, azure sky.

'It looks like the shady jerk-off I met yesterday was actually telling the truth about the magic beans!' Jack thought. 'Oh well; I guess that's the end of poor old Milky White. Say, that's what I also call my damned ejaculations!'

Since the colossal beanstalk had grown right past Jack's window, all the boy had to do was climb outside and latch onto the tremendous vine and then clamber-up to the majestic clouds. And so, the intrepid lad initiated his great adventure.

'I gotta' remember to first open the window before I grab onto the beanstalk,' the not-too-bright kid considered. 'If I'm not careful, I could break at least one window a day ascending and descending this extraordinary piece of vegetation.'

So, Jack hastily opened the window, gripped the beanstalk with both hands and then the dimwit closed the window with his right palm and fingers. The explorer shinnied and shinnied up the abnormal plant until the ascender arrived at the cloudy blue sky. Jack found a wide cumulus road that had somehow fluffily accumulated there, so the nutcase walked along the wide cottony path, not realizing that he might accidentally plummet down to earth at any time. Soon the dunce reached a gigantic house and was greeted by a huge woman that could have been an ogre herself if she had a penis and a set of testicles between her legs instead of a pair of disgusting sagging tits attached to her massive chest.

"Good morning Mrs. Whoever the hell you are," Jack audaciously articulated without a trace of normal courtesy. "Could I have some breakfast? I haven't eaten in eighteen long hours so I would like to break my fast."

"So, my young illustrious, mischievous trespasser, it's breakfast that you want!" the mammoth Amazon answered. "I assure that you'll be breakfast yourself if ya' don't swiftly get your ass off of this private property at once. The last boy up here disguised himself' as a tax collector and wound-up chopped-up in my husband's bowl of stew. My spouse Stuart is indeed a formidable ogre, and there's not a thing up here that my hubby savors more than little dismembered English boys mixed into his stew, especially when my' husband's stewed after drinking two hundred gallons of potent red wine."

"Don't give me your standard line of bullshit!" Jack haughtily squawked. "Your husband obviously discriminates against English boys when the big punk thinks he's *eatin'* young lads from *Eton*! What an absolute, total disgrace! And if that's the damned case, I'd rather be dead and eaten than have to starve to death before being eaten. Do ya' get the message I'm sayin', ya' nasty old dragon-faced bitch?"

"Well, if that's your attitude, come into my kitchen and I'll give you some putrid goat's milk, a stale slice of bread I've made into junk toast and a big chunk of rancid cheese so that when you fart, my greedy husband will be able to easily discover your cheesy hiding place and then squeeze the livin' shit out of your foul intestines with his brawny bare hands!"

When Jack was just finishing about half of his not-so-exotic feast, the obnoxious fool heard a very loud and disconcerting "Thump, thump, thump!" and felt the enormous home's floor and walls vibrate and tremble as if an unprecedented skyquake were in progress.

"Is the moon crashing into the earth's atmosphere?" Jack shrieked in horror. "What the fuck's goin' on out there?"

"Holy stromboli!" the warty-faced, immense, alarmed bitch hollered. "It's my old man come home to have his meal. Quick Junior Asshole; hop into the oven where you can safely hide."

"Do ya' think I'm a mini-brained dunce?" Jack vehemently protested. "I might just as well hop into a meatgrinder or into a steaming scalding cauldron! I might've flunked nursery school thrice, but I'm nobody's fool when it fuckin' comes to recognizin' danger!"

"Do ya' have a better fuckin' idea?" the twenty-foot-tall, vitriolic bitch staunchly argued. "Hop into the oven, and I guarantee you that you'll feel home on the range."

Jack caught a glimpse of the fifty-foot-tall giant approaching just as the bellicose ogre's wife swiftly closed the oven door. The gargantuan husband had three calves strung around both of his calves, which added up to six about-to-be slaughtered baby cows all together. The awesome Goliath unhooked the squealing animals, cruelly smashed their heads-down against the mammoth table (until each had been knocked unconscious) and then strongly bellowed, "Here Martha Stuartess; broil me some delicious meat for my breakfast. How come we never eat lunch or dinner in this damned story? Hey, what's that odd smellin' odor I'm detectin' with my nostrils?

Fee-fi-fo-fum,
I smell the perspiration of an Englishman,
Fingers, toes, ankles, thumb,
It's not a man, but a British boy' scum,
Be he alive, or be he dead,
I'll soon eat his friggin' head inside my bread!"

"You must be dreaming my dear!" the wife unconvincingly replied. "Or perhaps you smell the remains of the little boy from Liverpool you had eagerly devoured yesterday. Now please go wash and tidy-up, and don't forget to brush your teeth because your mouth and throat smell like a Birmingham garbage dump. I've left out a thousand-gallon bottle of rubbing alcohol for you to gargle with," the nervous wife communicated. "And by the time you freshen-up and take your daily morning shit, your delectable breakfast will be ready and waiting for you on the table."

So, the monstrous ogre paced-off to the only downstairs' lavatory where he kept water in the closet. Then the wife opened the oven door and instructed her trembling captive, "Wait in here you little scamp until he's asleep! He always dozes-off right after consuming a satisfying breakfast."

"Don't ya' have another death chamber I could hide in?" Jack strenuously objected. "Do ya' have a razor blade I could leap onto and slice myself' in two, balls and all? Such an imaginative suicide would be quick-but-messy, but cleaning-up the messy part would be *your* damned problem!"

The suspicious giant returned from his bathroom activities, and Jack noticed through a crack in the oven wall that the behemoth had stepped over to a massive chest and removed several bags of gold. Of course, Jack just assumed the sacks were bags of gold because the imbecile couldn't see inside them, and the cloth objects certainly weren't transparent.

Then the titanic homeowner counted his numerous shiny coins until his head began to nod and his mouth started yawning, and at that particular moment, Jack thought that *he* was going to be sucked right out of the oven by the strong vacuum caused by the behemoth's inhaling. And soon thereafter, the immense sky resident began sleeping until the walls shook and expanded and contracted with every rhythmic exhalation and inspiration.

Next, frightened Jack slid past the now partially opened oven door and deftly leaped-down onto the wood-planked floor. And when the fearful interloper came to the ogre's foot, the youth stooped-down and picked-up a fifty-pound bag of gold coins, his behavior following a genetically transmitted social trait because the kid's ancestors on both sides of his family were notorious bandits, burglars, purloiners, thieves and robbers. The anxious boy briskly dashed out of the enormous dwelling with his precious plunder tucked under his left armpit; his bold actions transpiring right before the old antagonistic Bitch returned from taking a hefty shit herself.

When the boy again arrived at the beanstalk's summit, the young robber tossed-down his heavy bag of gold, hoping that it would land on his mother's noggin so that he could enjoy the new-found wealth all to his greedy self. And then the naughty lad laboriously climbed-down for a full half hour, and when his exhausting descent finally reached his bedroom window, the larcenist methodically rolled himself into his room, forgetfully breaking the closed glass pane in the process.

"Well Mother," Jack stated upon entering the shack's kitchen, "wasn't I correct about the fantastic beans? The things were really magical, and I'm glad I hadn't eaten them. Holy shit! I could've been killed and could've died instantly from internal bleeding when that son-of-a-bitchin' beanstalk would've begun to wildly sprout inside my tender stomach."

So then, Jack and his now-grateful mother happily lived-off of the stolen bag of gold for around a year, but when the last coin had been spent on vegetables and dildos, the avaricious boy determined that he should ascend the awesome beanstalk a second time and rob the giant again. On the one-year anniversary of his first grand larceny, Jack daringly clambered-up the impressive beanstalk (which incidentally no one else in the village ever noticed, marveled at, or cared or gave a peasant's shit about) until the juvenile delinquent again located the cloudy white path, and on this second jaunt, Jack nonchalantly approached the giant's monument-sized abode.

The ogre's grotesque-looking wife was busy sweeping the front doorstep when Jack again solicited her with another dose of his insincere, inane, juvenile bullshit. "Good morning Mrs. Stewartess!" the trespasser began rather brazenly. "Could you possibly be inclined to give me something good to eat?"

"Hit the road Jack!" the despicable, humungous, bitchy bitch coincidentally yelled. "My husband does not take kindly to impudent, over-curious English boys investigatin' around. But I must say you do look awfully familiar! I do believe the last time you had visited us my lax husband reported one of his bags of gold missing," the erratic wife related. "He was so pissed-off that the ignoramus filled the entire fifty-foot-deep cesspool while taking an hour-long leak!"

"That's really weird lady!" Jack audaciously replied. "Your husband sounds like a real pisser. Perhaps I can clarify matters if ya' cordially invite me in for a little chow." And then the boy ruminated, 'Perhaps I should change my name from Jack to Rob!'

The big bitch was so interested in Jack's valiant words and in his confident, egotistical demeanor that the Amazon invited him inside to enjoy and savor a scrumptious meal. But the young visitor had hardly started swallowing his hot soup when his ears discerned a most frightening "Thump, thump, thump!" So according to past practice, Jack once again obediently concealed his tender body inside the wife's drafty oven.

The next events were a rerun of what the predictable giant had done before. The inimitable Stuart Stewartess sat-down, scratched his testicles and then killed and ravenously ate his booty of six calves that had previously been strapped to his leather boots. And then the monstrous hulk boomed, "Wife; fetch the hen that lays the golden eggs!" as if Mrs. Martha Stewartess was a faithful hound-dog commanded to retrieve a simple stick. And when the especially talented chicken was brought into the kitchen, the powerful human anomaly yelled-out "Lay!" sounding a lot like ear-shattering verbal thunder. And after the intimidated hen produced a beautiful golden egg, the appreciative giant nodded his head in approval a dozen times and then dozed-off into dreamland.

Jack immediately sprang-up and dashed to the giant's chair, and much to the astonishment of Mrs. Stewartess, the inhospitable thief snatched-up the unique hen, and before one could say Jack Samuel Richard Philip George Jeffrey David Stephen Robinson, the junior felon was fleeing out of the front door and soon sprinting down the clouded road with the cackling hen in his grasp.

"Wife!" the awakened giant vociferated. "Where is my ordinary-looking hen that lays the lustrous golden eggs?"

"I had placed the magic hen at your feet just before you began your daily napping!" the wife casually answered from the adjoining room. "Maybe you ate it by accident in your sleep, thinking that the hen was a savory calf. Have you ever considered Transcendental Meditation as a viable therapy for your failing memory?"

In the meantime, Jack frantically dashed to the now-familiar beanstalk and carefully-but-speedily exited the sky path and was soon headed in the direction of good old terra-firma. Upon entering his shack's front door, the pilferer showed his new possession to his astounded mother, and much to her astonishment, every time the lad yelled-out the word' "Lay!" the ordinary-looking chicken produced a shiny golden egg, even though everyone from here to Jupiter is aware that a hen only lays one egg per day.

The productive hen supplied enough eggs for Jack and his mother to acquire all new furniture and kitchen appliances for their modest domicile, and soon the residents both forgot all about how wonderfully resourceful Milky White really had been. Then one morning while being bored (as most rich kids usually are), Jack decided that his life needed to experience another exciting exploit. 'I think I'll return to my old *bean-stalking grounds* and risk my fabulous luck one more time! Who the hell knows what other marvelous things the belligerent ogre keeps in his house besides gold coins, a very skilled chicken and a repulsive-looking wife that could scare the shit out of a colony of adult gorillas?'

The next morning, Jack followed his inclination and again ascended the wonderfully sturdy beanstalk. But the boy was clever to bypass the giant's wife when she stepped outside to fetch a pail of water instead of searching for another highly talented hen to amuse her obnoxious, demanding husband. The brave youth hid behind some tall bushes, and when the colossal, bulky wench had her back to him, the bold lad sneaked into the house and then stealthily hid in the pantry. Soon, Jack's ears detected the familiar "Thump, thump, thump!" that signaled the approach of the incomparable giant, who was being accompanied by Mrs. Stewartess. The horrible ogre addressed his subordinate wife by saying:

> "Ho-ho-ho! Fi-fi-fo-fum,
> I smell the flesh of an Englishman,
> By tit, by testicle and by prized gonad,
> This English cad smells like a British lad,
> Little puppy dog, tiny pussy cat, the typical runt,
> This lousy English punk smells worse than your cunt."

Although quite offended, the giant's tolerant wife feared that her husband's wrath might be next directed toward her, so she deftly switched the focus of her spouse's vehemence to a more favorable subject. "I believe the little rogue was hiding in the oven the last time when he stole the magic hen from you!" the wife claimed. "He had left a wet, snotty handkerchief in there just before your gifted chicken was maliciously purloined."

The immense ogre was terribly disappointed upon inspecting the oven's vacant interior. And then in an effort to prevent the gruesome monster from flogging the eggs out of her ovaries, the fearful wife invented some rather credible fiction.

"Husband, I believe that the Leatherhead boy you had sampled for breakfast was the one that your excellent olfactory nerves still smell," the huge, towering wife imaginatively fibbed. "Your keen nasal and mouth taste buds are simply detecting lingering residue from the boy's already eaten body. That problem generally comes with the territory of you being a dedicated cannibal."

And so, the prodigious giant sat-down at his humungous table, scratched his psoriasis infected crotch seventeen times and uttered, "Well Martha, I could've sworn I smelled a boy's sweaty skin along with also his dirty asshole." And then the colossus stood and opened the cupboard to examine its burgeoning contents, but fortunately for Jack's sake, the gargantuan investigator failed to remember to search in the pantry.

Feeling frustrated and depressed, the fatigued ogre called for his enslaved wife to feed him his standard high-protein breakfast, and after the husband swallowed-down three more cooked calves, the husband insisted that Martha Stuartess fetch for him his Golden Harp, which also sang opera besides playing (music) with itself.

And within a half-hour after the melodious music had commenced, the master fell *fast* asleep, which actually here means *slowly* into a deep-sleep. And when the subservient wife left the room to take her morning crap in the outhouse (she preferred an outhouse to the giant's abominable-stinking bathroom sanctuary), Jack leaped out of the pantry, confiscated the Golden Harp, but the worried, inanimate instrument hysterically cried-out, "Master! Master! Save me from this delinquent, dysfunctional, junior jerk-off!"

The callow felon bolted left and dodged right, hurrying as fast as his scrawny legs could, but the visiting thief's strategy proved to be ignorant because Jack had to remain on the twenty-foot-wide, white cottony road all the way to the infamous beanstalk, still a distant three hundred (parking) meters down the gray lane. And then the pursuing monster witnessed the young desperado disappear down into one of the large clouds where an arrowed sign read: "Porno' Shop: Giants Only" had deliberately been planted by the ogre's whoring wife (who had been secretly having an affair with another little, horny oven boy from earth).

"Help me Master! Save me from this belligerent little thug!" the Golden Harp frenetically cried-out. "This little perverted rogue is more than a little perverted, and the lunatic creep wants to fondle my G-string!"

The incensed giant awkwardly maneuvered himself down from the beanstalk's summit, and upon peering-downward toward earth, his covetous eyes perceived his screaming Harp being held in the boy's clutches. But the rascal was by then only several hundred feet above the ground when Jack neurotically hollered, "Mother! Mother! Get me my axe, you old battle-axe!"

And the escaper's diligent mother, who had been impatiently waiting for the anticipated "axe command" for hours, came rushing with the dangerous cutting tool in hand, and when she arrived at the beanstalk's base, the woman looked upward with her mouth agape as if she were about to administer a super-blow-job to the swiftly descending ogre.

Jack jumped the last five feet to the ground with not a moment to 'spare', or even a propitious moment to make an incredible bowling strike. The boy quickly handed the harping Harp to his stunned Mother, pulled the axe from her clutches and began industriously chopping away at the beanstalk as if he himself' were a European Paul Bunyan. The vertical vegetation shook and vibrated from the first ten blows because it was an inferior quality plant despite the fact that it had been both magical and stupendous in size.

After two-dozen walloping hacks, the beanstalk finally severed, and its unbelievable form toppled and then collapsed to the ground, generating a tumultuous thud. The ogre also fell off the plummeting vine, and soon landed on his head, breaking his crown even though he had never been a king and had never aspired to be one.

Jack then enthusiastically presented the paranoid singing harp to his now-enthralled mother, and the wondrous instrument shrieked-out: "Fuck this goddamned shit! I'm not singing one fuckin' note for either of you two retards!"

And in the end, Jack and his proud Mother became very rich from selling the golden eggs from the phenomenal plain-looking chicken and by touring all of England (including Leatherhead) and exhibiting the amazing "Bitching and Foul-mouthed Harp" to applauding crowds at circus sideshow venues. People with nothing better to do gladly paid a pound apiece to listen to the Golden Harp's incessant cursing and continuous condemnations, which made the audience members feel good about their own major and minor aggravations in their own miserable, mediocre lives.

"Hansel and Gretel Dumkoff"

Hansel and Gretel lived in a small hut near Germany's mammoth Black Forest with their parents Gunther and Gertrude Dumkoff. The poor Dumkoffs resided in a deep, deep forest in a deep, deep valley, and the frivolous, adult assholes were always in deep, deep debt when they weren't in deep, deep trouble. Gunther was a woodchopper but never had the courage to give mean old Gertrude the axe. The wife despised Hansel and Gretel because they were products of Gunther's first marriage to Ingrid, who had gratefully died from complications of a double-breech birth.

The times were very hard for the hardheaded, bad-luck Dumkoffs. The price of wood had astronomically skyrocketed, and even toothpicks cost more than chickens, tampons or condoms in the raucous village marketplace. Many people all over Germany were starving and couldn't even afford to drink beer or eat stale hard pretzels at the annual Munich Octoberfests, let alone afford the luxury of quality chopped wood. The Dumkoffs were no exception to those very difficult times that especially brought adversity to Black Forest native residents and especially to transient illegal aliens.

"Our government is so poor that it can't provide welfare for people like us, even if the politicians in Berlin were smart enough to invent welfare," Gunther complained one rainy evening to Gertrude. "Why can't we Dumkoffs live in Ireland where the fortunate folks there only have occasional potato famines and plagues?"

"And there are no orphanages or kiddy insane asylums here in Germany to put our bratty children Hansel and Gretel in," Gertrude woefully sympathized. "And environmentalists are always breaking *your* stones about you destroying the natural environment. Gunther, why don't you simply change professions, join the opposition and become a bossy powerful environmentalist?"

"Let's get serious!" the aggravated husband admonished his generally sarcastic and abrasive-tongued, faultfinding wife. "I fear for the four of us. All of our potatoes are gone from the kitchen shelf, even though we don't live anywhere near fuckin' Ireland. And all of our tasteless cabbage has been consumed or stolen by forest marauders. And we destitute Dumkoffs just have sufficient rye to make maybe three more loaves of bread before we starve to death. Why couldn't we be born in another damned century? Maybe we can start a quasi-religious cult, make a secret pact and end it all by participating in a mass suicide."

"The asshole children are putting a definite strain on the family resources," Gertrude bitched although she never did a blessed thing all day or ever lifted a finger to earn a copper coin. "I'm too lazy and my well's too dry to even do a little prostitution on the side. I suggest that we take Hansel and Gretel deep into the deep, deep forest and lose them so that the little juvenile delinquents will have to fend for themselves."

"Gertrude, I just thought of something relevant. Everybody in Germany gets laid tomorrow!"

"Why is that?" the wife curiously asked.

"Because tomorrow is fuckin' Wednesday!"

But Gunther truly loved his snotty, defiant kids, even though the sadist would beat the shit out of them every night after getting drunk guzzling-down a pitcher of sour homemade beer. But since the father's beer supply had become exhausted from a lack of barley and hops, the child abuser could no longer abuse his kids after excessively drinking his nightly brew, obviously because he had run out of nightly brew.

"Gertrude, do you realize what your fat ugly lips have often suggested?" the husband instinctively challenged. "I could never have the heart to leave Hansel and Gretel in the forest without first drinking a full case of queer beer. I would prefer eating cement and shitting concrete rather than abandoning my frequently molested son and daughter deep, deep in the mysterious Black Forest."

"If you don't agree to abandon the little twerps in the darkest part of the deep, deep forest," Gertrude hypothesized and stated, "then we'll all have to go hungry and watch each other dying from starvation, just like the hungry people in Hungary are doing. Honestly Gunther; I wish that my damned pussy wasn't so dried-up, or else I would try making black market money whoring around the Munich suburbs and putting-out at the all-year-long Octoberfests."

Finally, the stubborn, dominant stepmother's will prevailed, and old Gunther Dumkoff conceded to honor Gertrude's unreasonable demand pertaining to abandoning *his* two obnoxious offspring. "May the angels protect the children from harm and foreign sodomy," the husband reluctantly assented. "On second thought Gertrude, the angels might themselves need adequate protection from our fucked-up, irascible kids!"

Hansel and Gretel had stayed-up all that night from hunger pangs, and the pair of discipline problems listened with intense interest to their parents' loud babbling and scheming in the adjoining room. The nosy brats were lying in their trundle beds inside their tiny room, which was so small that even the field mice and the cockroaches stayed away from it. The sister began whimpering and then crying, so Hansel left his flea-ridden bed and massaged Gretel's petite nipples to comfort her.

"Don't worry little sister," Hansel whispered in a soothing tone of voice. "Now let's see if you have any new fuzz growing around your nifty tiny crack."

"Why do you keep all of those white pebbles in your pants' pockets?" the mentally disturbed and emotionally apprehensive sister asked. "Do you plan for us to stone mother and father once they take us into the woods? Why don't we just stone them now inside the house so that we don't have to go through an entire saga attempting to survive out in the cold dark woods? Hansel," the concerned sister insisted. "I say let's stone our retarded parents right now and eliminate the possibility of us getting lost deep in the deep, deep Black Forest!"

"Gretel, I just like collecting pebbles," Hansel defensively uttered, "and the stones in my pants' pockets are too small without a slingshot to do any damage to our worthless father and stepmother. Ooh, ooh! I think a feel some new fuzz between your legs. Here Gretel. I'll now let you touch and fondle my private junk, and that little thrill will make *you* feel much better!"

When dawn broke over the remote valley (the valley was so remote that the sun had trouble finding it), the harsh stepmother violently woke-up the repulsive children. "Get up, you lazy, unproductive good-for-nothing dependents!" Gertrude screamed while grabbing and shaking each child separately. "We're going-off into the forest to help your father gather wood and to see if we could find any nourishing termites or lice to eat. Now, here are two pieces of bread for you two delinquents to munch on," Gertrude indicated. "Save your slices until noon because we might catch some yummy cockroaches so that you two asinine kids can improvise and make yourselves delicious sandwiches."

Since Hansel's pants' pockets were filled with stones, which when rattling-around nearly broke *his* tiny stones, Gretel carried both pieces of bread in what she imagined to be her "ape-run" (apron). Gertrude also toted a pitcher of swamp water, and Gunther actually had his axe tilted against his shoulder as if he was an intrepid soldier marching into battle. But then Hansel stood still, looked back at the family hut and wished that it were a small, edible pizza hut that the brother could chew and swallow.

"Move along Hansel!" Gertrude imperatively ordered. "Don't be so damned sentimental about leaving your disgusting, rat-infested home. Why else would you be phlegmatically loitering behind?"

"I'm looking at my little white pussy up on the roof, and I'm waving goodbye to her," the boy answered his stepmother.

"You're too young to be thinking about pussy," the old bitch criticized. "And in fact, your unfaithful father is too old to be thinking about pussy, too!"

"Hansel," Gunther stated in a much milder tone than his wife had been exhibiting, "that mirage only the reflection of the morning sun off of the chimney you're seeing. And why are you awkwardly bringing along all of those heavy stones in your pockets? You might have pebbles in your tawdry pants, but I think you also have rocks in your head! Sorry son, but I just felt a need to break your stones!"

'If the little jerk-off had half a brain,' Gertrude conjectured, 'he would drop the stones along the shady forest path and eventually find his way back to the shanty. But luckily for Gunther and me, Hansel has the intelligence of a moronic, jungle chimpanzee with three massive brain tumors.'

After three grueling hours of walking deeper into the deep, deep forest, the children became quite fatigued from their arduous ordeal. "Okay kiddies," the heartless stepmother sternly commanded. "Sit-down on those rocks over there while I gather the wood he'll be chopping. And please take a long nap if you two degenerates feel sleepy. Maybe if you're both nice and still," Gertrude sarcastically declared, "a family of bears will come by and devour the two of you repulsive pain-in-the-asses so that you'll be able to escape your mortal existence upon this horrible planet."

Hansel and Gretel sat on the assigned rocks and ravenously gobbled-down their moldy bread before their parents could return with ants, termites or other disgusting crawling insects for the siblings to creatively put into their already horrible sandwiches. The children soon believed that their ears perceived their father's axe penetrating trees in the distance, but what they falsely conceived as the felling of timber was actually a virile man vigorously pumping the poop out of his neighbor's accommodating wife a mere two hundred feet away.

And soon the brother and sister became quite drowsy from their long forest trek, so the brats laid their fatigued bodies-down on the moss and dried leaves and got algae and fungus all over themselves when the kiddies tossed, turned and rolled around the area slime in their sleep. When the ornery pair finally awoke from their prolonged slumbers, the stars were shining in the night sky and a new moon signaled almost total darkness throughout the Black Forest (which was even and always black in the damned daytime).

"Don't cry little sister!" Hansel advised his distraught sibling. "You'll feel much better once I fondle and caress your tiny nipples and rub your little, fuzzy love tunnel, which is now a little fuzzy."

"That particular sensation would feel much better if your tiny fingers were longer and thicker!" the sister critically remarked. "It's too bad Hansel you haven't achieved your first erection yet! And with you being nervous about being left stranded here in the forest," the naughty girl added, "your dingle will never get hard under these bizarre abnormal circumstances! And if our bodies begin turning purple, we'll then know for sure that we've been marooned."

At dawn, the children managed by chance reach their family home, which was quite extraordinary because the two idiots thought they had been traveling in the opposite direction in a dedicated effort to "run away from home". When Gertrude observed the wandering duo standing in the middle of the kitchen's dirt floor, the normally antagonistic stepmother was astonished and rather shocked at viewing the unexpected spectacle.

"Why there you are, you insolent, disobedient children!" the stepmother yelled while exposing her hyperactive tonsils. "Where have you two little shitheads been hiding all this time? Your father and I were at wits end searching the hinterland for the both of you, looking all over creation, and also then worrying about your fates! We were even contemplating that you two dumb-shit Dumkoffs were foolishly considering running-away from our nice, tidy, respectable home."

"We were playing doctor in the woods!" Gretel truthfully stated. "Hansel was pretending to be a world-famous gynecologist, and I was role-playing being a prostrate prostate specialist. Stepmother, you wouldn't believe how hairy his smelly asshole is!"

Gertrude wasn't much pleased or impressed with the aspiring future physicians' testimonies, but on the contrary, Gunther Dumkoff tearfully welcomed his children back with open arms.

"Father, why are you weeping so?" Gretel curiously asked. "Have you learned that you have testicular or prostate cancer?"

"No, my dear Gretel," the forest pop sobbed while repetitiously gesticulating to his second wife with his middle finger. "I now realize that I must work even harder to responsibly feed four mouths instead of just two."

The following several weeks, things seemed to be getting better for the bad-luck Dumkoff family. Gunther was able to earn some money by chopping wood and then building a "Cabin of Prostitution" for a few local sluts down near the village grist mill located ten miles to the east, but then after getting drunk, abusing his children and sending them off to bed, Hansel and Gretel overheard from *their* tiny room their dysfunctional parents conspiring once again.

"I tell you Gertrude," the inebriated husband prefaced, "our money is again dwindling-down to nothing. And since the well in your smelly love garden is now all dried-up, you cannot possibly work and earn money at the new Cabin of Prostitution participating as a filthy slut. But the quixotic owners have informed me that they do have a vacancy for an experienced blowjob specialist."

"Nonsense!" the wife fired-back without any hesitation. "We're down to a single loaf of bread, so *that* drastic circumstance means we're again going to have to abandon Hansel and Gretel inside the deep, deep woods. We can't sell them to anyone because nobody in this forsaken forest has any damned money to squander on brassy, out-of-control kids. I wish that a severe great depression would come along here in southern Germany so that things could get better!"

"But I love and adore my children when I don't get drunk," Gunther maintained, "and since I no longer have coins to buy lousy sour beer or visit the new Cabin of Prostitution, I now find that I'm loving Hansel and Gretel even more than I did before; in fact; much more than I care for you, you washed-up, wrinkled, bossy old bimbo!"

"Curb your arrogant tongue!" jealous Gertrude abruptly warned. "Or else I'll tie you to a chair and then burn the damned hut down with you and the children in it. But then I figure why should I live in misery while you, Hansel and Gretel have happily escaped into the hereafter?" Gunther's second wife then snarled and shouted. "Why should I punish myself by killing you? Shit! Life is so goddamned unfair!"

The next day, everything happened almost exactly as it had on the first family excursion deep into the deep, deep dark forest. But again, Hansel deliberately lagged behind, mostly because the wayward punk had been a worthless laggard and a foolish, impractical, idle dreamer his entire life.

"Hansel, why are you again straggling behind?" Gertrude immediately chastised her stepson. "Don't tell me you're thinking about a little pussy again?"

"No, my warty-faced stepmother," the supersensitive lad instantly responded. "I'm now waving to my pet dove sitting up on the roof, and the bird's singing a sorrowful goodbye to me."

"You're without a doubt a ridiculous, idiotic dreamer!" Gertrude rebuked. "You're more worried about your bird than your horny father cares about *his*! What your eyes see is simply the sun shining off the stone chimney and nothing more!" Gertrude nastily insisted. "Only fools, simpletons and an occasional visionary see things as they are not!

And you, young fellow must be a real dolt believing that cats and doves are your personal friends. What sheer fucked-up fantasy your fucked-up mind imagines! You Hansel might call your mental illness 'imagination', but we adulterous adult Dumkoffs are above such a ludicrous wasting of time and energy."

Hansel was so distressed at being reprimanded that instead of eating his crusty bread, the loafer broke-off pieces and left them at thousand-yard intervals to mark the trail. However, if the boy were a trifle more intelligent, he would have used the four-dozen white pebbles in his pockets as landmarks along the maze of trails that intersected and meandered throughout the deep, deep forest. All in all, Hansel was doing a rather crummy job walking along and casually discarding his crummy breadcrumbs.

On that lengthy trek, Gertrude and Gunther led the children even further into the deep, deep forest than the scheming parents had the time before, hoping that some wild hungry animal would pounce on the kids and devour every morsel of the unbearable egotistical tykes. At noon, Gretel generously shared her bread with Hansel, even though both children were not well 'bred' to begin with. Then the lazy, indolent kids went-off to sleep because all they ever did with their lives was eat, sleep, crap, defy their criminal-minded parents and occasionally attempt performing the art of masturbation individually or on each other.

When the siblings finally awoke from their siestas (even though the aberrant kids were in Germany and not Spain), the two nutcases realized that they had again been deserted inside the dark forest and that nightfall had arrived all over that fucked-up part of Germany. Hansel revealed to his sister that he had cleverly dropped breadcrumbs all along the trail so that *they* could find their way back home, but after they frantically searched for the first several crumbs that the brother had discarded, the duo soon realized that famished birds had descended from the trees and had eaten the markers that had been designated for *their* safe arrival back to Gunther's nondescript hut.

"Little birds ate-up all of the crumbs!" Hansel regretfully theorized and stated. "And there's not a morsel left for us to chew."

"If you could train *your* little bird to do the same thing and eat crumbs," Gretel speculated and articulated, "then we could make more money at a carnival freak show than the well-to-do owners of the Cabin of Prostitution do operating their prosperous new business."

The disconsolate, fucked-up children ambled aimlessly all night, and the entire next day the nomadic pair were monotonously walking in virtual forest circles around their point of origin. The itinerant boy and girl only managed to discover some tart berries to swallow-down after tripping over a termite-infested log along the narrow, dark trail. And so, lacking initiative and determination, the lost trekkers-plopped-down upon the slimy moss and went to sleep, dreaming about what it might be like to have and to implement mental qualities such as ambition and motivation.

On the third morning of frustration, the starving, incompetent kids futilely penetrated deeper into the deep, deep forest. The wanderers felt rather diminutive among the towering tree canopies, and the two were completely enveloped in the dense underbrush, which happened to rival the density of their minuscule brains. Then Hansel noticed a little white bird sitting in a tree that, from a distance, resembled his own little white bird. Soon, the creature spread its wings and soared over their heads seemingly saying, "Pitiful lost assholes! Follow me!"

The brother and sister found inspiration in the little white bird's odd behavior, so the undynamic duo scampered after the erratically flying creature until the twosome arrived at a forest cul-de-sac where their pupils perceived a strange-looking cottage that was surrounded by fragrant flowers even though winter had been setting-in and encroaching upon *that* fucked-up area of Germany.

"That's the prettiest damned house I'm ever seen!" Gretel gasped. "I make that observation even though I've only ever seen five or six other houses in my entire rather-restricted life!"

"The home looks like it's good enough to eat!" Hansel marveled and mentioned. "Perhaps it's only an evil illusion haunting our distressed minds, tempting our hungry eyes and giving my fadorkenbender a noteworthy erection."

Upon examining the delectable-looking dwelling, the curious trespassers immediately comprehended that the cottage's walls were indeed made of gingerbread, its roof was constructed of chocolate cake and its chimney was composed of solid homemade pudding and not of stinky 'cottage' cheese as one might suspect. The unique structure was trimmed and adorned with assorted tantalizing cookies, candy, popcorn and pretzels, and its glittering windowpanes consisted of pure translucent sugar.

Forgetting all about the dangers of high cholesterol and fattening food calories, the encroaching children impetuously honored their primitive survival instincts and began biting into and digesting gingerbread mouthfuls as if the interlopers were scavenging vultures attacking a dead animal's carcass.

76

"I don't give a shit if I get diabetes, diarrhea or the gout!" Hansel ecstatically hooted. "And if my stomach aches and if I suddenly feel nauseous, all the damned better! Long live my digestive tract"

All of a sudden, a flowery, sweet, melodic voice floating-out from the cottage's interior vibrated through the air.

> "Nibble, nibble, munch, chew, knotage,
> Who the hell's digesting *my* sweet cottage?
> I hope your foul intestines ache till you moan,
> Asshole kids, leave my confections alone!"

And then Hansel and Gretel both shared the exact same thoughts and remarkably answered the anonymous voice back in unison:

> "The sound you hear is only a breeze,
> Simply blowing its breath through the trees,
> And so, you' old nasty, grotesque-sounding bitch,
> Go fly your damned broom into the nearest ditch!"

After the bitchy, wrinkle-faced woman heard those defiant words being uttered, the cottage front door was magically flung open. In seconds, out pranced a bent-over old hag who looked like she belonged in either a geriatrics convalescent home or in the nearest cemetery grave. Hansel stopped gnawing-away at his confiscated chocolate cookie, and Gretel ceased her teeth crunching on the delicious candy-cane that she had just raised to her mouth.

The trespassing children gazed in wonder at the old hag, who possessed a long sharp snout, a whiskered chin, wrinkles and warts all over her hideous-looking face, despicable hands and a bizarre-looking body. The elderly, ruby-eyed bitch also sported three yellowish-brown teeth, two uppers and one below, displaying a terrible-in-appearance mouth analogous to that of a jack-o-lantern.

When the old bag hag noticed that her two frightened guests were about to sprint-away into the forest, the spellbinder addressed them in a phony, sugary, enticing tone of voice. "Aye, my little ones! My petite angels; come back so that I may tantalize you with candy and then cradle and wildly fondle and caress your personals! Come inside my delicious house and stay a while with me! I'm lonely and will give you abundant goodies until you' punk assholes puke your guts out. All I need now are two gullible children to love and to occasionally molest at my discretion!"

"Who do you think you're shitting?" Hansel vehemently protested. "Do you think you're talking to Jack and Jacqueline Beanstalk? We both weren't born yesterday, ya' know, ya' old wily bitch!"

"Come inside and I'll show you some drawings of naked men and horny women," the witch promised in what constituted a definite sugarcoated verbalization. "Then you can both eat sweets and cake before showing me your smooth, soft, angelic bodies. I might even be inclined to make a real sacrifice and take a damned shower with you two dimwits, and if my faulty memory serves me correctly, I believe it will be my first damned crotch washing in over a century!"

While the visiting children were gobbling-down all sorts of sweet treats, the old conniving witch prepared two beds for the pair to sleep in because *she* naturally realized that the lethargic kids only knew how to eat, snooze, shit and piss just like other simple-minded kiddies and ordinary animals chew, doze, crap and whiz. And after fluffing-up the beds' downy pillows, the old hussy said to the naïve kiddies, "Here you are my little guests, a soft comfortable nest for both of you fragile, delicate prepubescent nincompoops! Tumble in and snore away to your hearts' content, but make sure that your lily-white asses are clean because I deplore having brown shit-stains blemishing my nice satin sheets!"

As soon as the Dumkoff' kids were sound asleep, the "Old Bitch" stood above their cherub-like anatomies and lowly mumbled while egregiously rubbing her greedy hands together, "These two tender critters are mine; exclusively all mine, ha, ha, ha!"

Naturally, the "Old Bitch" was not half as decent as she artificially pretended to be, and the wonderful gingerbread house she had deviously constructed to lure wayward children was very similar to a spider's web that entrapped non-suspecting flying insects. And although the evil-minded Hag could hardly see out of her dastardly-looking ruby eyes, the witch could smell a fart ten miles away with her very long nose, which was twice as long as the average male erection. And so, while rambling Hansel and Gretel were wandering-around lost inside the huge forest that very morning, the Old Bitch knew of their presence since she had smelled their dwarfish asses incessantly passing odorous intestinal gases. "Ha, ha, ha, my juicy morsels!" the female sorcerer uttered to herself as the ugly enchantress stood-over and admired her most recent, prized acquisitions.

And then with an absence of ceremony or monologue, the crazed, whiskered woman pulled Hansel out of bed and tugged the vulnerable lad outside where the victim was then locked inside the malicious witch's goose-coop. And next, the demented Old Bitch entered her gingerbread home (which she couldn't herself' eat because she was allergic to sweets and because she was exclusively carnivorous) and shook Gretel so hard that the poor girl's brains rattled inside her dense cranium. "Wake up you Dumkoff!" the Bitch coincidentally and accurately yelled. "Cook some food for your shit-faced brother so that he may soon fatten-up. Then take the high-carb' stew out to the goose-coop where you can take a brief *gander* of your numbskull brother. And stop you're goddamned shrieking this very second! Get kindly your lazy legs synchronized and fulfill my urgent command!"

Each day Gretel had to prepare big kettles of fattening food for Hansel to consume since the stupid "Old Witch Bitch" didn't understand that the candy treats of the gingerbread house would put additional weight on the boy more readily than Gretel's lousy meals would. And logically, Hansel would stuff himself' silly with cake and with sugary carbohydrates more so than the miniature glutton would with what presently is called the "Atkins Diet".

Every day the old Hag would stray-out to the dilapidated goose-coop and sternly demand, "Hansel, let me feel your finger so that I can evaluate how corpulent you're becoming." So when the "Old Witch Bitch" stuck her gnarled hand around the corner inside the dark coop, she would feel Hansel's skinny pecker (which he gladly and voluntarily offered) and wondered why the imbecile was not becoming more portly even though the vernal prisoner had actually blown-up to a colossal three hundred pounds.

When four weeks of the same bullshit had eventually passed, and Hansel's "pathetic finger" had remained drooped and slender and felt like a tiny shrimp, the intolerant, impatient Hag bellowed at poor Gretel, "Now heat-up a big cauldron of water. I don't give a shit if Hansel is chunky or if he is lean and slender. I'm going to enjoy your fucked-up brother for supper one way or the other!"

The Old Bitch then built a blazing fire inside the chimney hearth and boomed, "Gretel; first you'll make some bread from the dough I've meticulously kneaded, which as you might know needed to be kneaded. Now Gretel my dear," the conniving Witch resumed her deceitful rhetoric, "do you believe the oven is warm enough to bake the bread? Please stick your lovely little head inside the inviting stove and make *that* important determination, you beautiful little creature!"

But at the same time as the Witch had suggested the exotic idea to the youthful female Dumkoff, a small white bird landed atop the chimney and chirped-down in a weird-sounding trill that resonated throughout the gingerbread house. "Beware Gretel, if you care, don't dare look the hell in there!"

Gretel adamantly refused to stick her noggin inside the hot oven. She spun around and yelled at the Old Bitch, "Well now, you old scummy geriatric snot; I really don't know how to open the damned oven and satisfactorily fulfill your direction. Why don't you simply show me exactly how I should burn the damned skin and attractive features off my precious face?"

"You dumb, fucked-up, egocentric little girl!" the Old Bitch scowled. "It's as damned easy as sticking your sticky finger up your little slit hole! Just do it like I'm about to show you!"

When the old Hag inserted her head into the hot oven, pretending that her skull was a huge penis ramming into a wet, pink vagina, Gretel mustered-up sufficient courage to shove the Old Bitch's obese ass into the enclosure, and then the alert girl promptly and effectively closed the hinged door. And when the courageous Dumkoff' child bolted-out of the house of horrors, the Old Bitch shrieked from the stove's interior, "What the fuck happened?" But then the wicked enchantress sizzled and fried as if she were Kentucky-fried chicken meat, but no one heard her distressful shrieks, and the Old Bitch quickly incinerated and then disintegrated inside the oven. So, who the hell in this pathetic, apathetic world cares one iota about such a repulsive, selfish, cannibalistic antagonist?

Without wasting a moment's time, Gretel rushed to the 'goose-coop' and when she opened the mechanical lock, her horny, fat brother felt compelled to pinch her ass and then aggressively goosed her again. "You are free Hansel!" Gretel euphorically exclaimed. "We are free!" she impulsively yelled. And then the ecstatic, reunited children overtly demonstrated their gay tendencies by throwing their arms around each other in celebration, symbolically wishing that *the other* sibling were a member of the opposite sex.

The brother and sister's excessive jubilation was soon accompanied by a pleasant whirring sound permeating the air. The vigilant and very helpful white bird could be seen fluttering and flapping its splendid wings overhead. And then a whole flock of rambunctious cardinals (not dressed in red ceremonial robes) appeared above, the contingent of twittering, thrilling, trilling birds landing on the gingerbread house's roof. The feathered assemblage enjoyed the confectionary feast of their lives now that the wicked Old Bitch had been justly cremated inside her very efficient oven.

The congregated merry birds also provided food for their attentive human audience, so Gretel held-out her dirty apron and Hansel pulled-out his scruffy pants at the belt as the delightful, tasty treasures from the gingerbread house obeyed the laws of gravity and collapsed onto the euphoric kids below. The Dumkoff' children now had more than sufficient food to undertake their perilous and fatiguing journey home.

And mixed in with the sweet treats was a surprising assortment of lustrous gems and jewels. The intelligent talking white dove (who had attended the *University of Guttenbird*) then chirped-down to the ecstatic siblings:

> "Thank you for the crummy crumbs of bread,
> Here's some gems for you instead.
> You gave *us* much needed food along the path,
> And now it's time to live well, on our behalf!
> You two idiots have nothing more to fear,
> So now you both should get the hell out of here!"

And while the appreciative birds flew away to some unknown destination, Hansel and Gretel realized that gems and stones meant a lot less to birdbrains than almost worthless cheap breadcrumbs did, for birds could not eat or shit large fantastic diamonds, rubies, emeralds, pearls or sapphires.

"I'm so homesick that I feel like being home sick!" Hansel smartly declared to his illiterate sister. "I want to be sick in bed so that we can play doctor!"

"Me too!" Gretel promptly agreed. "I can't wait to see the expression on father's face when we present him with some marvelous candy and cake. But let's be greedy and realistic and keep the damned gems and jewels all to ourselves!"

And the cooperative little white bird led the children out of the precarious, mysterious, dark woods and in the direction of the ordinary green meadow that was situated right next to their father's humble hut.

Upon reaching home, Hansel and Gretel were quite happy being reunited with their occasionally wonderful father, who relentlessly fondled them both that night and never once slept a minute. But the children were especially delighted to learn that their grumpy, grouchy, bitchy stepmother had permanently left their aging father to earn an immoral living by giving lousy blowjobs to perverted clients at the distant-but-popular Cabin of Prostitution.

"Now that we know that our stepmother is never returning," Hansel gleefully announced, "here you are father. Here are many fabulous jewels Gretel and I had found buried in the Black Forest! Let's now all go to the Octoberfest in Munich so that my sister and I can get drunk and laid for the very first time!"

"Little Ebony Sambo"

Once upon a time somewhere in mysterious India, a young boy named Little Ebony Sambo lived with his parents near the fringe of a vast jungle. Little Ebony Sambo was not called Little Black Sambo because insidious civil rights groups in distant America objected to "racial references" that discriminated against Afro-Americans, even though Little Ebony Sambo lived with his loving family somewhere in India long before there ever existed civil rights groups.

Little Ebony Sambo's mother was Black Mumbo, his huge father was Black Jumbo, his older sister was Black Mambo, and his half-brother was Black Sambadude, so the boy always felt like he was being alienated from the rest of his estranged family by having a peculiar, fucked-up appellation. Why the hell all of the Indian rain forest's family members had different last names remains an unsolved mystery even to this very day!

One day Black Mumbo stitched for Little Ebony Sambo a small Red Coat so that the tiny thug could imitate a *Revolutionary War* British soldier. And his father Black Jumbo visited the local bizarre Bazaar and purchased for Little Ebony Sambo a splendid Green Umbrella and an attractive pair of gay Purple shoes with Scarlet Soles and Scarlet Linings, just in case the young lad would ever have the opportunity to attend and participate in the New Orleans *Mardi Gras* or the Philadelphia *Mummers Parade*. And his Mother Black Mumbo presented Little Ebony Sambo with the cute little Red Coat and a pair of pretty Blue Trousers after saying a litany of arcane Mumbo Jumbo to the very impressionable, slow-learning jerk-off.

Little Ebony Sambo finally succumbed to temptation, and the next morning clad himself in his new festive clothes and bravely stepped-out into the dangerous jungle (against his parents' perpetual wishes and warnings), looking like a totally gay, freakish circus clown. Soon the aberrant lad confronted a soothsaying Tiger that almost knew *his* name and ferociously asked, "Say, aren't you Little Black Samba?"

"No big, cool cat! I hate to dance. I'm Little Ebony Sambo!"

"Well, whether you be Little Ebony Sambo or Little Black Samba, in either case I'm going to eat you up because I'm thoroughly pissed-off that your name isn't Little Black Sambo like it should be!"

Little Ebony Sambo was afraid that he might be in a dilemma way over his head by grabbing a fierce tiger by the tail, so the jungle ambler apprehensively answered, "Please Mr. Tiger. I promise to move to Detroit and play baseball if that's what you insist upon! If you choose not to gobble me up," Sambo proceeded with his narrative, "I'll give you my charming Red Coat so that you can pretend being a British soldier marching in the bloody *Revolutionary War*, which happened over two-hundred and twenty-five years ago in a fucked-up, distant land called Massa-two-shits!"

The greedy Tiger eagerly confiscated the magnificent Red Coat and proudly announced, "Now I'm the finest tiger living in the entire jungle, and I'm even more terrific than any tiger playing baseball in Detroit! Just a few more stripes and I guarantee you; I'll become a British captain! 'Don't fire until you see the whites of their eggs, that's all I've got to say'!"

And being greatly relieved that *he* had not been voraciously devoured, Little Ebony Sambo, like a complete ignoramus, continued further down the isolated jungle path when soon the wanderer encountered a second even fiercer clairvoyant Tiger that greeted threateningly, "Little Ebony Sambo, my intentions are to eat you up and shit what remains of you out of my big, fat, furry asshole!"

And Little Ebony Sambo abruptly responded, "Why don't you go to Cincinnati and play football for the damned *Bengals*?" Then the behavior problem child diplomatically added, "Oh please don't chew me up Mr. Tiger! I'll give you my custom-made colorful Blue Trousers. I don't want to appear *black and blue* after you violently beat, maul and pulverize the living crap out of me!"

"You stupid, little, arrogant shit!" the Tiger belligerently scolded. "I don't have to accept your irrelevant gift because I could easily kill and then consume you and still possess your silly cute Blue Pants. But because I believe in noble courtesy and often practice aristocratic etiquette," the second, obviously well-educated Tiger qualified, "I'll just graciously receive your token of tribute and let you live this time! But the next time around that we meet, you might not escape death so fortunately or so easily!"

After the highly intelligent Tiger possessed Little Ebony Sambo's gay-looking Blue Trousers, the sophisticated beast suffered from delusions of grandeur and anxiously left the vicinity muttering, "Now I'm the finest-looking Tiger in all the jungle! Just a few more stripes and I'll become a goddamned, friggin' colonel."

The not-too-brilliant Little Ebony Sambo proceeded strolling onward and five minutes later, the impossible imp was accosted by a third even more ferocious, clairvoyant Tiger that desired to brutally maul and mercilessly ravage him. "Little Black Sambo," the Tiger mentalist began his salutation. "I'm going to savagely mutilate you and then swallow you piece by piece for dinner!"

"Oh please Mr. Tiger; you look swell enough to sell frosted flakes or maybe premium gasoline at petrol stations!" Little Ebony Sambo falsely flattered. "I'll give you my exquisite Purple Shoes with Scarlet Soles and accompanying Scarlet Linings if you'll benevolently show admirable compassion by sparing my life!"

"What use would your ridiculous-looking shoes be to me?" the third vicious-looking Tiger skeptically questioned. "I've got four legs and feet if you're bright enough to count that high, and you Ebony Sambo happen to have only two walking appendages! You haven't got enough shoes to accommodate my wonderful feet!"

"But you could hang the shoes from your stunning ears or wear them on your most impressive, dangling testicles!" Little Ebony Sambo promptly suggested. "They make great decorations and will attract all kinds of gay and lesbian tigers."

"Not a bad proposal, and it's worthy of my utmost consideration," the third haughty Tiger honestly admitted. The great carnivore then latched onto the Purple Shoes with Scarlet Soles and Scarlet Linings and left the meandering jungle trail uttering, "Now I'm the finest Tiger in the entire jungle! Just a few more stripes and I'll become a goddamned major!"

Ten minutes later the aimless boy, who had absolutely no constructive direction in life, was stopped and threatened by a fourth gigantic, auguring Tiger. "Little Ebony Sambo," the amazing and formidable beast gruffly enunciated, "I'm going to eat you up because I'm exceedingly hungry and have nothing better to do right now except maybe take a very healthy shit!"

Little Ebony Sambo, after immediately shitting a wet turd inside his underwear yelled, "Oh please Mr. Fourth Immense Gargantuan Titanic Imperial Tiger, you look like you could beat the shit out of King Kong, Godzilla and Barney the Dinosaur all at the same time! I'll gladly give you my gay Green Umbrella if you change your mind about tearing me to shreds and leaving my damned red blood, yellow urine and black flesh all over this friggin' tiger-infested jungle trail!" the intimidated lad replied. "Then you could win first prize in the New Orleans *Mardi Gras* or perhaps even in the gaudy Philadelphia *New Year's Day Mummers Parade!*"

"Do I look like a ludicrous, queer dunce?" the humungous Tiger challenged in a heightened rage. "How can I possibly carry your gay-looking Green Umbrella when I don't have a friggin' hand or wrist and require all four of my pawed pads to permanently walk-on all around this desolate sector of India?"

"You could form a knot on your talented tail and then raise, lower and lift the Green Umbrella as if you were doing a very nifty strut, and you'll be amazed how this simple jungle trail could then become your personal boardwalk promenade!" the dark-complexioned boy slyly recommended.

"Okay, you've convinced me even though I still believe you're nothing more than a weak-minded, feckless, incompetent imbecile!" the fourth awesome Tiger reluctantly acceded. "Now I'll certainly be beyond the shadow of a doubt the finest and most handsome Tiger scurrying around the entire jungle! Just another stripe to go and I'll become a goddamned famous general!"

Instead of sprinting away overjoyed at salvaging his precious life, Little Ebony Sambo dejectedly strolled back along the trail, sobbing deliriously because the fair-minded, noble Tigers had cruelly taken all his worthless clothes and had callously left him stranded in the jungle's interior wearing only his smelly, shit-stained underwear. Soon the thick jungle environment turned into a thinner clustering of side-by-side trees, the new scenario indicating that Sambo was gradually approaching the *lunatic fringe* and was almost safely home.

Two minutes further down the dusty jungle trail, Little Ebony Sambo came to a neck of the woods where a recently painted sign distinctly read: "Tiger Woods." 'Oh, my word no!' the short, dark-complexioned lad in his smelly brown-stained underwear thought. 'I'm not exactly out of the damned woods yet!' Thirty seconds later, the boy's sensitive ears heard a very audible "Gr-rrr-rrrr-rrrr! Gr-rrr-rrr-rrr, Gr-rrr-rrr-rrr!"

'Oh, dear me!' Little Ebony Sambo fearfully realized. 'All four Tigers I had negotiated with are now converging on this very spot to rip me apart and then fight over possession of my skinny bones! How can I save my dumpy, ebony ass from certain extinction? I'll try scooting-over to that tall palm tree and peep from behind it. What else can a pea-brain like me possibly think of?'

Looking out at a nearby clearing, Little Ebony Sambo keenly observed the four conceited Tigers disputing over which one looked the finest. Then the four incensed animals began clawing the colorful clothes and special gifts (that Sambo had cleverly bartered for his life) off of each other's possession. The powerful cats' long sharp teeth were quite visible as the incensed animals endeavored bullying one another in a weird display of carnivorous ostentation. Soon a wild and wicked full-scale fight ensued as the extremely antagonistic quartet rolled and tumbled all the way to the aforementioned palm tree's base.

Little Ebony Sambo was then absolutely horrified to witness a most incredible event. The four enraged Tigers caught hold of each other's tails, and the battlers rushed in a frantic race around the tropical palm tree where the astounded young observer had been hiding, but none of the agitated predators took notice of the hapless, petrified boy that had rapidly shinnied up the tree. All the while in the remote distance, a 1940ish American big band touring the hinterlands of central India was playing a lively rendition of "Hold That Tiger!", even though the year was only 1889.

The four crazed and stubborn Tigers would not let go of each other's tails as the preoccupied beasts sped around the aforementioned palm tree, totally ignoring Little Ebony Sambo's presence and presents. So as the Tigers pursued their nonsensical maniac activity, the dark-skinned spectator climbed-down the palm tree, reached-down, grabbed his discarded clothes and gifts, waited until the four beasts had momentarily exhausted themselves running around in circles, and then the pesky observer stealthily left the protective safety that the palm tree had provided.

Soon the exhausted Tigers again became obsessed with showing each other which vicious cat officially ruled the jungle. The creatures persisted in biting into each other's tails and again pursued their objectives, running in maddening circles with even greater anger and intensity than before. The four fatigued-but-determined combatants were whizzing-by and whirling-around so speedily that Sambo (now wonderfully camouflaged inside the dense, jungle foliage) could neither distinguish their legs nor their damned captain's, colonel's, major's or general's stripes.

After another minute of frenzied rotation, the four obstinate Tigers all melted into a pool of thick butter around the huge palm tree's base. Seeing the delicious liquid splattered all over the ground, the amazed boy scampered home and summoned his father Big Black Jumbo, who had just purchased a ticket to visit America on a jumbo steamer ship before apathetically listening to Little Ebony Sambo's frenetic and incomprehensible Mumbo-Jumbo.

"Oh, what lovely melted butter is around this palm tree," Big Black Jumbo loquaciously mumbled. "I'll use one of my favorite smear tactics and butter-up Black Mumbo, and then we'll have some kinky, perverted sex together. And after that pleasure transpires, my Little Ebony Sambo," Black Jumbo continued his boring oratory, "the family will all sit-down to enjoy a late breakfast and consume some delectable buttermilk pancakes. Your pregnant older sister Black Mambo's tits will provide the rich milk for the sumptuous hotcakes."

Pregnant Black Mambo generously provided the necessary breast milk to complement the pancake batter, and Black Mumbo conscientiously stirred the milk with ovary eggs (donated by local village woman), with brown sugar, the entire process using the excess of butter her husband had discovered. Eventually, the clan's mamma prepared a marvelous batch of the most heavenly pancakes ever tasted or devoured. Sambo's half-brother Black Sambadude ate a dozen pancakes, Black Mumbo ate thirty-one pancakes, Black Mambo forty flapjacks because she was quite pregnant, Black Jumbo fifty-three, but Little Ebony Sambo ate not a single one since the curious adventurer was so neurotic and so upset from his morning jungle interactions with the brutal, ruthless, pugnacious jungle Tigers that had inadvertently melted themselves into a ton of juicy, mouth-watering butter. 'My poor stomach is still *churning* from me witnessing the remarkable butter incident!' the diminutive punk silently acknowledged.

"Rapunzel's Draping Hair"

A little German shepherd named Heinrich Duncedorf lived in a little German village and occasionally spoke a little German to other little Germans of other little-known occupations. Heinrich and his wife Ingrid wished for a child but never realized that the dull-minded couple had to first have sex in order to produce an offspring nine months later. But now alas, the Duncedorfs innermost hope stood a chance of finally being granted their wish by the fickle whim of fate.

Heinrich and Ingrid Duncedorf had a rickety, old shed in their backyard that looked like it had rickets. The miniature barn overlooked a sinister neighbor's property, and Ingrid both admired and envied Mother Mary Goethel's attractive garden very much. The splendid garden featured beautiful flowers fit for any funeral parlor wake, and the old lady's backyard also grew handsome and tantalizing vegetables that made poor Ingrid's mouth water daily.

"Mary, Mary, quite contrary, how does your garden grow," Ingrid hollered over the stone wall to Mother Goethel, who everyone in the vicinity claimed was a real mother who once was a Mother Superior.

"With tinker bells and cocker shells and a great big fuckin' white eggplant situated right in the middle, you stupid asshole!" Mary Goethel yelled back rather boisterously. "And furthermore, Sweet Cheeks, in this case the white eggplant happens to be my patch of gray pubic hair found nestled somewhere between my wrinkly, aged legs!"

Mother Mary Goethel was reputed to be an authentic witch according to the heavy gossip generated by the local, illiterate village idiots, all of whom could not read, write, spell, draw, do arithmetic, piss or shit right, or think. But one August day while the noon sun was shining brightly, Ingrid Duncedorf jealously gazed over at Mother Mary's terrific, exotic vegetable garden. The viewer coveted the long tender beans, the succulent summer peas, the hard, firm lettuce and the massive cucumbers that could have conveniently served for much-gratifying dildos. But besides the magnificent array of carrots and turnips, Ingrid's craving eyes fell-upon a well-tilled bed of rampion, a special plant that in Germany was also called "Rapunzel".

"I need to have rapunzel salad mixed with olive oil and vinegar," Ingrid avariciously mumbled to no one in particular. "The rampion looks so crisp and so fresh that I just have to have it regardless of the imminent risk or consequences." But then the scheming woman had second thoughts about pilfering the tempting vegetable. 'If Mother Goethel is indeed a foul, malicious witch as everyone in the village tavern insists she is,' Ingrid cautiously considered, 'then the wicked bitch might cast an evil spell on me and my ass and tits might fall off my body, or something even worse than that horror might happen. I'm scared totally shitless just thinking about it.'

Ingrid however could not stop desiring and lusting for the wonderful rampion, and the weak-minded woman even had a sinful dream that she had lost her virginity inserting the fantastic vegetable into her pink love cave. Heinrich noticed that his nasty wife had suddenly lost her appetite, which was Ingrid Duncedorf's scheme to get her spouse to steal the neighbor bitch's rampion and face possible death or terminal illness from the witch's diabolical curse.

"Oh Heinrich," Ingrid began her canard. "I have a strong passion for some of that luscious rapunzel growing in Mother Mary Goethel's tidy garden, and unless I have some to eat, I'm afraid that I'll die a skinny virgin wench like Joan of Arc or some other chaste, maniacal personage like that."

"You ought to have a passion for my erect dick instead of for that vile vegetable flourishing over in yonder garden!" Heinrich nastily scolded. "But since I don't give a shit or a rat's ass about living another mediocre minute on this despicable goddamned earth," Heir Duncedorf continued, "I'll merrily risk obtaining some rare rapunzel for you just to shut you the fuck up. And in conclusion Ingrid, I hope it's poisonous rampion that will rot your smelly asshole along with your smellier vagina from the inside out!"

At dusk Heinrich dutifully clambered over the ancient, irregularly shaped stone divider that had been inferiorly built by several of Attila the Hun's gay, drunken, barbarians many centuries before. The husband speedily dug-up several of the enticing rare plants and immediately hopped back over the wall and brought the rapunzel to his ailing, failing wife, hoping all the while that *she* would choke to death while swallowing the vegetable.

Ingrid Duncedorf ravenously ate the tasty vegetable in a big, highly-seasoned salad, which she gulped-down with great relish, mustard, ketchup and mayonnaise. But like the proverbial Eve in the *Book of Genesis*, Ingrid's curiosity about rapunsel and her intense desire for the irresistible, forbidden food were overwhelming.

Heinrich noticed that the cheeks on Ingrid's anemic-looking face and also the cheeks on her skinny ass were now rosier than ever, and even Mrs. Duncedorf's pubic hairs were turning from gray to black. And in addition, Ingrid's dried-up crack was changing from ugly gray to a succulent pink. 'Holy Heidi in Heidelberg!' Heinrich imagined. 'If Ingrid continues to eat the rampion, her snatcheroo will become more pink, wet and juicy, and who the hell knows what the heck will happen next? I gotta' admit; this rapunzel phenomenon is becoming all-too-wonderfully exciting!'

But after a week of not consuming the rampion, Ingrid's face again appeared gaunt and sickly, and her skin was once more becoming ashen in color. 'I'll have to stealthily go over to the witch's property and grab some more rampion for Ingrid,' Heinrich reckoned. But after the husband surreptitiously climbed over the stone wall and then stooped-down in the center of the neighbor's vast garden, Mother Goethel intercepted the amateur thief right in the middle of his clandestine activity.

"Oh, Mother Mary!" the little German twerp timidly exclaimed in un-germane German. "Please don't hex me, for I have a very fragile heart that thinks it's a diseased kidney. I'm not really a petty robber but only a caring husband attempting to save my wife's life because all she'll eat to stay alive is your garden's most superlative rampion. I fear that Ingrid will perish if she does not have her fill of your miraculous vegetable!"

After hearing the rather interesting confession, the witch replied, "Okay Heinrich Duncedorf. You may take as many of the plants you need every day to rehabilitate your nosy wife back to a healthy state like New Hampshire or Vermont, for instance. But I must stipulate two essential conditions."

"What are they?" Heinrich fearfully asked. "Please go easy on me Mother Goethel! I have hemorrhoids all over my friggin' body!"

"Number one, when your first child is born a year from now, you must surrender it to me," the nasty, evil woman indicated. "I'll tend and care for your baby daughter as if I was a loving mother, a loving Mother Gothel, ha, ha, ha!"

"And what is your second relevant provision?" Heinrich dreaded knowing. 'I trust that it's even more malevolent than your first excessive demand."

"Secondly Heinrich Duncedorf, you gotta' vigorously screw *me* twice a day before you go home and pump your old lady! And I insist on no false orgasms, do you completely understand, Asshole?"

"I'd rather sodomize Satan himself' rather that squirt my warm sperm up your stinky twat!" the irate man protested. "What a horrible nightmare my wife's flagging health has generated!"

"It's either those two conditions or else Ingrid painfully dies within a week!" Mary Goethel eerily cackled. "Now be off Heinrich Duncedorf so that you can figure-out how you're going to get and sustain three illustrious erections a day and how you're gonna' be able to shoot-off your flimsy cannon that many times too! Ha, ha, ha, ha, ha! What dumb fuck neighbors I got! Ha, ha, ha, ha!"

Heinrich was so nervous and tense at that particular moment that the traumatized fellow had to shove his dirty thumb up his ass to prevent a hard, rectangular, fecal brick from accidentally plopping-out. 'Mother Goethel has a green thumb and now I have a filthy brown one!' Duncedorf deeply thought. 'And during my time of trouble, Mother Mary came to me, speaking words of bullshit, so let it be! What a goddamned lot of ugly, pathetic lyrics those words are!'

Ingrid's stressed-out husband had to drink four gallons of water a day to replenish the sperm juices he had to use in servicing Mother Goethel ("That mangy mother fucker") twice daily and also his wife's now-vibrant love canal once. But remarkably a year later, as was predicted, Ingrid delivered an adorable child, but the sex-starved Mary Goethel still wanted to get wildly laid twice a day. Then the witchy neighbor came to the Duncedorf residence and claimed ownership of the daughter, calling the newborn girl "Rapunzel" after the nauseous vegetable that Ingrid loved consuming.

Twenty years later, Rapunzel had grown into a gorgeous woman with exotic, long, fabulous, golden tresses that dangled-down way past her feet, even when the vivacious maiden stood on a high toilet. The old Hag had built a tower the first ten years of the blonde girl's life and kept the comely vixen captive in it every day after Rapunzel had her first monthly period at age eleven.

Rapunzel's tower did not have a staircase, and since the structure had been constructed of stone, the girl never had to worry about evacuating the odd-looking edifice during a fire drill or a fierce terrorist bomb threat. The tower only had a little room at its top and a tiny window for the confined girl to look out of. And the closet-sized room also had a Lilliputian seat with a miniature hole in it for Rapunzel to leak and crap into. The hideous Mother Goethel would daily visit the tower and bring Rapunzel a stale loaf of bread, a small jug of water and a delicious, nutritious rampion plant to eat. And every morning at the base of the tower the old Hag would predictably call-up to its sole occupant:

"Rapunzel, Rapunzel,
Throw down your hair."

One day Rapunzel was in an antagonistic, defiant mood and yelled-down to Mother Goethel, "I can't throw-down my hair you old whoring bitch! I just shaved my bush off yesterday!"

And the old Hag angrily hollered-up, "Don't give me that irrational horseshit! You know I meant the freakin' golden hair growing out of your scalp, you ornery, complaining prevaricator!"

The young lady then complied with the Witch's strict command. Rapunzel lifted her long braids that had been roped in circles upon the small room's cluttered floor and flung each length at a time over a hook and out the window a whole sixty feet down to the ground. The wicked Witch then used an inconvenient ladder to climb-up to the tower window and finally deliver the daily groceries to the lonely, psychologically depressed girl. This peculiar practice continued every day in summer, fall, winter and spring for eight long years, and Mother Goethel developed arms and legs that rivaled those of any muscle-bound woman on the championship German Olympic Weightlifting Team, steroids or no damned steroids.

There was one principal problem that both the Witch and Rapunzel had to deal with. The tall stone tower smelled like shit! After eight years of solitary captivity, the stone tube had become a sixty-foot-high vertical cesspool filled with stenchy urine and accumulated fecal matter, and the abominable Mother Goethel was lucky that the structure was so remotely located that no environmentalists knew where the hell it was situated, so the dedicated conservationists couldn't impose their standard "excessive pollution violation fines".

One day a naïve, idealistic lost Prince, who knew nothing about earning a living or about any type of physical work, was riding his white stallion through the isolated German forest. Soon the royal fellow heard melodious-but-melancholy lyrics being sung in the distance. 'That must be Bertha Dee Blues!' the Prince immediately and erroneously concluded. 'She's a renowned, contemporary legend right now all over Germany!'

Rapunzel was once again endeavoring to lighten her feelings of desolation and despair with delivering her disconsolate singing voice and very haunting tune. The enchanted Prince followed the sound of music to the forbidden tower but could not find any door or staircase leading-up to the small room at its summit. 'I want to catch a glimpse of the babe doing the singing, and if she's pretty and has a nice set of supple breasts, I intend to pump her crotch like there's no tomorrow and hear her sing out 'Yes, Yes, yes'!' the stupid, delusional Prince foolishly speculated.

The visitor on horseback (whose nose was stuffed-up so he couldn't smell anything including the building's cesspool stench) espied the little window at the tower's top but never once thought of yelling-up to the maiden singing inside in order to get her attention. So, the imbecile camped-out in the nearby woods to resume listening to the haunting song because the wealthy playboy bastard had nothing better to do with his time or with his spoiled, aimless life. And as the Future King was strenuously jerking-off behind a hemlock tree, the royal idiot observed Mother Goethel hobbling up to the tower, and the regal asshole immediately lost his erection just before the "stick worker" was about to ejaculate an enviable load. Then the old Bitch yelled-up to the window:

<blockquote>
"Rapunzel, Rapunzel,
Let down your golden tresses."
</blockquote>

"I can't! I shaved my bush again yesterday!" the fair damsel monotonously replied with the only joke in her comedy repertoire. 'I wish the hell I knew how to read so that maybe my neighbors Ingrid and Heinrich could lend me a damned jokebook to amuse myself with,' the voluptuous, imprisoned babe lamented

The Prince, holding his now-limp dick in his wet, sticky hand, then observed the magnificent golden braids drop-out of the high window one at a time and fall sixty feet down from the window to the forest ground. The old Hag adroitly climbed-up the dangling "hairy ropes", which no full-fledged, muscular Parris Island Marine recruit could ever accomplish, during or after basic training.

'Well, if that's the way to access the lovely voice I hear, I'll have to get into shape to be able to haul my lazy ass up into the window,' the royal visitor decided. 'But gees. That horrible odor originating from that tower's interior smells like shit!' the intrigued Prince reckoned as he began getting his nose working properly again.

But soon the regal trespasser forgot all about the putrid malodor and exclusively concentrated his eyes on the lovely girl, who was now visible in the window conversing with diabolical Mother Goethel. 'Wow!' the Prince thought as his pupils expanded to their maximum diameter. 'Judging from the hair on her head, that luscious chickadee must have one hell of a blonde bush!' The royal one's erection instantly returned to its former grandeur, and the enraptured jerk-off prematurely popped a load that shot fifteen feet across the meadow straight into his unappreciative white horse's face. The victimized animal snorted several times to demonstrate its intense displeasure, and the young royal traveler had to wipe the gook off of his equine's face with the sleeves of *his* immaculate white shirt to effectively calm-down the greatly perturbed beast.

94

After Mother Goethel hobbled back to her house to be screwed a second monotonous time by the thoroughly disgusted Heinrich Duncedorf, the Prince eagerly approached the stone tower and proudly stood at its foundation, his attention looking upward. Then the wannabe' King deftly imitated the Witch's squawky voice and yelled-up to the golden hair beauty:

"Rapunzel, Rapunzel,
Throw down your goldie locks!"

The fabulous blonde braids (thicker than hemp) were tossed out the window over the hook one at a time, and the Prince realized that it was time for him to "learn the ropes" of tower climbing. The imperial personage then carefully tugged at and next rapidly ascended the improvised ladder, his effort scaling the tower like an inexperienced but very determined mountain climber.

When the horny Prince finally arrived at the hard-to-reach window, his general appearance shocked the fair maiden, because Rapunzel had never before seen a handsome young man, or for that matter, a handsome young man's wet limp dick still hanging out of his stained satin pants. But the amorous royal guest smiled with pearly white teeth and soothingly mumbled, "Please don't be alarmed lovely maiden! When I heard your sweet singing from afar, I could not rest until I would see your gorgeous face. All I can tell *you* right now is that I'm really glad that the old Bitch Witch doesn't have a marvelous singing voice like yours!"

Despite the horrendous, lingering cesspool malodor, the daft Prince was so stimulated by Rapunzel's pulchritude and by her exposed shaved, bush-less crotch that the august lord immediately grew and sustained another huge erection, which instantaneously scared the shit out of his very pretty host.

"If you're thinking about sticking that big ugly red thing inside me, then you've got another thing *coming*!" the appalled maiden fearfully declared. And after uttering those exact words, the fair damsel got down on her knees and gave the grateful Prince the best blowjob he had ever experienced, or could ever imagine.

And after receiving the best blowjob he could experience or ever imagine, the Royal Fuckhead forgot all about getting laid and impetuously proposed marriage to the now-shocked Rapunzel. "Look Blondie, I don't believe in long unnecessary courtships. I'm more of a love at first sight type of guy, if ya' know what the hell I mean! Will you marry me so that I could get your ass the fuck out of this unbearable, stinking tower?" the trespasser asked while wanting Rapunzel's special oral skills for the rest of his life and not necessarily her shaved crotch or unknown screwing ability.

The maiden was reluctant (out of fear of Mother Goethel's reprisal) to immediately answer "Yes", but the enamored Prince was very handsome and his polite words were gentle, and his erect dick had been quite impressive, so Rapunzel thought about her shitty existence living inside her shitty tower and also about her forced allegiance to shitty Mother Mary Goethel, and within a Munich minute, accepted the young man's premature solicitation for matrimony.

'Unlike Mother Goethel or me,' the blonde-haired girl surmised, 'at least this handsome hand-job smells okay, and he even seems to take an occasional bath now and then.' Next, Rapunzel laid her right hand in his and courteously replied, "Yes my Prince. I'll surely accompany you away from this dreadful, inferior, smelly, stone tower. But it's obvious that *you* can get out of here by climbing-down my lengthy braids," the fair damsel stated, "but I'm trapped with no stairway, and I only have this tiny window as an exit to a sixty-foot plummet. What the fuck can we do to resolve my terrible plight?"

"I'm not a carpenter or a handyman, so I don't know anything about building a tall ladder," the useless, impractical Prince confessed. "But I can bring you a cotton bathrobe and some silk I've transported to this forsaken land with me. Rapunzel, you could then make a suitable rope out of the splendid material I shall provide. I've heard that certain convicts have readily escaped their high prison cells while employing a similar method of departure."

Each day the Prince tenaciously came and brought silk and material to his lover, which she secretly concealed inside her tiny living quarters. He even showed admirable ambition and turned into a notorious forest bandit, robbing traveling merchants of their clothes and forcing the surprised victims to ride naked between villages in their rented donkey carts.

And as Rapunzel assiduously and imaginatively fabricated her escape mechanism each day, a little at a time, Mother Mary Goethel was coincidentally so happy and so preoccupied getting pumped twice daily by poor Heinrich Duncedorf that the wicked whore never once suspected the ongoing plot that her beautiful ward and the young nobleman were meticulously enacting. But then one day Rapunzel accidentally spilled the beans to her grotesque-thinking mistress by being entirely too garrulous about her recent activities.

"Why is it Mother Goethel that it requires you so long to climb-up here to my window encumbered by food and water when my suitor the

Prince can ascend the tower in less than a minute?" Then the fair maiden fully fathomed her impulsiveness and enacted her bad habit of speaking before thinking. 'Oh no, I really blew it this time!' Rapunzel realized while the doll had foolishly contemplated her lover's long firm erection as she had been addressing the extremely nefarious Mother Goethel.

"What!" the dastardly Witch screeched in an inharmonious tone. "A man is visiting you? Why that damned cheating Heinrich Duncedorf! How much sperm juice could the idiot bastard have? Is he the secret philanderer that I suspect you've been seeing? Answer me girl! Is it our fucked-up neighbor Heinrich Duncedorf?"

"No," Rapunzel honestly sighed after a brief hesitation. "It is a traveling, fucked-up Prince Charming I'm seeing and not our fucked-up neighbor, Heinrich Duncedorf."

"Why, you deceitful mortal sinning child!" the Witch plainly admonished. "I believed all the while I had kept you chaste and safe up here in this smelly stone tower only to hear you now, at this precise moment, arrogantly proclaim that you're seeing a studly Prince! What's this fuckin' crazy, mixed-up world coming to anyway!" the old Bitch ranted. "If he's taken your virginity, I'll lose my black arts powers right away. But if you've only serviced him with oral sex, then my powers will diminish gradually. And if he's kissed or touched you," the cantankerous Witch revealed, "then the warts on my face will migrate and immediately infect my already sore vagina! What a lot of cruel, vindictive punishment your careless, reckless abandon will have inflicted on vulnerable little old me!"

The reprehensible old Hag was so furious that she grasped the two braids of Rapunzel's golden hair and with the aid of black magic, skillfully looped them twice around her trembling left wrist. Next the despicable Bitch reached for a pair of scissors that had conveniently been stationed nearby (when actually she required a heavy-duty chainsaw to perform her desired task). And then the snippy old Bag severed the maiden's incomparable tresses and laid them in circular formations (like ship mooring ropes) onto the tower's floor. And with the use of her incredible black arts' knowledge, the livid sorceress transported the tampered-with damsel to a desolate part of the forest and then shuttled herself back to her cozy shack waiting for Heinrich Duncedorf's aging dork to massage and scrape against *her* new-found, irritating vaginal warts.

The next morning, the sly Witch tethered Rapunzel's sheared braids to the window hook and waited for the naïve Prince to return to the tower to aggressively court his lover. The dumbass jerk-off soon appeared at the structure's base, holding ten pounds of neatly folded sheer Chinese silk.

"Rapunzel, Rapunzel,
Throw-down your hair!" he requested.

The hoary, old Bitch complied with the callow Prince's entreaty and promptly flung down the girl's severed golden braids. The happy-go-lucky royal heir euphorically clambered-up, adroitly using the tower wall as a suitable foot-brace between ascending hops. But the unsuspecting Prince's testicles nearly evaporated into his abdomen when the stunned ascender detected the singular presence of the wretched old Hag standing inside the open window.

"Ah, so there you are!" Mother Mary Goethel exclaimed in a scary, hoarse, haunting voice. "You've come for Rapunzel, but I hate to disappoint you. The pretty, petite sweet-singing bird is no longer occupying her nest, and *your* bird will not be occupying *her* wet pink nest, either. So that means only one thing dear Prince!"

"What's that?" the callow fellow incredulously asked. "What could that drastic consequence possibly be?"

"You'll have to stick your boner into my gray-haired pubic slit and cause some intense friction against my very distressful itching vaginal warts!" the Witch insisted.

"Do you think I want to contract venereal disease from an ugly, old scumbag like you?" the Prince insolently yelled. "No way! Not even any kind of foreplay! I'd rather shove a rotten ear of corn up my ass and rivet it in and out five hundred times a minute!"

"If that's your type of pleasure," the infuriated Mother Goethel screamed. "Then Your Highness; you're to have the worst case of hemorrhoids in medical history; plus you'll be blinded by my wrath and left meandering around the forest with a triple hernia as a well-deserved punishment until you either die from starvation or are eaten by wolves, whichever deserved fate you encounter first!"

The baffled Prince looked into a wall mirror in the small tower room and saw that he was *beside himself* in a rather distorted double-vision reflection. His heart, being laden with despair, the grief-stricken idiot plunged out of the stone tower and landed in a briar patch where two thorns penetrated his pupils and immediately blinded the completely disillusioned, dysfunctional fool.

The blind royal jackass wandered all over the forest for months calling out Rapunzel's name, but not knowing exactly to where the beauty had been banished, all of the Prince's frustrating efforts at locating her were in vain. The Prince was not aware that twins had been born to Rapunzel and that dastardly Heinrich Duncedorf was the dirty-old-man biological father.

After a half year of trekking through the gigantic forest, and eating squirming insects, sour berries and rotten roots, the blind nobleman (now a nibble man) heard in the distance a familiar, sweet voice singing a mournful refrain. The spellbound trekker advanced closer to the sorrowful melody, and when Rapunzel saw her true love staggering forward through dense brambles and trees, the beauty dropped her twin boys onto the ground, wept with joy, and soon raced toward her chosen mate. Several of the young woman's tears trickled onto the Prince's lugubrious face and into his blinded eyes, and quite amazingly, the royal asshole's optic damage was spontaneously totally healed and his acute vision remarkably restored.

Then the ebullient Prince picked-up the twin boys and accompanied Rapunzel fifty miles back to the smelly, raunchy, stone tower. He chucked the infants (as if they were rag dolls) one at a time up into the air until the crying babes' trajectories each entered the high room passing through the tiny window and landing upon the wooden planked floor in two distinct thuds. And then the horny Prince seduced Rapunzel and pumped her now-hairy crotchola silly until her majestic blue eyes crossed.

"Heinrich Duncedorf never put it to me like this!" Rapunzel shrieked to her sex mate during their very wild dual organisms. "Yes! Yes! Yes, my wonderful Prince! Herr Heinrich Duncedorf never exploded inside me like this! Oh my God; yes, my Prince! Yes! Yes! Harder! Harder! More! More! Yes! Yes! Yes! Yes!"

"Tom Thumb's History"

In the era of the legendary King Arthur, who ate three *square meals* each day at the famous round table while the monarch's pissed-off knights had to sit quietly and watch and wonder why His Highness didn't eat any round meals at the round table, a most exceptional event was about to occur not far from the royal castle. Arthur's fabled court magician was a wise wizard known as Merlin. The conjurer was the most 'gifted' enchanter of his time because if any *Knight of the Round Table* neglected to give Merlin a present at least once a week, then that crusader was immediately converted into a piece of food on King Arthur's famous table. And that's why Merlin was regarded as more *gifted* than talented among the king's knights, bishops, prostitutes, rooks and pawns.

One fine day in a village not far from *Camelot* (where King Arthur had plenty of horses and also sold dromedaries on a camel lot), the famous magician was traveling the countryside incognito dressed as a common pleasant peasant without any pheasant. Merlin stopped at a yeoman's country cottage to rest his out-of-shape, weary body and requested some victuals (to consume in order to replenish his waning strength), which was the custom of mendicant journeymen at the time.

The good-natured countryman cordially welcomed the oddly-dressed stranger inside *his* modest abode, and the ploughman's wife brought the shabbily dressed itinerant a bowl of rancid milk that the family cat had refused to drink and also some coarse, brown pumpernickel, which her husband ordinarily ate before pumping his spouse's snatch through the bottom of the mattress. And the appreciative wife only asked for a five-pence prostitution service charge fee before spreading her flabby, varicose veined legs.

Merlin was very pleased and satisfied by the couple's extraordinary hospitality. But the sagacious visitor perceptively noticed that the countryman and his dairy wife looked rather remorseful and depressed. "Why are you both so damned despondent?" the traveler disguised as a medieval vagabond asked. "Has some evil sorceress taken away your lackluster sex lives?"

"We are without children," the husband remorsefully attested. "I pork my wife three times a day and then twice at night, yet no pregnancy has resulted from our dedicated efforts. I must be shooting damned empty blanks out of my fluid ejector, or maybe there's something amiss with my wife's egg dispenser!"

"Yes," the sobbing wife with the flabby, varicose-veined legs concurred. "I would be the happiest woman on the face of the earth if I could proudly produce, or please excuse me sir, I should say *reproduce* a son for my screw-happy, sperm-less husband. Even if the lad were no bigger than the average thumb, I would be perfectly appeased by the mercy of fate's decree!"

Merlin was much amused by the suggestion that a boy be no taller than a thumb, so the magician resolved to make the woman's special wish materialize in a matter of nine months' time. "I predict that next March you' dear, plump lady will give birth to a miniature baby boy, who will never ever be big enough to play midget football or dwarf rugby," the famed alchemist disguised as a ragpicker confidently augured. "And you both shall call the tiny tot Tom Thumb, who you will easily hold in your hand when attempting to hitchhike a donkey cart ride to a neighboring village!"

Nine months later, right after Tom Thumb was born no bigger than an embryo or a zygote, the Queen of the Fairies visited *his* cute little nursery (situated next to the farmer's nursery) and commanded that her subordinate fairies dress the miniature child in gay clothing to rightfully accentuate *his* future sexual preference. The whimsical Fairy Queen then presented her attendant underlings with a *little queer* rhyme:

"An oak leaf hat Tom has for a crown,
And a jacket woven from a fairy's gown,
His shirt be webbed of spider's spun,
And with his minuscule penis, he'll enjoy gay fun.
His stockings will consist of apple-rind,
The socks will reach from his ankles up to his behind.
His shoes be made of mouse's skin,
They will warmly keep his tiny clodhoppers in.
And while I'm still on the lousy topic,
Tom Thumb's dick will be microscopic!"

Tom never grew any larger than his father's often sore right thumb, which was one third as big and long as his father's often sore erection. But for what the gay lad lacked in size, the youngster more than made up for in performing a myriad of tricks and pranks.

Tom once lost all of his cherrystones when playing with normal-sized straight boys, so the lad would creep into their bags (and even sometimes into their pants' pockets) and very effectively break *their* stones. So, the tiny tot proved that not only could he be a major pain in the ass but also a giant pain in the testicles too! 'I'm going to play this fucked-up game with girls!' the tiny gay fellow creatively thought. 'I'll then be able to break their cherries and their friggin' stones too all at the same time! Ha, ha, ha, ha!' And next Tom pensively considered another distinct possibility. 'I've heard that older girls have bearded cherrystone clams, but I don't give two flying shits about that heterosexual fact! Frankly, I'm quite proud to admit that I'm a tiny gay son-of-a-bitch!'

But one day Tom was caught emerging from a boy's bag of cherry-stones when the alert eyewitness yelled, "Ah ha Tom Thumb! I've caught you breaking my stones and you shall pay a hefty price for your blatant audacity!" The aggravated punk then pulled the string at the top of the bag and shook the sack quite vigorously, bruising the two-inch occupant inside and giving the mischievous Tom Thumb a broken leg, a lacerated scrotum, a severe ass rash and finally, a really bent, minuscule penis.

A month later, the tiny child's mother was mixing some pudding batter when the ultra-curious Tom Thumb fell from the overhead kitchen lantern directly into the middle of the wooden blending bowl. The diminutive kid was stirred and mixed and swooshed around until the freak-of-nature nearly drowned. And then, his dipshit mother poured the pudding from the bowl into a copper pot, which soon was set on the stove and eventually began to boil.

Tom kicked and coughed and wildly waved his arms in an attempt for his dilemma to get noticed, but his focused mother kept on stirring while looking out the window at her tall, handsome neighbor. But soon Mrs. Ploughman saw short waves rippling-out from the hot pudding's center and thought that the concoction was either bewitched or that she was actually having a dreadful, paranormal hallucination. And so not realizing the cause of the perplexing aberration, the disgusted woman then opened the kitchen window and threw the pudding outside with her victimized son frantically thrashing about inside the rejected mass.

The village tinker ambled-by and scooped up the discarded pudding, put it in his tin cup and then ambled down the lane to see what other rejected treasures he might find. But then Tom managed to let out a shriek that even the nearly deaf tinker could hear. The superstitious old man believed that the pudding was indeed haunted by demons and so, the old geezer immediately dropped his cane. Tom and the substance were roughly flung-up into the air, landing in a rain gutter as the old tinker forgot all about his myriad afflictions and sprinted like an obsessed maniac into the village whorehouse. Fortunately, a tremendous thundershower happened later that afternoon. Tom rode the pudding mass like a raft, his mode of transportation tumbling over a small waterfall directly into a rainspout. And after exiting the house's twelve-foot-high drainpipe, the exhausted adventurer finally reached ground level with an inaudible thud.

The gooey pudding had broken into fragments from the harsh impact, so Tom left the mess behind and trekked the entire fifty yards home, a hike that took the already fatigued phenomenon a full thirty-seven minutes to complete. His hysterical mother cleaned the tot up and placed him in a teacup to dry off and adequately recuperate from his most recent travails.

'I wish I could be as tall as a dwarf or as a regular midget!' the boy woefully regretted. 'When I take a decent shit in the pasture, even the dung beetles ignore my crap or don't even take notice of my turds, or don't even seem to care!'

The following Tuesday, Tom's overprotective mother took her wee son outside where she walked to the meadow to milk the family cow, since the household was too poor to own a damned government approved barn in which to keep the pathetic animal. The wind was swirling in lusty gales that spring day, and the only thing Tom Thumb feared more than being blown right up into the stratosphere was being blown by an experienced hooker and having his microscopic pecker permanently detached from his very fragile body. Such was the horrible recurring nightmare poor Tom frequently suffered. 'A blow job from a woman!' the gay tot disgustedly thought. 'What a horribly repugnant idea!'

His responsible mother tied Tom to a thistle with a length of thread to securely anchor him down, but the nearly blind old family cow spotted Tom's unique oak leaf cap and thinking that *it* was appropriate grazing food, the animal instinctively took the hat into her mouth along with young Thumb and the thistle too. Tom roared out "Mommy! Mommy! Save me! Save me! I've never been to Texas, and I'm not a goddamned cowpuncher!" as the old blind bovine maneuvered the frightened fellow from one side of her gum-infected mouth to the other, and during the ordeal, nearly decapitated the tiny tot with every back and forth oscillation of the cow's mouth and tongue.

Tom's mother futilely attempted extracting the lad from the cow's mouth, but the stubborn animal curled-up her wet tongue, causing the creature's captive to nearly choke to death from breathing her terrible bad breath. But then the aggressive cow had to indulgently sneeze, so Tom Thumb was sucked-up into one of the moo-moo's nostrils and then snorted-out like a bullet being blasted from a shotgun. Tom fortuitously was emitted from the cow's snot compartment, zooming directly into his mother's bosom. The airborne tot had a softer landing than expected as he rattled-around between her soft fleshy breasts. So, Tom had two nice, brown, succulent, varicose-veined nipples to toy around with on his mother's trek all the way back to the family's modest country home.

Tom's concerned father carefully manufactured a barley straw whip that the incomparable two-inch-tall boy could use to prod the cow with, but while out exploring anthills in the verdant pasture, the boy tripped and fell into a furrow, which to young Thumb felt like plunging into a bottomless pit. An alert raven perched overhead noticed the boy's grave predicament, so it soared-down from a nearby tree and plucked the still dazed kid from the trench's bottom. The fickle, inquisitive blackbird soon lost interest in its acquisition while flying over a nearby coastal harbor, so the raven decided to let go of its object, and Tom tumbled from the blackbird's beak and plummeted fifty feet into the cold sea below.

Well then, a large, far-sighted sea bass thought that Tom was a corpulent, misplaced bug, so the fish swallowed the boy up whole just before the intended prey was caught by an adventurous knight's fishing line, and the little imp was fortuitously brought to King Arthur's table at *Camelot*, which as you already know, had a lot of camels instead of a lot of horses at the time. When Arthur's chef sliced opened the huge fish to fillet it, both the chief cook and the King were utterly amazed to discover the little tyke remarkably still breathing and cursing up a storm inside.

Tom Thumb soon became a favorite source of entertainment for King Arthur, Queen Guinevere, Sir Lancelot, Sir Kay, Sir Gay, along with the other renowned homosexual *Knights of the Round Table,* who always drank enumerable rounds of beer while reveling or quarreling. And when Arthur rode his horse all around the land looking for horny harlots and filthy sluts to screw, the Ruler took Tom along in a pouch, and if it rained, young Thumb was allowed to keep dry inside the Monarch's great waistcoat until the storm finally subsided.

But Tom did have his paranoid frustrations about being so tiny and was always apprehensive about being possibly eaten by a dog or a kitten, or if that wasn't the case, the lad was very concerned about having his picayune body crushed as King Arthur pounced and bounded up and down upon his incredibly swift steed, or when the King would be pouncing and bounding up and down riding a horny harlot or a kinky, filthy slut he had just mounted.

'I hate being only a mere thumb's length in height,' the tiny tot sulked while being jostled about inside King Arthur's leather pouch while on a country sally. 'If only I could be as tall as King Arthur's three-inch erection! And when the *Knights of the Round Table* make fun of my size, I can't even insult them by giving the idiots the middle finger because not one of the poor-sighted imbeciles can see my damned hand let alone view my emphatic gesture of defiance! That damned Merlin's balls should immediately turn to heavy brass testicles so that the crazy bastard could no longer be able to saunter around and cause innocent people like me accursed hardship! What a haughty. naughty asshole that clownish magician has turned out to be!'

One Thursday afternoon, King Arthur asked Tom about *his* parents' social and economic status and if they were also as diminutive in height as *he* was. The Monarch was quite astounded and equally embarrassed by the opinionated lad's blunt response.

"My father is twice as big and muscular as you are, and my mother could kick your fat, raunchy ass too if she ever had the opportunity," Tom boastfully related to Arthur. "But unfortunately, my parents live on the perimeter of your oppressed kingdom, are taxed to death, and mom and pop can't even afford a new wooden outhouse in which to shit and piss. You ought to be ashamed of how you exploit your loyal subjects and predicates with excessively high taxes!" the tiny lad reprimanded and criticized his chagrined king in a high-pitched voice in front of the thoroughly amused *Knights of the Round Table.*

Arthur was so humiliated and felt such massive guilt about the boy's stinging remarks that the King guiltily articulated, "Tom Thumb; I truly feel ashamed at how I've grossly exploited my countrymen. You may carry all the money you desire from my bankrupt treasury," the shrewd Ruler promised while thinking that the little tyke had the capability of transporting only one silver coin back to his impoverished family's shabby farmhouse. But Tom Thumb was definitely smarter than the average wise wizard, so the little fellow hired the biggest cart in all of *Camelot,* and much to the King's ire and mortification, the boy had Sir Lancelot drive the loaded wagon filled with the Monarch's entire treasury back to the primitive London suburbs escorted by all of the *Knights of the Round Table*, who gladly offered their loyal protection and mercenary allegiance for twenty-five silver coins each.

Young Thumb's parents were thrilled to see their son arrive back home safe and sound, and the couple was even more delighted to learn that the Ploughmans were now the wealthiest family in all the land. Sir Lancelot dubbed Tom the "Littlest and Bravest Knight Errant", and the boy's creative mother made the lad a special bronze coat of armor out of a junked copper cup, and his father then mounted the boy onto a tame house mouse that was imaginatively ornamented exactly like a knight's black charger. "I'll go hunting for ants, slugs, insects and cockroaches," the boy proudly announced to the delight of his royal spectators and parents. "And woe to any termite or spider that dares to challenge my valiant audacity!"

Sir Lancelot was so pleased with Tom's amazing courage (here bravado) that the famous knight made the pipsqueak loudmouth a "little throne," which was an appropriate synonym for a tiny toilet upon which young Thumb could park his ass and "take a royal shit whenever you like". The boy's now rich parents had a small castle of gold made for Tom to reside in. The model fortress, complete with a drawbridge and towering ramparts, had a three-inch-high swinging door and a platinum closet in which the boy could privately "jerk-off his junk" without any annoying disturbances or interruptions from bothersome curiosity seekers.

And when Queen Guinevere heard the news that Tom also had a magnificent golden carriage drawn by six large, white, valet mice, the Queen became very jealous and enraged. Since Arthur's wife's weekly allowance had been chopped-down from a handsome ten gold coins to a pittance of three pence every week, the wily Guinevere clandestinely traveled to Tom's country home, kidnapped the gay lad back to *Camelot* and cruelly kept him hostage inside a hermit crab's abandoned shell. Poor Thumb almost starved to death during "those worse of times", being the object of the Queen's relentless acrimony and of her implacable need for 'sweet revenge".

One day the incarcerated lad seriously contemplated escaping from his terrible ordeal, being secluded inside the jail-like hermit crab shell. 'It's time for me to finally come out of my shell!' Tom Thumb realized. 'I'll just pretend I'm a nude clam, snail or turtle.'

Tom astutely observed a carefree butterfly land near his shell-cell domicile, and demonstrating noteworthy stamina and admirable dexterity, the easily distracted boy exited his shell and just as the butterfly ascended, Tom latched onto its *mothballs* and was elevated high up into the air.

The confused and weighted-down butterfly flew out an open window and then flittered from tree to bush to tree, and after ascending above all neighboring fields, it returned to *Camelot* and King Arthur's court where the Monarch and all of his drunken *Knights of the Round Table* tried catching the elusive, flying, "rival monarch". During *their* frantic pursuit, Tom still was clinging to the butterfly's mothballs, and the crazed chasers (dressed in full battle armor) were especially jovial and making merry during their frenzied enterprise after consuming seven *rounds* of potent ale. And because of *their* commendable drinking escapades that particular evening, that's really why Sir

Lancelot and the rest of his colleagues are historically referred to as the Knights of the *Round* Table. But the men's raucous amusement was destined to be short-lived.

When Queen Guinevere entered the boisterous out-of-control "stag party", she became so livid at seeing Tom Thumb the center of attraction and also the source of the men's raucous merriment that Her Highness immediately banged a huge gong and got all of the revelers to momentarily settle-down and be quiet.

"I want Tom Thumb 'beheaded' at once!" the Queen yelled to the boy now situated in the palm of her right hand. "That is the essence of my royal decree!"

"I don't want to have a bee head, nor a wasp's head, nor any damned ant or insect's head either!" Tom indignantly yelled-up at the astonished Guinevere, his blunt language representing total disregard for her assumed authority and influence. "I want to keep my big, intelligent brain remaining as an appreciative prisoner inside my little thick skull!"

King Arthur and his jubilant knights all raised their goblets to salute the triumphant genius along with the undaunted integrity of Tom Thumb, much to the flabbergasted Queen's ultimate dissatisfaction. "Hail to Tom Thumb, who is anything but dumb!" the ecstatic men all chauvinistically yelled in unison, and then the jolly ballbreakers (or in this case tit busters) repeated the description at least fifty times until aggravated Queen Guinevere rapidly left the clamorous chamber insulted and livid.

But the peeved Queen's intense animosity for the sensational Tom Thumb was not to be denied. A month later, the royal lady unleashed her pet venomous spider on vulnerable Tom, and to show good sportsmanship, Guinevere barbarously provided Thumb with a miniature sword with which to awkwardly and symbolically defend himself. The brave lad fought the arachnid quite honorably, but the vicious tarantula emerged victorious and killed the tiny fellow, then lapping-up all of the blood out of the lad's body, starting with Thumb's microscopic, limp pecker.

When King Arthur and his knights found-out about Tom Thumb's tragic demise, the gents all went into mourning, which meant that they drank ale', beer and wine all night until the next morning. And to show his appreciation and remembrance of the sensational "tiny court jester", King Arthur had a splendid white memorial erected over the brave lad's grave with the following inscription as a relevant epitaph:

"Here lies Tom Thumb, King Arthur's knight,
Who had bravely died by a poisonous spider bite.
Tom was well-received in the King's noble court,
Where he provided entertainment along with good sport.
The tiny champion rode a mouse into a castle vent,
And everyone laughed when *his* dick got bent.
Tom filled the court with great joy and mirth,
Tom died a bold knight, even though born a serf.
And even though the boy's apparatus was microscopic,
Tom Thumb's heart remained philanthropic.
Wipe your teary eyes and shake your head,
The wonderful, young knight, Tom Thumb is dead!"

"Peter W. and the Wolf"

Peter Wolfenshlieglesteinerbrennerhusendorfer opened the gate to his parents' front yard early one morning and darted-out to cavort around and prodigiously fart quantities of intestinal gas to his heart's content in a nearby meadow. A chirping, opinionated blue jay disgustedly peeped to Peter W., "Look here freak face. All was marvelously quiet out around this vicinity until your gaseous ass showed-up and polluted the lower atmosphere! Now tell me. How the hell did your retarded father ever get the ridiculous, idiotic last name of Wolfenshieglesteinerbrennerhusendorfer?" the thoroughly upset Canadian blue jay from Toronto protested. "Maybe your mother should sprinkle some 'shortening' on your damned last name the next time she bakes a damned loaf of her putrid, foul-tasting bread!"

Soon a duck in a blithe mood came expeditiously waddling by Peter, who had left the gate open so that the people-friendly creature could clumsily enter the yard. "You need a ten-foot-long mailbox to truly fit all of your last name," the very politically correct duck nonchalantly said. "Wolfenshieglesteinerbrennerhusendorfer sounds like a combination of every German immigrant's telephone book name currently living in all of downtown Moscow!"

As soon as the nosy bird spotted the garrulous duck, the blue jay flew-down from a limb to begin irritating its chief nemesis. "What kind of an ignorant bird are you since you can't fly worth a damn!" the troublemaking blue jay provoked. "Go take some flying lessons at the nearest flight school and learn to get airborne."

"Stop mocking me! You're a freakin' blue jay and not a goddamned mockingbird! And kindly tell me what the fuck kind of bird are you anyway if you can't swim thirty seconds to save your friggin' life!" the insulted duck indignantly criticized the cocky, hypocritical blue bird of unhappiness. And next, the affronted duck further broke the blue jay's tiny testicles by stepping into a small pond on Peter's property and then gracefully swimming out to its center.

As the duck and the bird continued trading derogatory remarks, a mongrel cat stealthily crawled through the tall grass and soon captured Peter's attention. "The stupid blue jay has gotten its feathers ruffled and is arguing with the equally idiotic duck," the amused cat snidely laughed. "I'll first maul the loudmouthed, glib son-of-a-bitch and then promptly eat everything except its feathers after I thoroughly and convincingly beat the living shit out of that bigmouthed blowhard! I promise that *that* preposterous azure bird won't do any more foolish blue 'jay-walking' around here."

"Oh Mr. Blue Jay! Look out!" Peter yelled. "Cover your rear end or my proud name isn't Peter Wolfenshieglesteinerbrennerhusen-oh, whatever!"

The grateful-but-conceited blue jay immediately flew-up into a tree while the safe duck rebuked the disappointed cat from the middle of the pond. "Go take a catnap you frustrated feline!" the duck haughtily quacked. "And Mr. Cat, I think that you should first hunt mice and then build your way up to more mobile blue jays and then finally to ducks after your infantile brain masters the basics of being an established predator."

"Go fuck a duck!" the cat loudly meowed to its annoying adversary. 'Hmmm,' the contemptible cat surmised. 'By the time I climb up the tall oak tree, the alert bird will tease me and then cravenly fly away! And the deplorable duck can swim, and I can't!' the discontented cat reasoned. 'Why the fuck couldn't I live on another much better kitten-friendly planet where hungry cats could fly faster than birds and could also swim swifter than loud-mouthed ducks could maneuver on water! This goddamned world the humans call earth really sucks!'

Soon Peter's neurotic old Russian grandfather anxiously came rushing-out of the house to address his grandson. But the dauntless lad intercepted his grand-papa's approach with a very relevant question that temporarily surprised the senile, old codger, who incidentally was incontinent on the European continent.

"Grandfather, why do we have to have such an embarrassingly long last name like Wolfenshieglesteinerbrennerhusendorfer? Our new mailbox with our last name spelled-out will have to extend way into the next village if not into the next damned time zone!"

"Well Peter, if you really want to know the gospel truth, then read the friggin' Bible," the grandfather stated with a trace of shame mixed with guilt. "All the males in our family have short fadorkenbenders, so our ancestors had to compensate for their short, abbreviated peckers by having a long last name. Does that stupid bullshit I've just expounded make good sense to you? That explanation never made much sense to me, even though it's a damned indisputable, proven, genetic fact!"

"No, it doesn't!" the confused boy vehemently protested. "My future wife is going to have to always be on the receiving side of the short end of my stick. And I'll never ever have to use both hands to work my tool into a wild climax!" young Peter bitched and complained about *his* one-inch-long peter. "What a lot of useless bullshit this cursed last W. name of ours actually is! I'd much rather have a short last name like Smithski or Putin and a corresponding long, firm, glorious dick any damned day of the year."

"Well Peter," the equally embarrassed grandfather slowly answered, "you'll never be Peter the Great, if ya' know what the hell I mean! And you'll always be petered-out before you ever stick your shrunken peter inside any horny hot female's love tunnel! But in a philosophical sense, evaluate the situation this way!" the erudite grandfather aptly continued. "Contrary to popular theory, women, especially teenage girls, like long last names much more than they prefer long fat fadorkenbenders. Does that fabricated fucked-up lie satisfactorily resolve and satisfy your piqued curiosity?"

"Not exactly!" Peter W. obstinately balked. "Now Grandfather, why did you come running out here? To erect our new enormous mailbox in our new home's front yard? We need two bona fide alphabets just to spell the sucker correctly!"

"No Peter!" the old Mr. Wolfenshieglesteinerbrennerhusendorfer adamantly replied. "I wanted to warn you about a mean-looking wolf I saw this morning patrolling the forest's edge! What would you do to scare away the big, bad wolf? Would you show him your shriveled-up fadorkenbender? That almost-invisible object would only make the wolf laugh his furry ass off!"

"I would tell the hungry son-of-a-bitch my last name over and over again until the pathetic predator laughed his balls off instead!" Peter humorously revealed. "And if it was a female wolf in heat, I would do the same damned thing until she laughed her hairy tits off! The whole strategy I'm describing would yield very favorable results anywhere in Russia or Alaska!"

Brash boys like Peter Wolfenshlieglesteinerbrennerhusendorfer are not afraid of voracious wolves, and in fact, act like mentally deranged wolves themselves when around aroused, big-breasted girls. So, the cautious grandfather grabbed the boy's right hand and roughly yanked him into the house, nearly dislodging Peter's arm from his shoulder in the process.

As a precaution, the wary grandfather again came outside and locked the two-foot-high front gate, which any nimble wolf could easily hurtle over with minimal effort. No sooner had the scatterbrained ancient human suffering from dementia reentered the house that the overconfident muscle-bound gray wolf exited the forest looking to kick some smaller animal's ass and then energetically swallow-down its vanquished prey for dinner.

The ever-vigilant, neurotic cat was the first to detect the wolf's encroachment, and the frightened scamp raced up the front yard's only tree. It occupied a branch on the oak opposite its principal tormentor (besides the dipshit duck), the totally obnoxious, rowdy blue jay. Realizing the approach of danger (in the form of the wolf), the devilish duck loudly quacked and frenetically departed the shallow pond in a most unceremonious manner.

But the squawking duck could not escape the hungry wolf's tenacious pursuit. The keen hunter was foaming at the mouth, anticipating its next delicious meal as it swiftly raced toward its prime objective. The duck soon realized that its only recourse for survival was that it must use guile to trick the wolf because speed was not an available advantage to be enjoyed. So, the scared shitless duck stopped dead in its tracks and addressed the wary wolf possessing the tremendous appetite.

"Excuse me Mr. Wolf!" the duck stammered and stuttered. "Are you a werewolf?"

"No asshole!" the wolf exclaimed with a wicked smile showing a mouth full of sharp fangs. "I'm not a damned werewolf! I'm a damned *is wolf* because I'm going to eat your tender ass right this minute in the present tense! Ha, ha, ha, ha!"

And with those prophetic words, the ferocious, ravenous wolf lunged forward and swallowed the garrulous quacky duck in one mighty hostile gulp, which indeed appeared mighty hostile. But the furry predator was still hungry, so the attacker next directed its attention up to the tall oak tree. It observed the cat sitting like a statue on one thin branch, and the petrified bird was standing like a mummy on another. The cunning wolf circled the base of the tree, slyly contemplating how it could acquire its next delectable ingestion. But Peter was scrutinizing the wolf's activities through a window from behind a parlor curtain, and the ignoramus bravely came outside to officially challenge the avaricious critter.

"What is your name mean old wolf?" the boy demanded. "Identify yourself! For example, are you male or female?"

"My name's Virginia!" the female bitch answered. "Must I repeat myself'! My damned name's Virginia!"

"Who's afraid of Virginia Wolf?" Peter recklessly-but-ingeniously hollered. "Nobody in their right mind including me is afraid of Virginia Wolf!" And after bellowing those most defiant words, the pusillanimous boy dashed into the house like a true coward to wipe the brown fluid off of his malodorous ass.

The dangerous wolf returned to the oak tree and again harassed and intimidated the paralyzed blue jay that was too frightened to even fly and then also the naughty cat possessing the arrogant personality. Peter

Vladimir Wolfenshlieglesteinerbrennerhusendorfer found a strong rope inside his bedroom closet, scurried outside with the newly acquired hemp and deftly climbed atop a stone wall as if he were a Russian version of Stonewall Jackson. The cat and the blue jay represented an effective distraction for the hostile wolf, who believed that Peter W. was but a craven asshole with a bad case of diarrhea that happened to be too afraid to go one-on-one with the determined carnivore, the best two out of three falls.

The imaginative boy proceeded to toss and loop his rope over one of the flimsy branches under which the wily wolf was intently pacing in circles around the oak tree's base. Peter W. then managed to successfully pull himself up onto a sturdier lower limb and instantly directed an instruction to the still-frozen blue jay.

"Look you totally despicable birdbrain; fly-down and zoom around the wolf's head, but make sure that you don't get too close or else you'll violently die whether that pissed-off predator is infected with rabies or not!"

The cooperative bird gathered-up sufficient daring and zipped-down at breakneck speed and furiously zipped around the preoccupied wolf's head, making the formerly formidable-looking creature dizzy and quite vulnerable to Peter's contrived deception. The livid wolf snapped its powerful jaws where it thought the blue jay would be flitting around next, but was always out of rhythm with the bird's very apparent agility. Soon, the emotion known as frustration set-in, and the wolf's addled head was momentarily crestfallen, which was body language that suggested to Peter that the creature was plagued with a bitter, defeated attitude.

In the interim (during the wolf's series of failures), Peter had formed a lasso that was very deftly lowered to the general area of the wolf's ass. The dangling loop caught around the animal's tail, and when the contemptible creature pulled forward and then incessantly jumped around to escape its snare, the knot tightened and further encumbered the surprised and now-alarmed carnivore.

At that precise moment, three very excited hunters who had been trailing the wolf by following, picking-up and smelling its stinking droppings, dashed forward from the forest's fringe. The enthusiastic, shouting men began shooting their guns and rifles into the air, and the unwary, shocked cat soon fell out of the oak tree, and in five seconds, lay dead on the front lawn.

Peter screamed at the overzealous interlopers from his position high up in the tree. "You stupid, dumb-fuck assholes!" the lofty lad vociferously shrieked at the inane trackers. "That egotistical cat you just accidentally executed could have been me!"

When the helpless wolf was gingerly lowered to the ground, the avid hunters beat the shit out of it with their rifle butts, first knocking the animal unconscious and then effectively sending it to "wolf heaven". The hunters next used knives to slice open the gray, furry creature, and the trio was positively stunned to find the nearly expired duck that had recently been swallowed whole. The dumb bird was still alive but barely breathing inside the deceased wolf's severed stomach.

"Young man," the first hunter forcefully announced. "I'm the local game warden and must file a comprehensive bureaucratic report about this unbelievable incident to the authorities. What is your name?"

"It's Peter Vladimir Wolfenshlieglesteinerbrennerhusendorfer!" the quivering boy regretfully answered.

"Shit! I'm sorry I even asked!" the amazed game warden replied with his pencil applied to his notepad. Then the local official suddenly stopped his intense scribbling. "How the hell do you ever begin spelling that challenging word demon?"

"I can't spell the damned thing either!" Peter honestly confessed. "You'll just have to wait for the answer until my father erects our ten-foot-long mailbox and paints the family last name on the side!"

"The Rumpelstiltskin' No Spin Zone"

A poor miller named Stephen lived on the outskirts of a hamlet, which was situated not-too-far from a village called Macbeth. The poor miller was just as poverty-stricken and just as destitute as any other poor miller in any other hamlet anywhere else in the piss-poor world. However, the scrawny laborer had a beautiful daughter just like all the other scrawny millers in all the other hamlets on all the known continents of the medieval world.

But this particular, insignificant miller was somehow good friends with the land's scumbag King, who happened to prefer the company of impoverished millers as opposed to associating with aristocratic noblemen, because the royal landowning assholes all had ugly, skanky daughters, and the bag-person miller had a gorgeous teenager that made all dicks in the domain instantly become erect and then involuntarily bob up and down at the mere mention of her name, Lady Bird Miller.

The transgender King approached the penniless miller in the marketplace and initiated a typical, ass-wipe conversation. "Stephen, I understand that your daughter just entered puberty and can spin straw into pure gold," the royal mental case began his commentary. "Now *that* wonderful talent is an extraordinary art that defies both radical science and fucked-up alchemy. But your daughter's special skill also goes against narrow-minded religious morality and would be condemned by all the sanctimonious deacons and priests that practice their brand of nonsensical bullshit on my brainwashed subjects, the gullible public. Man, do I hate the major competition! Anyway, poor miller," the insane monarch glibly continued lecturing to Stephen, "I want to protect your young beauty queen from the church's holier-than-thou hypocrites who are bound by stupid jealousy to accuse Lady Bird Miller of black arts' witchcraft once the dirt-balls learn of your child's practice and utilization of her dynamic propensity."

"Your first two names wouldn't happen to be Martin Luther, are they?" the frivolous miller innocently asked the haughty King. "Your corpulent Catholic body looks like it needs more than a Protestant reformation!"

"No," the chagrined Ruler curtly answered his destitute subject. "I was an avowed Catholic, but just last month I turned into a hedonistic atheist."

"Well then Your Highness, when would you like to see Lady Bird do her glorious thing?" Stephen the Miller curiously requested. "My beautiful daughter owns a large pet dromedary and is still waiting to find *the straw* that breaks her camel's back. Confidentially, Lady Bird owns the dromedary so that she can someday learn how to hump."

"Take Miss Miller to my castle at noon tomorrow so that I can put her to the test," the King imperatively ordered. "I'll evaluate her ability just like I had done with my personal LBTGQATS harem: Miss Goodhead, Miss Honeywell and Miss Jenny Tailya!"

At noon the following day the bankrupt father escorted Lady Bird Miller into the royal throne chamber. Soon the King's personal ass-wiper conducted her to a tower room that was loaded with common straw and with an expensive-looking spindle wheel located in one dark corner.

"Now Lady Bird Miller," the King's personal ass-wiper solemnly declared. "His Majesty demands that you either spin this smelly straw into gold by dawn tomorrow or else you'll be put to a most excruciating "Death by Gigantic Dildo" experience. Of course, Miss Lady Bird, the King might make other specific arrangements, but I can't speak for his many dumbass edicts at this moment," the royal ass-wiper elaborated. "Now I recommend that you start spinning the pile of common straw into pure gold or else face an embarrassing love-tunnel execution with the entire kingdom's population mocking and jeering your presence as you stand stark naked on a platform in the center of town with your head facing a gallows rope. You'll be standing before the infamous, gargantuan termite-infected dildo, which will then be violently inserted up your fragrant love tunnel! What a totally stellar way to lose your fuckin' virginity!"

So, Lady Bird Miller, who was only capable of spinning lies and fibs and tall tales, didn't have an Inca's inkling as to how to go about transforming the cheap mound of ordinary straw into a fabulous king's treasure. The petrified maiden was so stressed-out that the fair teenager began to weep and was soon so bent out of shape that she couldn't even masturbate or take a healthy shit.

Then without any notice, the room's squeaky, wooden door swung open and in stepped a little, twisted-looking dwarf, who appeared to be a peculiar mixture of a Mexican midget and a queer-bait jerk-off. "Good evening young gorgeous lady," the distorted troll-like humanoid energetically greeted. "Why are you crying your eyes out? Has some nefarious individual stolen your tampon supply or absconded with your clit massager? Did you accidentally lose your virginity by not getting laid? Did you run out of sanitary napkins during your last supper?"

"Oh no kind freak!" the abashed girl sadly exclaimed. "I've been instructed by the King's command to spin straw into gold or else I shall be put to death, which really isn't such a bad idea once you really think about it. Anyway," the thoroughly anguished girl lamented, "I don't know shit about the business of spinning anything into anything. Are *you* some sort of weird magician who can assist me in my monumental endeavor?" anguished Lady Bird Miller inquired. "I don't have any money with which to show my appreciation, but I do have nice firm breasts, curvaceous hips and a juicy brown-haired pussy I could gladly share with you."

"Well," said the somewhat interested dwarf, "I *am* a magician of sorts because every time I go home and enter my house, I walk down the hall and then I 'turn into my bedroom'. Ha, ha, ha! But seriously young lady," the freaky-looking fellow persisted, "I can easily spin straw into gold; no problem whatsoever. What kind of compensation besides your vivacious-looking body could you offer me?"

"I do have this personal necklace," the miller's daughter indicated. "I won it as a prize playing Bingo at last summer's annual village carnival."

The little, physically distorted asshole (who was more than a little physically distorted) confiscated the cheap piece of "costume jewelry" and then sat himself next to the wooden spinning wheel, and then the rotary spun three times around and the catch basket (which normally was full of shit) was quickly filled with pure gold. And so, the dwarf merrily continued his assiduous labor all through the night while Lady Bird went to sleep and dreamed about marrying the strange little man and having an assortment of queer-looking elves, fairies, leprechauns and deformed trolls for bratty children.

When Lady Bird Miller awoke from her turbulent slumber, the grotesque-looking little man had already evacuated the tower premises, and now the money-hungry King was standing above her. "You must manufacture more gold for me from my massive straw collection," the avaricious royal asshole insisted. "Lady Bird, you must now spin all of the straw in the larger adjoining room into pure gold. And please be industrious and don't spin any yarns in there while you're enacting my imperial command!"

Distraught Lady Bird Miller didn't know what the hell to do, so after she began crying out loud as was her wont, ten minutes later the little circus sideshow freak again appeared in her midst. 'There must be some odd cause-effect relationship between me crying and this abominable tiny miscreant of nature showing-up as a result,' the very fair damsel hypothesized and concluded.

"What will you give me if I spin all of this putrid-smelling straw into gold?" the diminutive, chunky dwarf asked. "And it better be good and capable of stimulating my libido. And I must warn you. I hate straight sex with a passion!"

"How about a long look into my nice inviting open beaver?" Lady Bird Miller suggested. "You can even sniff my alluring love tunnel, but don't get too close or you might get pink-eye!"

"Maybe I'll attempt performing that particular project later in this story," the dwarf diplomatically answered. "Now Lady Bird, do you have anything tangible to give me that's comparable in value to that cheap carnival necklace you're wearing?"

"Yes, I have this inexpensive ring my boyfriend the shoemaker's son had offered me last summer," Lady Bird informed the long-nosed, stumpy-legged fellow. "It's much better than a bathtub ring I must say! My date had won it for me at the same carnival that had the exciting Bingo game."

"Okay honey buns, that's a definite *ringa*-ding-ding!" the dirty little man answered as the tiny magician raised and lowered his eyebrows three consecutive times. "It's much more delightful than a hemorrhoid ring, I must truly confess!"

The little imp quickly accepted the tawdry ring as adequate compensation for his extraordinary service, and again the fanatical maniac seized control of the wheel and by the following morning's twilight, spun *fifty thousand pounds* of gold (which was worth a hell of a lot more than seventy-five thousand dollars in today's deflated British to American money conversion).

Upon seeing *his* magnificent addition to the royal treasury, the King rejoiced and then required that Lady Bird next spin an even larger amount of straw (inside a much huger chamber) into a hundred thousand pounds of solid gold. "If you can accomplish that rather astounding feat," the King told the now-rattled miller's daughter, "then I shall have the present queen assassinated, and the next day I'll gladly take you for my lawful wedded wife. Well, young woman, is that a deal or what? Do you do platinum and uranium, too?"

"What if I refuse to comply with your treacherous whim?" Lady Bird insisted on knowing. "What penalty then? Will you painfully nude my beaver one pubic hair at a time? Please Sire, leave me the fuck alone! I'm presently going through a terribly difficult identity crisis, ya' know!"

"Much worse than the splintery giant dildo, if you fail to comply with my demand, I shall have a massive battering ram repeatedly shoved in and pulled out of your sensitive love canal until the object finally appears coming out of your tender mouth!" the sadistic King austerely vociferated. "My trustworthy body guards will gladly enact that responsibility with you lying spread eagle upon the castle's Maternity Ward operating table with your legs firmly planted inside the royal stirrups!"

"Well, if that's the case," the miller's daughter reluctantly assented, "show me the damned larger straw chamber. I'd rather have sex with a bull elephant than be thrashed to death with the King's infamous two-foot-wide, twenty-foot-long battering ram!"

As soon as Lady Bird Miller was left alone inside the colossal third smelly straw room, the fair maiden considered that the crazy King might make *her* his wife and then compel the girl to manufacture straw into gold every night for the remainder of her lackluster life. And *that* very disturbing thought made the miller's daughter whimper and then openly sob.

As soon as the beleaguered girl began crying aloud, the obnoxious, disfigured, sex-starved twerp again appeared at the doorway and volunteered to complete the King's preposterous bidding. The miniature fellow cut right to the chase by declaring, "Do you have anything else that had been won at the summer carnival to trade for my exceptional services?"

Lady Bird made a reply in a very disappointed and depressed tone of voice, which somehow touched the dwarf's heart. "I have nothing tangible left to trade you except my soft, cuddly feminine body," the girl sadly communicated.

"Because I've been castrated and my severed dick is presently visiting relatives in Germany, you might call me a Munich eunuch," the cute freak incomprehensibly answered. "But I'll make you a tempting proposition. Lady Bird; I shall spin this roomful of smelly straw into gold if you promise to give me your first child after you become the new queen."

"How do you know I'll be capable of producing a child?" the astounded girl volleyed back. 'Do you have a fortuneteller's diploma from a certified and accredited European mail order university?"

"When the queen moves from the queen sized-bed and then sleeps with the emperor in the king-sized bed, a child appears on the scene nine months later. That's normally what the fuck happens!" the little rascal most logically and convincingly replied.

The next morning, the covetous King entered the immense chamber's portal and delightfully observed that all of the stinking straw had been miraculously transformed into radiant gold. "I shall honor my promise and marry you," the transgender King informed the well-proportioned Miller girl. And Lady Bird," the royal toilet-mouth added,

"I command that you don't have to necessarily sleep in the queen-sized bed if you don't want to."

Consistent with the dwarf's incredible prediction, the faggot royal asshole married the miller's daughter and remarkably, Her Highness gave birth to a baby boy within the next year, even though the couple never had actual sex. But the happy Queen soon forgot all about the little man that had spun straw into gold and also about her solemn pledge to the pipsqueak gold-maker. But one fine morning, the repugnant jerk-off showed-up inside the palace and demanded that Mrs. Lady Bird King hand-over her newborn progeny, who by far was no prodigy.

"Now give me the infant, or I'll feel compelled to spin *your* tits and ass into straw!" the now-emotional dwarf dramatically threatened the now-bewildered Queen. "I know how to perform all sorts of wondrous bull-shit, ya' know, your royal High Ass!"

The determined dwarf's unanticipated demand extremely 'upset' the mercurial Queen, who immediately was seen standing on her head. "Mr. Troll, I'll give you all of my greedy husband's gold if you do not take little Barfthouamew away from me," the regal lady answered. "You could be the richest dwarf in all of dwarfdom and could even purchase the world's biggest yacht and could go *trolling* for little queer bait pearl divers if you'd like."

"No thank you," the pesky hand-job maintained. "Even though little Barfthouamew is enough to make anyone puke, a deal's still a deal, and I prefer to own your *living* son to have and to hold rather than count all of your demented husband's inanimate gold over and over again. And Lady Bird," the irascible-but-persistent dwarf emphasized, "please consider this. Gold doesn't breathe, think, feel, care, or love, and it also doesn't shit or piss in its cotton diapers!"

The bewildered Queen began incessantly crying and wildly gesticulating, as was her bad habit whenever Lady Bird had promised what she couldn't deliver; her reaction being just like what had happened with her absurd claim that she could readily turn the King's worthless straw piles into lustrous gold. The little rogue felt pity for Lady Bird's predicament and made a major compromise that departed from his original inflexible demand.

"I'll grant you three days' time to correctly guess my name," the zany dwarf uneasily related, "and if you cannot deliver an accurate answer, I shall take what is deservedly mine and then spin *you* into an ordinary-looking haystack."

The beautiful new queen hurried to the royal library and researched and memorized all of the male names listed in the appendix of a well-organized and sophisticated dictionary. And then Queen Lady Bird King sent a royal messenger along with her ninety-seven-year-old father all over the mountainous kingdom to ask the names of the land's ten thousand or so impotent male citizens.

And when the little rogue returned to claim his unusual prize, Lady Bird King bombarded the small character with her entire repertoire of fucked-up names that she had recently amassed. "Are you Elvis Sinatra, Willie Mantle, John F. Eisenhower or Abraham Washington?" she asked in rapid succession. But before the coy dwarf could say "No," the impulsive Queen continued her impressive litany. "What about Caspar, Balthazar, Melchior, Simon, Theodore, Alvin, Peter, Judas Iscariot or Dasher or Prancer?"

"None of those appellations meet my essential criterion," the dwarf indulgently laughed. "You aren't even close, even though you're standing right next to me!" And after each additional statement that the very worried Queen advanced, the little runt aptly stated with emphatic conviction, "That is not my damned name!"

Then the troubled Queen glanced at the dwarf's nametag, which instead of a series of letters forming a standard name, the little white badge consisted of four drawings of a person's ass, an apothecary tablet, a little man standing on tall wooden sticks, and last but not least, an illustration of an uncircumcised limp penis. "I'll now need precious time to contemplate your bizarre riddle overnight and then I'll give you a more adequate and accurate response tomorrow morning!" the now-paranoid Queen nervously declared.

That night, before hopping into the king-sized bed with her trans' husband, the flustered Queen mentioned the strange dwarf to her royal spouse who then told her, "I'm scared shitless of that little fucked-up magician's powers," the wimpy Ruler disclosed in a rare display of honesty. "That's one little mother-humper that I don't want to ever mess around with. If I would threaten to have him beheaded," the King expressed and then paused, "the vindictive dwarf would awesomely spin my ass into grass before I could ever give any damned orders to the royal executioner."

The woebegone Queen realized that her faggot husband could be of no help, and the beauty suspected that the tiny man with the gnarled nose had somehow made her become pregnant because Lady Bird never once had sex with the fucked-up King (or with anyone else for that matter) in either the royal queen-sized bed or in the regal king-sized sleeping accommodation. When the disfigured imp predictably showed-up at the palace the next morning, the apprehensive King hid his ass on a hopper inside a turret bathroom while the more courageous

Queen proceeded to interrogate the tiny all-too-frequent, annoying visitor.

"Is your name Socrates, Aristotle, Plato, Pericles or Thucydides?" the queen asked. And after each name the diminutive jerk-weed answered, "That is not my damned name!"

"Well then," proceeded the frustrated royal lady, "what about Ernest Steinbeck? John Hemingway? Edgar Allan Poet? Cervantes Shakespeare? John F. Jefferson?" And to each of those possibilities the little instigator confidently replied, "That is not my damned name!"

Then the under-pressure queen remembered the little twerp's nametag with the fat ass, the apothecary tablet, the midget on high walking sticks and the uncircumcised penis. "Is your damned name Asspillstiltsdick? Asstabletstickscock? Hineypharmacypolespecker?"

And after each of those outrageous references, the little agitator nastily responded, "No, that is not my fuckin' name!"

On the third day of the dwarf's cryptic riddle caper, Lady Bird King's aged and still-poor father excitedly entered the palace and yelled out just before collapsing onto the floor, "My lovely daughter Lady Bird," the old-coot miller began all out of breath and showing signs of an impending coronary attack. "Last night I came across an extraordinary little house near the edge of the forest. A campfire was ablaze, and I noticed a queer-looking dwarf who was dancing and hopping all around the flames singing:

> "Asshole, pecker-head, bullshit, twin,
> Tomorrow morning the child I'll win.
> And the queen will lose our little game,
> For Rumpelstiltskin is my name!"

The Queen was so elated upon learning the vital information that she raced into the adjacent chamber, leaving her faltering father lying in a coma on the cold, black, marble floor. And so, when the arrogant dwarf entered the room to claim his rightful compensation, the Queen altogether destroyed the little fuckhead's confidence.

"Is your lousy name George W. Clinton?" the Queen inquired. "What about Madonna Spears?" the regal lady joked as she deliberately crossed genders.

And after each of those distinguished names were humorously recited, the weird visitor cockily laughed, "No; I'm sorry Lady Bird, that is not my goddamned name, you stupid cunt!"

The scrupulous Queen then again casually scrutinized the short fellow's nametag and surprised him by inquiring, "Perhaps your silly name is Rumpelstiltskin? Yes, I shall say it very declaratively. Your damned fucked-up name *is* Rumpelstiltskin, you mutant midget!"

The suddenly incensed three-foot-tall mage got even more bent out of shape than his bad case of scoliosis previously had allowed. "Satan, or perhaps one of his evil agents told you the correct nomenclature!" the irate dwarf cried-out in apparent despair. "You've wickedly accepted malicious knowledge from Lucifer! The village priests will have your lily-white Caucasian ass burned at the stake, yes they will!"

And to demonstrate his total exasperation, the livid dwarf stamped and pounced and leaped and back flipped all over the throne-room. And then the irate nutcase continued his psychotic behavior out the door and somersaulted backwards four times into the royal courtyard. When the fit-to-be-tied dwarf finally flipped and reached the King's favorite garden, the aggravated fellow acrobatically leaped so high that when the dwarf eventually landed in soft turf, the little sorcerer's fat, stumpy legs implanted themselves into the soggy ground.

And all the amazed palace courtiers that had witnessed the unparalleled event were stumped when they observed with great fascination that Rumpelstiltskin's stumpy legs and visible torso had amazingly converted into an inanimate tree stump in the shape of a petrified dwarf, visible from the waist on up. Queen Lady Bird King wanted to honor the inimitable dwarf's memory and dedicate the petrified wood monument to his legendary feats, so she declared to everyone assembled in the garden, "From this day forward let it be understood that this botanical terrace shall be renamed the 'Rumpelstiltskin No Spin Zone, and all spinning wheels are hereby declared off-limits within a hundred feet of the deceased dwarf's unique wooden statue."

"Beauty and the Beastly Beast"

In the venerable olden times, when adventurous assholes and perverted jerk-offs first roamed the world (because they had no houses or caves in which to live), an immensely wealthy merchant had six spoiled sons and six doted-on daughters that were used to experimenting in whatever their insatiable pleasures desired. But the old merchant fell upon hard times and had difficulty coping with his new-found devastating, bad luck skein.

First, the ill-fated merchant's mansion caught fire and burned to cinders, and next, his fleet of seafaring vessels had been raided and plundered by pirates, and the remaining ships were destroyed by whales on drugs or became shipwrecked on jetties, or wound-up stranded on coral reefs. And finally, the elderly merchant's agents and accountants conducting his business in foreign lands robbed him blind, even though the old geezer remarkably still had twenty-twenty vision.

The formerly influential but presently shamed old merchant now lived in a dilapidated house several miles from the nearest town's limits. The lustful older daughters were too lazy to attempt something requiring a degree of effort such as prostitution or couch dancing, and the unproductive females hoped that their friends would support them through their "time of travail". But soon the young ladies all realized that their acquaintances had all abandoned them and were not really friends at all but selfish, greedy and spoiled lesbian assholes just like the destitute sisters were.

The twelve children all now worked for former servants that had elevated themselves above poverty by stealing, skimming and hoarding excess profits from "our kind-hearted father". But the twelve offspring (especially the older gay girls) craved the luxuries of the past but never once regretted the extravagant amusements and expensive habits they once enjoyed, pissed-away and had fancifully took for granted. Only the youngest and prettiest daughter remained cheerful and aspiring, for she had been the least exposed to the family's former "high-on-the-hog" lifestyle, and the innocent girl had shunned the general decadence that accompanied her siblings' decadent extravagance. The eleven other brothers and sisters called the youngest of the brood the nickname "Beauty".

One summer day the elderly, about-to-croak father heard word that one of his ships (after years at sea) had safely returned to port from the Orient, and its substantial hull contained a fabulous cargo that had been traded for in Japan and China. But Beauty was wise and practical and did not impetuously leave her job selling sailors brandy and peel-off tattoos at a popular seaport tavern. The old decrepit merchant's other eleven offspring immediately demanded that their benevolent father give them exotic mansions and expensive clothing when the senile codger would trade his imported Oriental merchandise for cash, but Beauty asked for not a single favor.

"What gifts should I allow for you, my dear?" the hoary Methuselah asked his favorite and youngest offspring. "A superb palace, good furniture, a platinum bathtub, elegant evening gowns, comfortable morning gowns, dancing male transvestite faggots, or perhaps several dozen bisexual prostitutes acting as servants at your beckoned call?"

"The only thing I wish for is to see you returning safely from the city with your newly reported treasure," gracious Beauty courteously and respectfully answered. "Dear Father, I don't want to see you harmed by treacherous, ruthless thieves or held against your will for ransom. And please beware of your traitorous, two-faced, disloyal employees. This warning I wholeheartedly caution you because your international representatives are almost as untrustworthy and virtually as deceitful as most of your scheming children are."

The other five sisters were angry at Beauty's pure and simple request that she had made to *their* dispirited father, and sensing animosity developing among his children, the old curmudgeon reiterated his sincere intention. "Beauty, I feel obligated to bring you something valuable as a token of my recent good fortune, since my ship has come in, so to speak. What will it be?"

"If you insist and persist with your endless fantasizing dear father," the knockout maiden replied as she dreamily massaged her erect nipples in a simulated trance, "I would like you to bring me a red rose and nothing more. I've not had one in my possession for many years, and since my aberrant sisters are constant thorns in my side, and in yours too, I do believe that a red rose would symbolize more than adequate compensation for me."

The resolute merchant set-out on horseback and reached the seaport city a day later, only to learn that his former "partners" had assumed he was dead and had greedily divided-up (and had already squandered) the ship's bountiful cargo. The distressed victim was too old and too weary to beat the shit out of his younger, ingrate, playboy affiliates, so not having sufficient money to enter either a hospital or a sanitarium, the feeble old gent rode his plough-horse back toward his country shack, all the while having a trace of pneumonia infecting his frail lungs. A wicked snowstorm descended upon the area, much to *his* bitter consternation, since the official calendar date was July 15th, the height of summer.

'I must find a suitable shelter to rest my tired bones, or else I'll certainly die from frostbite or starvation, or perhaps a combination of both,' the old half-frozen coot thought. 'Maybe I should just fall off my faithful horse, break my neck and get it all over with. I'm a failure and am also too weak to simply stab myself to death with a penknife!' the emotionally distressed old fart accurately reckoned and concluded.

The disconsolate importer awkwardly fell off of his lazy plow-horse and rapidly rolled into the hollow of a great fallen tree where the doddering patriarch spent the frigid night protected from wolves and insulated from snowdrifts. At dawn, the bad luck geezer awoke, being quite surprised that death had spared his mortal existence. 'Not even the on-the-prowl Grim Reaper gives a shit about my worthless life!' the disgusted fellow surmised. 'He probably walked right by me and deliberately ignored my unimportant soul!'

But upon rising to his feet, the old man noticed that the snowflakes had ceased falling and swirling and that the forest trees had changed from summer to a resplendent autumnal appearance. Beauty's old man hobbled-over to his trusty plow-horse and carefully mounted it, thinking all the while how he used to mount his wife three times each night in order to produce eleven of the most deplorable children on the planet, plus his treasured Beauty.

Riding on down an unfamiliar tree-lined lane, the old goat's steed soon came to a magnificent castle, which was too ornate and too well-maintained to be a hotel, motel or neighborhood forest brothel. After tying his nearly dead plough-horse to a hitching post, the old man slowly dismounted from his saddle, and his bloodshot eyes then beheld a most fabulous garden exhibiting a vast variety of colorful rosebushes. The aged viewer recollected his promise to Beauty to return with a fine red rose, so the sentimental fool snapped one off without thinking twice about committing his minor theft.

Upon entering the inimitable castle (which was not identified on any map anywhere in Europe), the old traveler found that the structure consisted of a labyrinth of rooms, all luxuriously well decorated and very appealing to his eyes. But as the fatigued interloper was about to explore another lengthy corridor to seek-out any inhabitant, a gruff voice bellowed directly behind the intruder, "Who the hell told you that you had permission to pilfer a rose from my personal garden? Is this the way you show your gratitude for being an uninvited guest in my palace?" the powerful voice bellowed. "Your audacity shall result in swift punishment, and I might even feel motivated to eat your tiny testicles for dessert after dinner. I happen to love Swedish meatballs prepared in hot Italian marinara sauce and am quite an authority on the subject, in addition to being an avid connoisseur!"

The senile merchant was terrified by the dreadful voice that sounded analogous to thunder, and upon seeing the horrifying beast's face and form, *he* dropped to his knees like a terrified suppliant. "Pardon me noble sir, I could not imagine that the absence of one rose would offend Your Excellency so greatly," the near-dead trespasser apologized. "I'm even too weak and exhausted to offer you oral sex. I have no teeth, which under normal circumstances means that my infected gums could give you the best blowjob for miles around. And you must be able to achieve one hell of an erection judging by those sagging furry lion's balls you're proudly exhibiting!"

The Beast was not at all impressed with the old man's flagrant flattery. "You've fabricated a half-decent explanation, and the notion of fellatio administered by a toothless, aged piece of shit such as yourself is rather refreshing, and as a matter of fact, it's quite intriguing!" the Beast evaluated in a booming voice several decibels lower than his introductory remark. "But old man, why did you steal my precious rose?"

The intruder retold the story of his pathetic life and all about his eleven egotistical children and how he had promised his youngest daughter Beauty a rose upon his return to his country shanty. "But now that my former partners whom I had trusted have taken advantage of my confidence and my naïve reliance, this ephemeral rose is the most valuable thing in my possession. Please have pity on me and respectfully show and extend your clemency," the old fellow begged the Beast. "As you can plainly see, I'm very near death, want to be reunited with Beauty, and finally, my intestines are so dysfunctional that I haven't taken a proper shit in over two weeks. You wouldn't happen to be a damned proctologist by any chance, would you Mr. Beast? If so, I require your services."

"Do you think that your shit isn't brown and that it doesn't stink?" the Beast growled and challenged in a threatening tone. "What's so special about your stupid feces deposits? Do they produce non-clinging dingle-berries?"

"Oh no kind Beast!" the old intruder admitted. "Even my constipation hard nuggets smell a little terrible! I think my large intestine is actually rotting away!"

"Well then, because you seem to be an honest and candid ignoramus, I'll forgive your trespassing violation on one condition," the Beast judiciously stipulated.

"You want two guaranteed blowjobs instead of only one?" the old knucklehead questioned.

"No, Asshole!" the Beast vociferously yelled. "This Beauty that you praise so much must willfully take your place and voluntarily live with me in my expansive castle. We lions have sex on the average of fifty times a day during mating season, so your Beauty must possess something better than a mere eager beaver, if ya' know what the hell I'm *driving* at."

"I'll go home and try to convince her to return in my place," the old merchant courteously offered. "And since I can't get my pecker to stand at attention anymore, would you mind having an old fart voyeur like me around to watch you get your huge rocks off fifty times a day. That kind of repetitious monotony might actually arouse my dormant libido. Yes Mr. Beast, that is my ultimate wish! If only I could get a fuckin' erection and fuckin' ejaculate one final time for old times' sake before my lungs and heart expire!"

"First, you must eat a meal packed with special vitamins, minerals, St. John's Wort and extra protein," the Beast ordered. "This nutrition will afford you the energy you'll need to ride one of my mechanical horses back to your ramshackle home. The metallic thoroughbred can race at a speed of a hundred kilometers per hour, which means that you should be home in around two minutes flat, give or take a few seconds. Now old man; go and eat your enriched health food in the adjoining room so that you'll possess the wherewithal to successfully accomplish your mission!"

The sumptuous supper of bull's balls' supreme and minced mouse ovaries was soon eagerly devoured, and both the old fuck's spirit and his aged body were miraculously replenished. And then the Beast entered the gent's private banquet chamber to give some last-minute instructions and to remind the old fart of *his* promise to return to the remote castle with his beloved Beauty.

"How was your supper?" the Beast asked in a less intimidating voice than he had used before.

"Excellent!" the old guest exclaimed. "What was in the red wine that gave it such an exquisite flavor?"

"Elephant semen!" the beast replied with a grin as the old asshole choked and unsuccessfully tried puking upon the dank, stone floor. "Elephant semen mixed with three varieties of rhinoceros shit!" the Beast eloquently elaborated.

Then the old dickhead, who was still too frail to vomit, had to listen to the Beast's final rhetoric. "Do not get-up out of bed tomorrow morning until you witness the whole sun above the eastern horizon and hear my untalented rap group the Beastly Boys singing outside your bedroom window. You will then reenter this deserted banquet chamber and consume your hearty breakfast, and I'm not going to divulge to you the contents of your next morning's food so don't fuckin' ask me *that* superficial question!" the Beast instructed. "And last but not least; take your rose to Beauty and return to my regal residence within a week on the swift mechanical horse I'm generously providing you with."

"And what if I don't return with Beauty on the swift mechanical horse that you're providing me with?" the old imbecile slyly asked. "What then Beast?"

"Then I'll hunt you down, kill all twelve of your children and make you commit incestual cannibalism having *them* all for dinner in one sitting! Does that explanation satisfactorily answer your fuckin' stupid-assed inquiry?"

"Okay, I understand your description completely and agree to comply with your particular provisions!" the old turd acceded. "And I'll show the remarkable patience of a saint and even suffer through that horrendous Beastly Boy serenade you've so provocatively alluded to."

When the old man raced home atop the sleek-looking, fleet-footed, black mechanical horse, his twelve children all rushed out of the ramshackle shack to greet him, but after learning that their father was still bankrupt and not worth a plug penny, the eleven ungrateful siblings insolently gave him the royal middle finger and yelled "Fuck off!" in unison. Only Beauty displayed any semblance of empathy and compassion toward her loving father.

"Here is the red rose that you've asked me to give you!" the penniless goods trader said to his all-too-sweet youngest daughter. "Be careful not to prick yourself. As you are well-aware, I'm an old prick and don't want to be pricked and then become an even bigger old prick than I already am!"

"It's all your goddamned fault that father had encountered the Beast's castle and picked the red rose!" the eldest sister blatantly accused Beauty. "If you'd asked for something materialistic like a trunk full of pearls, or a silo filled with rare gems, or a barn full of white circus horses, then daddy-cakes would've never been exposed to his debilitating ordeal. When it comes down to silly, impractical whims," the oldest sister alleged, "you've always been a real Beauty ever since you took your first shit after being born into this nonsensical, chaotic world!"

Naturally, Beauty felt responsible for being irresponsible and for causing her father excessive misery by making a very humble request for a red flower instead of an arrogant demand for opulent treasure. "Since I've caused our father who aren't in heaven yet his great grief'," Beauty attested to her disgruntled siblings, "I shall make amends for the misery I've unintentionally initiated. I'll go to the Beast's castle despite the horrible rap singing of the discordant Beastly Boys. And furthermore," Beauty continued her extemporaneous speech with sparkling eyes, "how the hell can we be sure that our senile father hasn't just imagined or hallucinated all of this dumb bullshit about a Beast living in an obscure castle, simply contrived to conceal *his* gross failure at not getting his fair portion of the ship's prized Oriental merchandise?"

The following morning, Beauty and her "delusional father" (who had seen better days despite his 20-20 vision) climbed onto the mechanical black horse, which immediately neighed, got a huge erection and then did not horse-around but instead bolted-off and sallied forth like a steed galloping out of *Dante's Inferno*. Two minutes into their fantastic ride, (like magic), day turned into night and the surrounding trees assumed autumnal hues, and then wonderful fireworks illuminated the entire forest.

"Is there an intense war going on between magical, forest creatures?" Beauty asked her numb-minded father, who had to be vigorously shaken to awaken from a deep sleep in order to respond to his daughter's perceptive interrogative.

"Er, no my precious spring flower. The Beast possesses such phenomenal wealth that the monster can afford to be impractically ostentatious by spending large sums of money simply to stage great spectacular pyrotechnics like those we are presently witnessing!" the knowledgeable guide fictionally related to his daughter. "The Beast is amused by excesses in frivolity, and his spirit and body are stimulated by the advent of the winter mating season, which according to the Gregorian calendar, the obsolete encyclopedia and the local farmer's almanac, begins tomorrow."

The mechanical horse sped down the avenue of colorful, splendidly leafed trees, and soon the discordant voices of the ill-talented Beastly Boys could be noisily heard in the distance. 'The Beast really has to get his eardrums broken before he gets his rocks off!' Beauty marveled and conjectured. 'And if the dreadful monster looks anything like the King of Beasts as my father has claimed, I have to wonder if *he* belongs to the local Lions Club? He's probably the damned District Governor if that exaggerated, exorbitant, pretentious fireworks' display is any kind of ego barometer. Perhaps he's the Lions Grand Wizard or Area Potentate?'

The well-trained mechanical black horse obediently stopped in front of the magnificent castle, and the two riders slid-down from the large black leather saddle. The farting father led Beauty up the marble steps into the golden foyer, and then through the spectacular maze-like corridors, and eventually the pair managed to find the banquet room where two meals had been prepared, waiting to be consumed.

But soon frightening roaring was heard from down the corridor, and the panicked father began trembling five times as much as he normally does when having his ordinary Parkinson's disease attack. But Beauty was determined to feign courage and not show any fear of the approaching awesome Beast, who incidentally was having a really bad day suffering from chronic constipation and severe abominable abdominal cramps before *his* undistinguished guests had arrived.

The fact that Beauty was unfazed by the Beast's formidable voice and ugly appearance pleased her host immensely. "Good evening old merchant! Good evening Beauty!" the Beast cordially greeted. "I'm happy to see you're both enjoying my hospitality. Indulge to your hearts' content! That was not the fire roaring in the fireplace. That was me' doing the roaring and I'm not lion (lyin')! Ha, ha, ha, ha!"

"Thank you, kind sir!" Beauty answered with discernible poise and confidence. "I was originally a little leery about coming here, but you seem no different than any other Beast I've had the pleasure or displeasure of knowing. Beasts such as yourself are quite common in my old neighborhood, but they seemed much more civilized than my many human companions, who all acted like absolute uncultured animals all the damned time!"

"Then I can deduce that you've come willingly to be your father's substitute at my palace," the Beast jubilantly concluded and declared. "And will you be satisfied to stay when your father departs my property? If he doesn't want to leave you, I'll shove a major piece of fireworks up his rectum and explode him directly home without employing my mechanical horse to transport him back. Ha, ha, ha, ha!"

"I'm prepared to do your *bidding* for my father's sake and welfare," Beauty replied. "Especially when you play poker or blackjack with other Beasts including the illiterate, incompetent and untalented Beastly Boys."

"I'm quite pleased with your daring and also with your singular pulchritude," the Beast conveyed to his targeted future blonde female sex slave. "And as for you, silly old man. I suggest that you stay overnight in the same room you had occupied last time. When the sun rises and then you hear my nephews the notorious Beastly Boys trying to harmonize their lousy larynxes, eat breakfast in a hurry. Then I have

134

something special to give you as a token of my appreciation for your magnificent compliance."

"I suppose you have a rocket filled with gunpowder to be shoved up my ancient anus? I hope I have the intestinal fortitude to endure you giving me the *works!*" the old coot laughed and challenged in a weird statement that reflected mild defiance.

"Beauty, kindly take your cooperative parent into the next chamber and select gifts that your fucked-up family might enjoy!" the Beast imperatively directed. "You'll find two large chests in the room's center. Fill them both with exotic presents and shimmering jewels that you might randomly select from my extensive inventory. But I warn you to leave the jeweled ribbed condoms alone. That's the only prize in the adjoining treasure trove room you're prohibited from stashing into the two golden traveling trunks."

Beauty uttered a sad, premature "Goodbye!" to her failing father and escorted him into the treasure room, where the lucky fellow could delight in romping-around amongst diamonds, rubies, emeralds, sapphires and jeweled ribbed condoms, which he could merrily play with but could not place into either of the designated chests. And it just so happened that the more precious stones and valuable objects the delighted merchant had placed into the two chests, the more empty each container became, and this ridiculous nonsense continued for five hours of diligent labor until all of the vast chamber's contents had been stored inside the two golden-but-ordinary-sized trunks.

'The Beast is mocking me and my very evident senility!' the old man realized. 'He thinks I can't carry these heavy bulky trunks home on either my own plough-horse or on his mechanical horse contraption. But I've cunningly outsmarted the dimwitted Beast,' the still-sly old-fart merchant reckoned with a broad smile. 'I've already instructed *UPS (Ubiquitous Postal Syndicate)* to send a special brown wagon out to this remote castle and cart the fantastic treasures away to my humble shack. The brown wagon company guarantees next day delivery anywhere in the damned kingdom.'

And so, the heavy-duty brown *UPS* wagon showed-up just as the shrewd, near-death merchant had cunningly planned, and soon the heavy trunks were meticulously loaded onto the buckboard's rear, and after the old gent signed a shipping receipt and an attached destination address, the two muscular delivery men hopped back onto their brown wagon, and their two faithful chocolate-haired horses trotted-off down the castle's entrance lane, heading due east to engage in additional medieval corporate business bureaucracy.

While the *UPS* wagon was leaving the castle's silver-coin-paved driveway, Beauty became very drowsy inside her assigned room and soon fell into a deep, deep sleep. The fair maiden dreamed that she was sadly strolling by a babbling brook and reviewing her terrible fate of living with the Beast when a vibrant handsome prince (who like most princes of that time was completely lost wandering about in a fog or a smog) approached her presence and amiably initiated a genuine conversation.

"Beauty, you're not so unfortunate as you think you are," the Beast stated to purposely cheer-up the obviously melancholy maiden. "I shall see to it that your every wish shall instantly transform into reality. No matter how you view this horrible external disguise I'm wearing, you must understand that I love you very, very much, and I have so much excess semen and adrenalin in my virile lion's body that I need to get laid fifty times right away. It's my mating season, ya' know!"

"Why must you talk in such ridiculous riddles?" Beauty demanded knowing. "Let's forget all about this farcical camouflage bullshit for a minute. Why can't you just tell me what the fuck's wrong with you without all of this secret disguise nonsense being used as some sort of artificial smokescreen?"

"If I tell you the whole story," the Beast solemnly confided, "then I'll never be able to seduce you properly, either in bed or in a damned wet haystack. It's up to you Beauty to use your intelligence and your sympathy to uncover the terrible secret that I must bear and can never share until *you* discover it."

The puzzled maiden then noticed that the Beast was stark naked, and her eyes studied with interest his swollen testicles from five feet away. "You're hairy, or should I say furry balls really look *swell!*" the young female blushingly praised. "But they appear to have too many layers of fat and also seem to presently require some sort of plastic surgery or necessary liposuction."

"I think that they really require *your* therapeutic liposuction," the Beast intimated. "Yes Beauty; a good blowjob from you will send my heart and my hairy testicles too into sweet ecstasy. That's exactly what I need more than anything else right now, Beauty. I tell you this truth because I expect that *you*'re still in *cherry* condition. I need to have some maiden head, *your maidenhead,* if you get the full gist of my suggestive statement!"

"What type of perverted drama is unfolding here?" Beauty queried. "This scene is somewhere between a very bad dream and a very traumatic nightmare!"

"Oh Beauty; do not believe all that your eyes perceive and most of all," the Beast adamantly pleaded, "don't desert my fidelity until you've effectively rescued me from my cruel and overwhelming penalty. It's both a curse and a liability!"

And just like in certain incredible fairy tales, the surrounding furniture and drapes miraculously disappeared, and the fair maiden found herself in another room with an elderly, maternal-looking woman pacifying *her* anxiety with a soothing gentle voice. The matronly old broad then addressed the awed young lady.

"Dear Beauty, you have my professed emotional support and also my profound total confidence," the anonymous dame acknowledged and promised. "I assure you that you're destined to experience a much better fate in the future than you've been jinxed with in the past. Don't be deceived by aberrations, apparitions or false influences," the benign-sounding old-bag woman advised. "And make sure you wipe your ass good every time you take a shit or before you hop into the sack to have some hot sex." And then the mysterious old lady in the vision supernaturally vanished, her form being absorbed into the room's many dark shadows.

Before Beauty knew or could remember anything else, she woke-up just as the big brass clock upon her bedroom mantel stuck twelve' noon. 'Holy shit! I don't even have time to find a scissors to cut my toenails and to trim my pubic bush!' she realized. So, after a late lunch the befuddled maiden sat-down in a cozy chair beside her drafty bedroom window and amply considered all the strange, fucked-up things that had recently occurred to her and also to her unfortunate father.

'The Beast disclosed that I had the potential to make him happy and gay,' Beauty seriously thought. 'I'd rather make him gay so that he would go outside and sodomize the Beastly Boys instead of having straight sex with me a horrible fifty times each and every damned night! Oh well; why should I trust or place any merit in dreams?' the girl skeptically wondered. 'Grim reality is all that really matters, and *its* ugly day-to-day lessons can never be altered.' And then the incarcerated maiden carefully studied her reflection in a wall mirror. "Let's face it," she said to her very attractive looking-glass image. "Having wild intercourse with a virulent animal like a lion or a gorilla is really the epitome of sexual perversion! Let's get it on!"

In the next several weeks, Beauty explored all sectors of the grand palace, wondering what the hell her captivity by choice was really all about. Each day her quandary expanded as the searcher investigated numerous formerly unexplored chambers, and the many enigmas of the gigantic castle seemed to proportionately grow in magnitude. And so,

Beauty intensely dreamed each night of her special, imaginary, handsome prince, and during one such odd mental excursion, the perplexed girl was portrayed in her vision as having a romantic dialogue with the frightful phantom Beast.

In her ghastly dream, Beauty heard the Beast approaching and considered if the brute meant to slaughter and eat her right at that moment, starting by lapping her nicely-trimmed blonde pussy and then biting into her fleshy, aroused clit after becoming sufficiently excited and nearing a wild, animalistic climax.

"Oh Beast," Beauty orally conveyed in the mental manifestation that seemed all too real and surreal simultaneously, "what should I say every time you insist that I marry you. Please wear some clothes, or trousers, or something in the line of attire, and cover-up those tremendous. furry testicles and your long flabby dick that also obviously needs immediate liposuction."

"Please say 'yes' to my proposal," the Beast explicitly begged in the dream. "Then I'll pork your wet, pink slit so thoroughly that you'll be yelling 'yes, yes, yes' until the day that your soul leaves your passionate body and passes into the high atmosphere, fluttering away from this vile and evil earth."

"Oh Beast, don't you have air conditioning in your capacious palace?" Beauty asked. "It gets pretty beastly in the hotter rooms every now and then."

"No, I have no idea what you mean by air conditioning," the Beast lowly growled. "But I can surely feed my gaseous nephews, the incomparable Beastly Boys, plenty of baked beans and the beauty salon quartet could spontaneously fart all night in your direction if that's your pleasure."

"Ah, no thanks," the girl (in her nightmare) smartly retreated from her former concern. "Here's what I really meant to inquire about. Do you too have erotic exotic dreams kind Beast similar to the ones I do?" Beauty candidly requested knowing.

"Yes, I do have certain dreams," the Beast disclosed, "but they're horrible sticky, white dreams. When I dream about your liposuction, for instance, I explode my white juices all over the ceiling and the floor, and my bed should really be a gooey swimming pool instead of a mattress on a wooden frame. Each night I wake up drowning in my own damned messy semen," the Beast complained, "and it's all because I'm dreaming of your stunning body and of your gorgeous face, in that damned exact order."

And next in her vivid dream, the fair maiden observed the Beast transform into the benign handsome Prince, and the fair girl felt compelled to ask a pertinent question of him. "Now I think I actually fathom the nature of this great conundrum!" she told the Prince in her bizarre mental manifestation. "But dear Prince, why are you so depressed and miserable?"

"Because I'm dick-less!" the royal one reluctantly admitted. "Because I'm dick-less, dear beloved Beauty; that's precisely what anguishes me and also makes me clueless!" the handsome Prince reiterated just before evaporating into another vague dimension.

"Now I fully comprehend what the hell's going on around this fucked-up palace!" Beauty yelled to the walls. "The Beast is really the unpopulated region's reigning Prince! I suspect that both the Beast and the Prince have been punished by some wicked enchanter or enchantress's curse. If I consent to marry the Beast," Beauty theorized and said to herself, "he'll turn into the Prince, and the Prince will then acquire the Beast's hairy balls and fatty pussy plunger. Then I'll definitely feel more comfortable administering liposuction to the young royal, and the Prince will again be happy in his existence, and the Beast will probably become a gay faggot without a dick, but he'll still find contentment from being porked up the ass by his naughty nasty nephews, the horrendous Beastly Boys. In other words," Beauty concluded and uttered to a spotless wall mirror, "my first blowjob will break the reprehensible, atrocious curse that has been bothering both the Beast and his alter ego, the Prince, who are actually one and the same damned personage!"

Suppertime arrived, but there was no sign of the Beast anywhere throughout Beauty's thorough explorations of the mammoth castle. Refusing to touch her wonderful food, Beauty dashed out of the palace but forgot that there were twelve marble steps leading from the ground to the building's massive chandeliered foyer. So, the damsel tumbled headlong to the driveway below, extensively scraping her hands, wrists, legs and tits. The fair lass then called for the Beast's assistance, but no palpable response was forthcoming.

It was then that the rosy-faced maiden realized that she had been standing outside in a gorgeous garden bordering a babbling brook, the same stream she had visualized in her marvelous-but-nebulous dream of the royal lost Prince. At the end of a palace entrance lane was a small cave, and inside Beauty chanced upon the Beast's figure lying prone upon a blue blanket. The wanderer slowly advanced and lovingly stroked the Beast's face and mangy hair, but no tangible response resulted. Then the intrepid girl stroked the lion's flaccid penis, which to her amazement grew to a length of two-*feet* even though it was an animal dick and not the lower part of any leg. And soon sticky semen was squirting all over the damned roof of the cave as if the Beast's thick, lengthy tool was a modern, efficiently functioning reproductive fire hose.

The Beast began breathing sighs of gratification as his eyes gradually opened, and the recipient of the rapid strokes thankfully beheld his exclusive heroine, benefactor and savior.

"Oh Beast, I was so frightened for your life!" the maiden joyfully cried. "Now I fully comprehend how much I really care for you. Wow! What a tremendous orgasm my right hand and fingers have generated! In fact, I actually do love you despite your totally wretched, grotesque, hideous, diabolical, carnivorous appearance. And if I may add to my poignant description, your facial hair and whiskers desperately need a sharp razor shave besides your furry balls."

"Oh, Beauty, I was near death because I thought that you would certainly abandon me," the Beast whimpered in a grateful-but-pouting tone of voice. "Will you marry me?"

Beauty thought about her theory that the Beast and the Prince would switch identities with the lion's huge sexual apparatus suddenly attaching to the Prince's dick-less, ball-less abdomen. Then the bankrupt merchant's daughter ruminated about the lion's fantastic penis that squirted rich white sperm juices all over the damned cave and about the Beast's ten-pound furry testicles and exultantly yelled, "Yes, yes, ohhhhh yes!" in a simulated orgasm.

An array of sensational fireworks soon lit-up the now-night sky, and cannons loudly boomed and a thousand rifles blasted in the distance. And next, across the avenue of autumnal deciduous trees, in the dark sky magically appeared an inspiring message: "Long Live the Prince, his Bride and the Fully Fucked-up Beastly Boys!"

And then the sophisticated, stately, aristocratic woman that had mystically appeared in one of Beauty's dreams (to comfort her in a time of sorrowful indecision) crystallized, and the elderly matron turned-out to be the Prince's devoted mother, who was praying for the day that a beautiful virgin would arrive to release her accursed son from an evil witch's diabolical spell.

"Well my Mother Queen of Phantasia," the joyful Prince announced. "I want to officially introduce you to my future wife Beauty, and Mommy, I promise not to try any advanced *S and M* tactics until *our* second official honeymoon night."

"How can I ever thank you enough my dear Beauty for returning my son to his natural form?" the Queen of Phantasia asked. "We're both greatly indebted to you!"

"You can invite my eleven self-centered brothers and sisters to the nuptial ceremony," Beauty suggested. "And the faggot Beastly Boys could sing two of my favorite songs at *our* upcoming wedding reception: "The Monster Mash" and "Beast of Burden," but only if the talentless Beastly Boys learn how to read music and how to play instruments other than having one of those numbskulls repetitiously banging on a snare drum," Beauty communicated. "And also, the rapping monotone dolts must satisfactorily master the art of singing four-part-harmony within the two-week span between now and the upcoming, gala, wedding ceremony."

"Cinderella's Fella"

In the old strange times when just like today, odd strange people abounded, three sisters lived in a stone house with their mother and the daughters espousing the interesting philosophy that people who live in stone houses should not throw glass. The sturdy stone house was situated only several blocks from the city's great square, mostly because architects and engineers back then were squares that knew nothing about designing or building circles, triangles, whorehouses, rhombuses, parallelograms or trapezoids. The King's palace was located on one side of the great central square, where other squares lived besides the ones that constituted the inbred royal family.

The two older hideous, insidious sisters living in the stone house were also ugly, bitter, sour, jealous, envious, distrustful and vengeful, but their youngest sister was only their half-sister, and nobody knew or talked about whom the girl's anonymous father might have been. But many neurotic citizens suspected that the biological dad might have been the King or his dyke-like perverted wife. Despite those sketchy circumstances, the young maiden was beautiful, passive, modest, humble and gentle, and that's why her bellicose older haggling, haggish sisters despised her with a mean-spirited passion.

While the two nasty bimbos sat in comfort in their well-appointed upstairs rooms, the younger half-sister had to live in squalor in the basement and had to share damp mildewed living space with rats, cockroaches, mice and vicious, rabid gerbils. But pristine Cinderella had to do the bulk of the cooking, sewing, scrubbing, cleaning, scouring and laundry while her dastardly good-for-nothing sisters taunted and ridiculed her at every opportunity.

Cinderella vigilantly (and without complaint) washed all the family linens, darned everyone's socks and stockings, mended their brassieres and corsets and performed all the family's grocery shopping. In fact, the exploited girl worked from dawn to midnight every seven days a week and labored extensively on *Christmas, Hanukkah, Kwanzaa, Easter* and *New Year's Day* too.

'I don't mind chopping the firewood and going to the well to fetch water with my neighborhood friends Jack and Jill,' Cinderella thought, 'but I refuse to wipe my sisters' dumpy asses or change their cruddy tampons. Those practices they'll have to do for themselves or perform for each other. That's where I draw the damned line!'

And despite the fact that poor Cinderella had little to eat, the girl sported a curvaceous hourglass 38-24-36" body that made her sisters cringe with envy and vomit from jealousy. And the two older, whoring sluts nagged, mocked, jeered, scorned and even beat Cinderella with the fireplace poker, but the wonderful virgin remained cheerful and optimistic despite *their* rancor, sarcasm and excessive physical abuse.

And the good-hearted teenager always faithfully said her morning and evening prayers and stayed refreshingly enthusiastic even though she lived a horrible slave-like existence. The medieval stones on the house's exterior were warmer than her sisters' hearts happened to be. But the adolescent's greatest joy was to sit by the cozy, inviting hearth after her many tasks had been completed, and because of the cinders burning away amongst the fireplace's embers, the maiden had obtained the unique-but-appropriate nickname "Cinderella".

The gorgeous girl's sisters hated her beauty, hated her positive attitude, hated her energy, hated her pleasant smile and hated all of Cinderella's other marvelous qualities that *they* didn't possess. And the mild-mannered virgin childishly believed that she had a fairy godmother with a humped back that was reputed to be a descendant of famed Quasimodo, although that delicate matter has been widely disputed, even by Victor Hugo.

The fairy godmother, even though deformed and a lecherous lesbian practicing absolute abstinence, had attended Cinderella's Christening in peculiar garb of the time, dressed in a high dunce-like, black hat and a garish green dress, and almost every guest that attended the solemn religious ceremony including the two older sisters called the old woman both a declarative phrase and an interrogative sentence: "Old Stumpy-Stump" and "Which Witch is She?"

The day of Cinderella's Christening, the old fairy godmother gave all of her vocal gossipy critics one long glare out of her emerald green eyes, and the other sophisticated women attending the event all got quite startled and farted quite loudly, stinking-up the whole damned dismal, Baptismal ceremony. And everyone in attendance watched in awe when the fairy godmother violently shoved the sanctimonious priest into a hard, wooden chair and then casually sauntered-up to the poorly constructed wooden cradle and touched the child's silky soft forehead while nodding three times to tacitly show her approval and full satisfaction.

One day, when Cinderella was about to enter puberty a second time, the girl mentioned her phantom "Fairy Godmother" to her two despicable loathsome sisters, and both of the scumbag whores became extraordinarily enraged at the mere suggestion that Cinderella might be favored by anyone, especially one so powerful and committed to and skilled in the mysterious black arts.

144

"That crazy old humpback you call a Fairy Godmother doesn't care one hoot about you, my Prissy Miss Slut Wannabe'!" the eldest bitch meanly criticized her pristine, innocent sister. "And any way Miss Goody-Goody Two Shoes, the old deformed witch is probably long dead by now, so don't you dare Cinderella imagine that this unidentified Grandmother could be of any assistance or comfort to you. Stop your idle daydreaming by the fire and go out and buy us some more tampons and toilet paper. My sister and I want to teach you several new body responsibilities."

"Use your middle fingers to plug-up each other's pleasure cracks and while you bitches are at it, use each other's big toes to seal-up your smelly rectums!" Cinderella aggressively fired back. "I'll go out and buy your tampons and your damned liquor-scented toilet paper, but I'll never stoop to changing tampons or wiping either of your smelly buttocks. And if I ever find a Prince Charming, I'm the lucky one that's gonna' be squeezing the Charmin'."

Around *Christmas* time of Cinderella's eighteenth birthday, the King sent-out his blithe trumpeters and his zany saxophone players (all wearing tight leotards and tutus) to proclaim that a Great Palace Ball was to occur on the Twelfth Night with much revelry, dancing, feasting, burping, farting and perverted and straight sex being indulged in. The celebration would eventually spill-out into the city streets with many bonfires, bomb fires, fireworks, falling meteors and comets, and the grand festivities also would feature marketplace stalls selling cakes, sweetmeats, pizza, root beer, hot dogs, hoagies, sex toys and ribbed prophylactics of various pastel colors. The great jubilation was to commemorate the young Prince's twenty-first birthday, and hopefully for the worried King and Queen, a fair buxom maiden would accelerate the physically immature lad to finally enter puberty, achieve a decent erection and then pop his first load either by getting blown or getting laid for the very first damned time.

The King's Lord Chamberlain (who always looked rather wilted) visited the old stone house, and the two older sisters, upon seeing his royal minister's arrival, locked-up Cinderella in the kitchen pantry so that the government official would not gaze upon or discover her exceptionally attractive face. The two greedy, fucked-up siblings enthusiastically greeted the Lord Chamberlain at the front door and deliberately kept the aristocratic visitor standing in the foyer.

"I see that *three* daughters are enrolled on my ledger who are eligible to attend the Grand Palace Ball," the King's representative observed and solemnly stated. "And I mean to tell you two bimbos that even ugly bitches like you dumb broads stand a decent chance of getting laid or sodomized once I deliberately trip the lights' fantastic. After the cotillion is over, the Grand Ballroom's candles will go out at midnight so that everyone attending can chaotically participate in the highly anticipated Grand Balling in total darkness!"

"But only *two* of us are left living in this household," the oldest and most wicked of the sisters attested. And so, the royal Chamberlain's dick wilted even more when the king's advisor learned *that* unfortunate misinformation, and soon the royal public ambassador courteously bowed to the two grotesque-looking, wart-faced hags and immediately left the premises to find the nearest bar and get as plastered as the tavern's walls.

The vile elder sisters talked relentlessly about the upcoming ball and about the lights going-out at midnight so that each of them might get porked in the dark by some adulterous government officials, And thereafter, the mean-hearted scabby-faced sisters persisted in antagonizing Cinderella mercilessly, taunting and mocking her and emphasizing how *they* had been cordially invited to the Great Ball, and how she wasn't even considered eligible, and how their clothes and gowns were of the finest fabrics while the half-sister had to wear rags and scarves mended together to look like rags and scarves. And when the contemptible, horny bitches weren't quarreling with and berating poor Cinderella, the harlots were arguing with and belittling each other. Such is the existence of psychopathic brow-beaters and of socio-path*etic* female vultures.

The two sisters were like queen hornets trapped in a small box. The more Cinderella tried satisfying their selfish personalities, and the harder the beauty diligently worked on command, the more the dual bitches resented her and the angrier they each became. The hostile filthy sluts dumped more bullshit on the young maiden than that which existed in all the pastures all over the lethargic King's expansive dairy and beef realm.

The night of the Grand Palace Ball, the city's streets and avenues were aglow with torches and bonfires at intervals of every fifty feet. Splendid tapestries and silk flags were draped from overhanging balconies, and the male citizens were all drunk and suffering from diarrhea obtained from all of the red and white wine gushing from the numerous contaminated water fountains.

Music and laughter abounded on all the avenues that were teeming with jolly revelers such as circus performers who deftly juggled midgets and dwarfs into the air and then abandoned the tiny beings as the fools began their downward plummets. And sideshow freaks were present everywhere, and in most cases it was difficult distinguishing the

146

city's raucous residents from the entrepreneurial, visiting, shit-eating lady giants, the bearded tit-less women and the freakish twin men that shared five testicles.

The elder sisters had bought and worn extra-large hairpieces so that they would appear as important *bigwigs* at the gala event. And the two wretched bitches wore so much powder on their faces that the sluts' looked like a pair of plump ghosts as the sluts snobbishly entered their rented carriage on their way to the Grand Ballroom where they hoped they each would be laid by at least two rich aristocratic, drunken, old fucks when the lights would go out at midnight.

Meanwhile, Cinderella was quite disappointed and in a very cheerless, melancholy mood. The inconsolable girl sat dolefully by the fireplace, and when the natural beauty bent over to stoke the flames, a tear fell from her eyes, and a sparkling sizzle resulted when the damp drop landed upon the hot cinders.

But then a discernible knock originated from the front door, and Cinderella couldn't imagine what ignoramus would be visiting the stone house while such a fantastic Grand Palace Ball was in progress only several blocks away.

When the sobbing girl wiped-away her tears and finally opened the front door, a certain green-eyed, humpbacked lady was standing outside in the frigid cold. "Good evening my precious one," the wrinkle-faced old dame politely greeted. "I see you don't seem to know who the fuck I am. But why are you standing here all alone when every fun-loving girl and lady is dancing at the Palace Ball in preparation and anticipation of getting balled in the Grand Ballroom when the lights go out at midnight?"

Cinderella felt lonely and alienated from society at that particular moment. She stared at the influential-looking spell-caster with the peculiar-looking hooked nose, imagined that the old lady's warty face was a weirdly ornamented dildo, and then out of courtesy, invited the old bat inside for a casual chat. The maiden informed the old Fairy Godmother all the pertinent details about the Palace Ball, which the nearly deaf, daft old woman had intermittently thought was rowdy peasants rioting for food and winter shelter in the distant streets.

"Ah ha!" the Fairy Godmother that had had lesbian sex with assorted fairies and with immoral homo' transgenders countless times exclaimed. "We have no time to lose. Night is rapidly speeding ahead on fast-forward. Put on your best gown young woman, and I'll promptly alter it so that your breasts will make every man at the ball drool, and then they'll all prematurely fire-off their anxious cannons into their dainty silk underwear."

Cinderella knew that her sadistic sisters had threatened to have her eating only bread and drinking only water for a full month if she ever dared leaving the stone house in their absence. But the damsel in distress fully knew from reconnaissance eavesdropping that *she* had also been invited to the "Grand Ball", and the fair maiden wanted to get balled so badly on that particular evening that she didn't give two flying shits about her cruel sisters' vengeance or about losing her damned virgin cherry to some drunken aristocrat who was capable of sustaining a hard on and porking her sweet honey-hole good.

"I have nothing to wear to the Grand Ball," Cinderella shyly confessed to her self-appointed guardian. "And I don't have the courage to go naked, even though I would definitely set the tone for later at midnight, and I'm sure that every male there would want to ravish and molest me. What should I do Fairy Godmother?"

"Don't worry my dear!" the old shrew (who looked something like a small, vertical humpback whale) assuredly answered. "I'll make you look like the finest high society slut there, even though I know you're still a stupid-ass damned virgin! Now duck-down and bow if you don't want to get knocked unconscious," the old bag sternly commanded. "You don't want to miss having a grand ball getting balled in the Grand Ballroom!"

Cinderella lowered her head just in time as a golden Arabian chest with ruby hinges came flying through the opened doorway, nearly decapitating her. The old fairy wretch then touched the box with her gnarled cane, wishing all the while that Cinderella would have the gumption to simultaneously touch *her* ancient, dried-up box. And beneath the trunk's lid was an Oriental gown that was so beautiful that Cinderella momentarily was disoriented and had to subsequently orient herself to admiring the magnificent piece of silk apparel.

"So, my dear, there's your fuckin' evening gown!" the fairy godmother cackled. "Now hop inside the damned thing before I can wink an eye. Notice how enticing your breasts and hips will be when this magical gown accentuates all of your fine femininity. My word; what a gorgeous firm ass you have!"

"Oh wonderful! Now I'm a damsel in *this dress!*" the girl joyfully jested. "But kind woman," Cinderella addressed in a sadder, more serious tone of voice. "Just look at my holey shoes. They appear to belong to a whoring pauper wench. My toes are coming through the fronts, and also Gay Fairy Godmother," Cinderella continued, "my walking arrangements are obviously in stark contrast to my elegant gown that makes me look like I've had wonderful breast, hip, thigh and ass enhancements done at an expensive plastic surgery clinic!"

The old witch indulgently laughed, bent-over and casually examined the scruffy-looking objects that the poorest of beggars wouldn't be buried in. "Shoo, you' old shoes!" the Gay Fairy Godmother screamed. "Out with the old, and in with the new!"

A bright, blinding light temporarily hid the old leather horrors, and when the illumination slowly vanished, a fabulous pair of glass slippers appeared in their stead.

"But wonderful magician woman," Cinderella remarked in absolute amazement. "I need stylish high-heel-shoes and not fancy glass slippers. And besides, I do believe that banana peels make the best slippers and not glass."

And so, the old woman wagged her crooked cane over the spun glass slippers (as if the walking stick were a magic wand) and remarkably, the well-crafted slippers changed into an exquisite pair of glistening spun glass high heels.

"Oh, Gay Fairy Godmother!" the maiden triumphantly exclaimed. "Now I'm truly and fully ready and willing to get balled in the Grand Ballroom at the Grand Ball."

"And how do you suppose we'll get you through the deep snow my dear, if you get the *drift* of what the hell I'm asking?" the eccentric Fairy Godmother rhetorically questioned. "If you walk the short distance to the palace, you might contract pneumonia, which at times could be just as deadly as ammonia after the stinking cleaning chemical is swallowed."

"Holy Shit Fairy Godmother!" Cinderella realized and gasped. "Certainly, if your magic could produce such an exotic dress and such stellar glass shoes, so too it could provide me with reasonable transportation to the Grand Palace Ball. Of course, I could sprint the two city blocks and be there in shorter time than a wet fart's smell lasts."

"Nonsense my dear!" the Madam Fairy (who was once a fairy madam at an exclusive lesbian brothel) shrieked in amusement. "I'll provide you a coach that's better than the one that manages the city's undefeated soccer team."

> "Never complaining, you're never awry,
> You'll make men's dicks get caught in their fly.
> Be patient Cindy, be vigilant, and be free as air,
> Just watch that fuckin' pumpkin, sitting over there!"

Cinderella peered at the orange late fall pumpkin (that was to be harvested to make a delicious early winter pie) situated next to the hearth and thought, 'My late uncle once told me he liked to *pump kin,* and believing in incest, he did.' The girl then lifted-up the plump orange vegetable and conveyed it to her incoherent Fairy Godmother as the maiden had been strictly instructed. The old woman again waved her curved cane, and the selected pumpkin amazingly grew and swelled into a splendid green and white carriage, which happened to be the same colors as the city's undefeated soccer team's uniforms.

And then a dozen anxious, pesky house mice came pattering out of their favorite wall and floor holes, and the hyperactive rodents immediately grew in stature and transformed into twelve silver antlered reindeer, all of whom immediately crapped egregiously all over the formerly immaculate floor. But impeccable Cinderella didn't give a shit about the reindeer dung because the prospective passenger was so fascinated with the astounding spectacles that her eyes had been witnessing.

And next, four gaily-dressed, gay coachmen came out of the side closet and publicly announced their homosexuality, even though Cinderella didn't recognize any of the pedophiles from Post Office "Most Wanted Posters" and finally comprehended that *their* identities were anonymous (at least to her).

"Oh, Fairy Godmother. I know I'm going to have a gay old time even though I really want to simply get seduced and laid in the prodigious Grand Ballroom and not sodomized by some demented dyke wearing a belted dildo! But being sodomized up the ass by a big erect, natural pecker isn't such a goddamned bad idea, either!"

"And now my dear, I must leave your company, even though you don't own any corporation," the visiting sorceress informed her thoroughly delighted hostess. "But I just gotta' tell you Cinderella to get the hell back home from the Grand Palace Ball by midnight or else you're going to instantly die a damned virgin and go to hell to be fucked for all eternity by Satan!"

"But then I won't be able to get balled or naturally sodomized in the Grand Ballroom when the lights dim and then go out at the stroke of twelve!" Cinderella emotionally protested. "Logic dictates I'd better religiously adhere to your austere directions."

"Haven't you ever heard of masturbation my dear?" the Gay Fairy Godmother answered with a wide grin as she crystallized and then vanished into thin air. "It's a terrific method of reducing stress and tension!" an echo from afar attested.

'My flighty Fairy Godmother in her haste forgot to place the carriage and the reindeer outside,' Cinderella noticed and mentally noted. 'Oh well. I guess I can't have it all!'

150

And so, the girl got the four gay coachmen to push and squeeze their green and white carriage through the stone house's narrow front entrance outside into the bitter cold, and then the mindless attendants methodically shoved each reindeer's ass one-by-one through the portal, too. After the animals were hitched-up to the stellar coach, Cinderella soon entered the shiny mode of transportation, and the four faggot coachmen acted like an out-of-tune barbershop quartet singing a lively futuristic number, "Gay sex marriage, gay sex marriage, go together like reindeer and carriage!"

Soon the loveliest of the King's invited guests arrived in her emerald green and snow-white dwarfed carriage, which the King assumed was the late arrival of the city's heralded, undefeated soccer team. When the shivering mendicants and bag-ladies that were demonstrating outside the Palace for more food, better shelters and the establishment of cleaner soup kitchens caught sight of the radiant damsel, the protesters alternately cheered the beaming girl and emphatically gave the royal middle finger to the apathetic, dimwit King and his entourage.

And when Cinderella finally entered the main Grand Ballroom, even the violinists stopped fiddling around and the guitarist began to fret, and then the musician vigorously scratched his swollen hemorrhoids with his right big toe while eagerly strumming his stringed instrument like a maniac. The entire chamber became as silent as the lunar surface as if the abashed girl had suddenly shocked everyone by imaginatively mooning her captivated audience.

The Prince came-down from the *head table* where he had abandoned a terrific blowjob being administered to him by a filthy slut on her knees, obscured under the draped counter (the King had hired the harlot kneeling under the table so that the twenty-one-year-old Prince could achieve his first erection and subsequent ejaculation, which would have been the greatest achievements of *his* lazy, worthless life). The royal son finally remembered to put his dingle in his saliva-stained drawers and button-up his silk pants (which had yellow piss stains and not white come stains) before he paced halfway to the vivacious angel presently standing in the majestic chamber's arch.

Everyone admired the new arrival except two skanky-looking bitches that jealously stood under the upside-down mistletoe, which was medieval symbolism representing the females' desire to get screwed before the stroke of midnight when the lights would suddenly extinguish and all the straight men would begin stroking their chosen women, and all the gay son of a bitches would be either giving professional blowjobs to well-endowed attendees or sodomizing anyone or anything (around the large hall) that had an asshole.

The Prince danced all evening with the lovely maiden with the glass slippers while her deplorable half-sisters (who couldn't figure-out who the mystery maiden was) were wholly envious of her charm and radiance. And right when the Prince was contemplating pumping his erect pecker into Cinderella's virgin pussy, precisely at the *stroke* of midnight, the great bell of the Palace clock began very slowly tolling, one, two three, four…"

"Oh Prince," the unnerved girl sighed. "I hear a bell chiming. Ring my chimes Prince, I implore you! Please go ahead and ring my chimes with your wild and crazy, bobbing, throbbing cuckoo bird!"

"Don't you worry my sugary darling," the not-too-alert Prince confidently replied. "After the clock strikes twelve, the lights will go out throughout the Ballroom, and I'll be pumping your honey-well so hard that torrents of semen will start squirting out of your ears!"

The color began fading from Cinderella's rosy cheeks (both on her face and on her well-proportioned ass), which unfortunately was concealed by her pure white, Oriental silk evening gown. In her fright, the nervous maiden withdrew from the Prince and bolted across the crowded Ballroom just before the clock's tolling finished recording the magic hour. And at the bottom of the staircase the girl twisted her foot in her hectic rush, just at the stroke of eleven chimes. Cinderella's right glass shoe came-off her dainty foot at the exact same time when the clock boomed midnight, and all kinds of moaning and groaning along with shrieks of ecstasy permeated (and was emitted from) the Grand Ballroom on the Grand Palace's second floor.

The next thing Cinderella knew, she was standing in the stone house's familiar kitchen, and the teen instantly observed the orange pumpkin lying at a corner of the hearth near the rusty hob. The stunned girl chased a lazy pigeon away and then plopped-down on her familiar wooden stool, which had previously been occupied by the stool pigeon. And as Cinderella gazed into the fire, she, for the first time experienced envy while watching an image of the royal family and their contented guests having a wild orgy in the hectic Grand Ballroom's dark shadows.

Cinderella looked-down in depression at the stone floor and beheld a glass high heel shoe on her left foot and a black tattered stocking on her right one. And the maiden waited in a dreamy state of mind for a full half-hour until she heard her diabolical, glib sisters returning home. The distressed girl popped-up from her stool and reckoned that she should attend to her overbearing sisters' needs.

"What a lousy, goddamned party that was!" the eldest wench yelled after entering the stone house and then slamming shut the front door. "I didn't even get a tit fondled let alone a hairy salami shoved-up my hungry love tunnel. Not even my raunchy butthole got penetrated. What a damned crock of shit that whole event was!"

"And all the Prince could do was cry over that Princess impostor who had crashed his glorious birthday celebration," the second sister screamed in a rage. "Who was that queer Princess who raided the ball before *I* could drop my drawers and get balled myself'. I mean shit; I didn't even get sodomized up my ass by a damned gay bishop or cardinal, or even by a faggot horny hummingbird! Where have all the pedophiles gone to? Gay Paris, to Amsterdam or maybe to saucy San Francisco, I suppose?"

"Not even a damned elf, midget or dwarf so much as touched either of my nipples in the dark," the eldest sister squawked and complained. "I hope you didn't throw my porno' animal sex magazine out, Cinderella. I need to look at a gorilla putting it to a donkey so that I could rub my little love button like crazy and achieve a decent orgasm!"

'It's a good thing my gossiping sisters are so friggin' enraged out of their senses that neither one of them has noticed my sole glass shoe and my other foot without any slipper on it!' Cinderella realized. 'I'd better scamper upstairs to the dressing room like a gazelle before the two ornery bitches both go ballistic on me!'

The next morning, before the first horse-drawn snowplow passed by the ancient stone house, the strumpeters and their husband trumpeters were blowing their horns out in the city square, heralding some sort of official government announcement. Then the King sent-out his seventy-six-year-old, really wilted Chamberlain (who had gotten laid in the Grand Ballroom seven times from midnight to three a.m. the night before) along with six attendant pages, the half-dozen shithead squires making-up the governing council of the local gay sex *chapter*.

The juice-less, useless old geezer was going from house to house desperately searching for the "special one" whose right foot exactly fit the elegant glass shoe, which was being gingerly carried around (in the still-raging snowstorm) on a wet, velvet cushion. At every house being canvassed, the most beautiful occupant living within was graciously requested to try-on the same glass high-heel-shoe, which was a size eight, the same size as nine-tenths of the seven-hundred-thousand Princess wannabes' residing in the whole, damned, lousy city wore on their stinking feet.

"Shit!" the wilted, sperm-less Chamberlain exclaimed to his six faggot *pages*, who represented half of the local gay *chapter* of "Queers Synonymous". "This damned glass shoe will fit just about everybody but friggin' Bigfoot!"

Finally, the wilted, juiceless Lord Chamberlain persevered and arrived at the stone house occupied by the three sisters. The two older sisters, who both wore size twelve shoes, had snipped-off all ten of their toes with a butcher's blade and had bandaged-up their bleeding feet to attempt fooling the royal agent by having the glass shoe fit perfectly. But even though "the miracle slipper" matched the sisters' foot length, it was far too narrow for either mentally challenged bitch to comfortably wear.

The wilted, fluid-less Lord Chamberlain next disgustingly looked at the pathetic, ugly, gross sisters and patiently asked, "Is there any other lady living in this house? If there is, I trust that she's not half as ugly and not half as incompetent as you two dimwits apparently are. Now I've noticed that neither of you has any toes on either of your damned, altered feet! How damned fucked-up can you possibly get? Do you two imbeciles think that you're dealing with an inept palace amateur here?"

The two black-hearted, toeless sisters hollered "No Fuck Head!" in unison, but then the wilted Chamberlain heard a sweet voice singing, and the marvelous melodious sound was originating from upstairs.

The totally exhausted Chamberlain dispatched two of his equally wilted pages up the steps to ascertain the source of the lovely singing. And the exploring scouts finally returned downstairs accompanied by Cinderella, dressed in her standard daily rags. But the innocent girl suddenly broke-out into hysterics upon seeing the "glass slipper" resting upon the soft, soaking wet, velvet cushion.

"Why are you smiling and acting like a simpleminded proletarian?" the prudish Protestant moral majority wilted Chamberlain mildly chastised the girl.

"Because my Lord," the happy young lady stated, "I have in my possession a glass shoe that's almost the duplicate of the wet one situated on that snow-laden velvet cushion. I've slickly hidden my prized possession from my ugly sisters' scrutiny inside the kitchen drawer farthest to the right."

And after the only sober gay page brought back the designated glass shoe from the specified kitchen drawer, the item was found to fit perfectly on Cinderella's left foot, and the shoe that was formerly on the velvet cushion fit perfectly on the maiden's right clodhopper.

Cinderella was immediately conducted to the Palace Throne Room to an audience with the King and Queen, who were still recuperating on their royal chairs from being sodomized up the ass by just about everyone in their kingdom that had a dick who had attended the Grand Ball inside the Grand Palace Ballroom. After screwing the kingdom's citizens with high taxes for many years, the Monarch and his wife finally were justly screwed in return by receiving myriad royal salamis up their sensitive butt-holes. But the aching, sore-assed, half-intoxicated royals received and accepted Cinderella as if she were their actual biological daughter, which she might have actually been.

In three weeks, (much to the chagrin of the elder sisters), the gay bishop married Cinderella to the mentally challenged, bisexual Prince, and the whole damned city's population was clamoring for another Midnight Ball celebration to transpire inside the Palace Grand Ballroom. Black pudding, meat cakes, electric eels that served as female crotch vibrators, rap rhapsody singers, hair pie samples and sticky buns were very evident and abundant all over the city, and especially smattered all over the friggin' main square.

And Cinderella's old maid of honor was not either of *her* despicable, bad-tempered, avaricious sisters, but instead, the principal bridesmaid was her humped back Gay Fairy Godmother, who arrived at the prodigious ceremony clad in an eerie, dark, green mantle. The old dame ate nothing at all at the gala banquet reception, and the outlandish witch continuously smiled at the other guests, exhibiting a mouth featuring two upper incisors and one lower-jaw, yellowish-brown. decayed tooth.

Everyone attending the merry feast was enthralled with the entertainment that had been determined and organized by the somewhat-kinky bisexual Prince, who incidentally finally entered puberty just at the right time. For everyone's amusement, Cinderella's two horrible half-sisters were stripped naked and then were forcefully manacled to stone chairs securely anchored into the chamber's floor. And then six donkeys and four stud bull elephants hilariously took turns sodomizing the two bitches up their asses until both notorious whores finally collapsed, going unconscious from suffering their embarrassing-but-animalistic, masochistic ordeal.

"Flakey Snow White and the Seven Midgdwarfs"

Once upon a time (because this kind of bullshit never happens twice upon a time), a winter storm's snowflakes were covering the ground, forming massive drifts. A young Queen sat stitching embroidery at a castle window and was occasionally staring-out at the swirling blizzard. The King's wife's needle accidentally pricked her finger, and three blood droplets fell-down into the snowbank below. Now how the blood drops got from inside the warm castle through the wall, or through the closed window for that matter, remains a puzzling fairy tale mystery until this very day.

'Hey!' the young Queen thought. 'If I could only be having my period right now, I could sit my ass out in the ice-cold snow and make a really big red area instead of three tiny insignificant scarlet spots.' And then the restive Queen had an inspiration to match her very foul perspiration. 'If I only could have a little child as white as snow, with rosy cheeks as red as blood, and with jet black hair the same shade as my bedroom's newly painted window frame,' the regal personage wished. 'Oh well! Such stupid shit only happens in grim fairy tales.'

Three days later a baby girl was born to the Queen, who incidentally had had her ovaries, Fallopian tubes and most of her uterus removed two years before the miraculous birth during an emergency hysterectomy. And then upon Flakey Snow White's "miraculous birth", the Queen unexpectedly passed-away (without any medical insurance) from internal hemorrhaging and also from external hemorrhoid hemorrhaging that together caused a rare, never-heard-of-before "body implosion."

A year later, the heterosexual King got over his grief about his wife's sudden death, became horny again and married another woman who then became the Queen of the Land. But the new spouse was arrogant and vain and desired to be the most beautiful lady in the entire ten-square-mile empire. The second Queen possessed a magic talking mirror, and one morning when she was admiring herself' in the looking glass, she selfishly asked:

> "Mirror, mirror, on the wall,
> "Who's the queerest of them all?"

And the honest-minded mirror truthfully replied, "You are, you big, fat, ugly, lesbian bitch!"

The vengeful Queen threatened to smash and shatter the mirror into microscopic glass bits if the talking wonder persisted in being "impudent and irresponsibly ludicrous". So, the haughty royal lady changed her strategy and asked the now-admonished mirror another more thought-provoking inquiry:

"Mirror, mirror on the wall,
Who's the fairest of them all?"

The inimitable loquacious mirror eloquently replied:

"Queen, thou great ugliness is quite easy to pass,
Because your tiny tits are accompanied by a huge, fat ass,
But Snow White having rosy red cheeks and ebony hair,
Is a thousand times fairer than you are queer!"

The Queen's face turned deep green with envy being reflected in the kooky wall mirror. And whenever the jealous, jaded Queen's beady, green eyes scrutinized Flakey Snow White after the honest mirror's very accurate descriptions, the miserable monarch despised the beautiful girl with an intense antipathy. The diabolical woman summoned the royal huntsman to convey the child into the deep forest and permanently dispose of her. "And you must bring me a token as proof that you've completed your assignment and as verification that you've obeyed my exact instruction!" the nasty Queen imperatively commanded Mr. Hunter.

The huntsman dragged Flakey Snow White into the mountainous forest, and the girl made a last-ditch sorrowful plea to the notorious child molester and convicted pedophile. "Oh Mr. Hunter, please have pity on me!" Flakey Snow White begged the child serial killer with tears forming in her eyes. "If you let me go and if I remain a virgin, I'll gladly wander into the bleak wilderness and never return to 'the Palace' again, regardless of what X-rated vaudeville show will be appearing there on stage!"

The huntsman had an important appointment to keep where he had to circumcise the royal bishop's puny salami, so he hastily said to Flakey Snow White, "Okay little maiden. Dash into the woods and may the wolves, wild boars and other dreadful carnivores have mercy on you. If it wasn't so damned cold out here, and if you weren't so damned frigid to begin with," the huntsman regretted and stated, "I'd let you toot my eager horn until it erupted and foamed with froth, and if ya' ever took *Sex 101* in advanced kindergarten, you'd know exactly what the hell I'm talkin' about!"

Flakey Snow White scooted-off into the rugged steep hills while the benign huntsman removed an arrow from his quiver and aiming at a fleeing wolf, accidentally shot a wild boar by mistake. The archer removed the fierce pig's heart and brought it to the pernicious Queen claiming that it was "Flakey Snow White's ticker that no longer ticks or tocks." After Mr. Hunter departed the castle to circumcise the royal bishop's pecker, the lawless above-the-law Queen sprinkled salt, pepper, vinegar, relish, mustard, ketchup, Catalina dressing and mayonnaise on the bloody organ, and quickly devoured the boar's heart raw, licking her lips with great evil insanity throughout her terrible feast. 'No more evidence! Ha, ha, ha!' the malicious bitch insanely mused.

Meanwhile, Flakey Snow White's mind was in a quandary as the girl wandered lost along narrow, dark, shadowy, forest trails. And then she childishly sprinted as fast as her ivory-skinned legs would carry her over seven large hills until finally at sunset the runner reached a very small hut situated in a grassy meadow. The fair trekker opened the enclosure's front door, but no one was home, so the girl entered and curiously inspected the tidy, clean, tiny residence. Seven very little plates decorated the central table with the same number of forks, spoons, knives and goblets meticulously set around the individual dishes. Seven chairs were tucked-in under the kitchen table, and seven neatly made beds were organized in a perfect row.

'What kind of nutcase brothel is this?' the trespassing girl imagined. 'Is it a bordello for midgets? The Queen's not the only fucked-up person in this illogical world, that's for damned sure!'

Since the encroacher was extremely hungry and thirsty after the exhaustive travails of her traumatic day, the forest wanderer removed from each of the seven plates a small portion of bread, and then the famished interloper didn't waste valuable time farting around while biting into seven foul-tasting pieces of broccoli. Next, Flakey Snow White sipped and sampled wine from each of the seven pewter goblets and soon became quite fatigued and intoxicated, so the home intruder tried 'lying' on each of the seven beds because it was always difficult for Flakey Snow White to tell the truth while resting in a horizontal position.

The first bed was too hard, just like the notorious huntsman's reputed spectacular erection.

The second bed was too soft, just like the lamebrain King's diminutive boner.

The third bed was too short, just like the holier-than-thou bishop's inferior hard-on.

The fourth bed was too narrow, just like the new Queen's diseased sex cave.

The fifth bed was too flat, just like the new Queen's reprehensible-looking breasts.

The sixth bed was too fluffy, just like the new Queen's big, fat hideous buttocks.

But the seventh bed was just right, just like Flakey Snow White's perfectly developed female sexual equipment. So, the narcissistic girl quickly entered dreamland to ponder and mentally admire her wonderfully symmetrical, well-proportioned body.

Soon the sun set in the west, and foreboding shadows crept over the seven woody hills. The seven occupants of the fascinating hut returned from their daily labor of prospecting for gems and gold and also searching for discarded Parisian porno' magazines that had been secretly buried all over the damned mountainsides. Upon entering their modest dwelling, the horny little Midgdwarfs all simultaneously lit their seven lanterns and noticed right away that their familiar environment had been evidently violated and tampered with during their absence.

"Who's been sitting and farting in my chair?" the first Midgdwarf with his supersensitive nose asked.

"Who's been eating and spitting broccoli chucks in my damned plate?" the second appalled Midgdwarf demanded knowing.

"Who's been munching my bread and not biting my tiny pecker?" the third disenchanted Midgdwarf questioned.

"Who's been tasting my putrid vegetables and not lapping my delicious sperm juices?" the fourth thoroughly confused Midgdwarf asked.

"Who's been eating with my fork and not eating my diminutive dingle raw?" the fifth offended Midgdwarf wondered and vociferated.

"Who's been cutting with my knife and not cutting the curly hair off my balls with nice sharp teeth?" the sixth exasperated Midgdwarf inquired.

"Who's been drinking from my wine goblet and not being intoxicated enough to lick my smelly, hairy asshole?" the seventh displeased Midgdwarf demanded knowing.

And then the first pudgy, rotund Midgdwarf advanced to his bed and under great duress asked, "Who the fuck's been sleeping in my bed?"

And the second Midgdwarf observed and stated, "Who the fuck's been sneezing in my bed? There's friggin' snot and dried-up boogers all over the freakin' clean spread and pillowcase!"

And the third disgruntled Midgdwarf yelled-out, "My bed is all crumpled and humped without me remembering humping anybody nor pleasurably slapping my tiny monkey around!"

And the fourth Midgdwarf shrieked, "My bed is full of wrinkles just like the new Queen's big fat ass!"

And the fifth Midgdwarf appropriately hollered, "My bed is full of crinkles just like the new Queen's foul-smelling, dried-up pussy!"

And the sixth fussy Midgdwarf boomed, "My bed is all jumbled and tumbled without any nice tits being fumbled or hairy snatch being rumbled or thumbled!"

But the seventh and most fastidious of the short, obese, bearded Midgdwarfs bellowed as the examiner carefully inspected and then smelled several black pubic hairs, "Well, someone's been sleeping and masturbating in my bed, and here the fuck she is!"

The other six near-sighted, dirty-old-man Midgdwarfs quickly moved to the seventh bed's vicinity and then each unsuccessfully grabbed at the three prized black pubic hairs to have a satisfying whiff. The forest miners then raised their little lanterns up high over their heads and noticed with awe and delight the very curvaceous young maiden soundly sleeping upon the seventh bed.

"You jerk-offs can all sleep in your own damned beds tonight," the seventh impish fellow declared. "I'm gonna' buddy-up with this slick bitch and hopefully, I'll get to feel some warm breast flesh, suck on some virgin nipples and lay down my pick-ax besides my bed and get to use my other tool for a change!"

In the morning, Flakey Snow White abruptly woke-up and was frightened to see a little man licking away at her opened crotch, so she lifted up the tiny asshole, looked him in the eyes and adroitly flipped the short stubby bastard out of the comfortable bed and onto the hard wood-planked floor. But upon covering-up her exposed soft, white, radiant breasts, the fair maiden quickly and intuitively sensed that her hosts were mostly bashful inexperienced virgin Midgdwarfs more interested in pornography and lapping juicy pussies than in actually getting laid.

"What is your name dear child?" the seven Midgdwarfs all asked in unison, for they all had exactly the same thoughts and expressed the exact same words most (if not all) of the damned time.

"I'm known as Flakey Snow White," the beautiful girl answered, "mostly because my ideas are a bit flaky at times. And oh yes, you gentlemen may keep my ebony pubic hairs as souvenirs if you'd like, and if you let me live with you, I'll shave my hairy black bush once every month and let you weird, perverted little jerk-offs sniff away to your hearts' content!"

"Yippee!" the seven psychopathic morons all simultaneously yelled. "Hooray for Flakey Snow White and her juicy, jet black, dandruff-less pussy patch!"

And then the charming visitor retold her complete autobiography, and at first the seven pudgy Midgdwarfs stroked their long hairy beards, and then the easily influenced neurotics anxiously stroked their short, hard, hairy dingles.

"Flakey Snow White, do you think you could sew, cook, knit and masturbate daily for us?" the horny seventh Midgdwarf asked. "If you become our dedicated domestic slave, we'll give you half of the gold we haven't yet discovered!"

"Oh yes, I'll most certainly do all of those perfunctory chores with all of my heart!" the maiden promised the horny little men. But every morning before the little freaks went out to one of the seven small hills to dig for gold that wasn't there, the prospectors emphatically warned their sexy guest about the wicked Queen that had evilly sent Flakey Snow White into the forest.

"We don't trust her as far as a liquid fart can travel," the first Midgdwarf cautioned. "Whatever you do, don't let anyone into the house, especially an ugly bitch with a nasty temperament soliciting to give free blow-jobs!"

Meanwhile, the wretched Queen approached her unique talking mirror just to verify that innocent, immaculate Flakey Snow White had been disposed of, just as the bisexual, cross-dressing huntsman had claimed.

> "Mirror, mirror, on the wall,
> Who is the fairest one of all?"

And the omniscient mirror declaratively replied:

> "Royal crown, jeweled regal dress, throne all clean,
> It certainly isn't you, you bitchy witch, whoring Queen.
> The fairest woman dwells within a mountain glen,
> Cleaning and masturbating for seven little horny men!"

The obnoxious, jaded Queen became exceedingly livid, and her green eyes again turned even greener with envy. 'That huntsman has deceived me, and I'll have his dick delivered to me on a silver platter, and I'll then feed the bleeding organ to the royal hound to snack on,' the atrocious, satanic woman imagined and decided. "And as for Flakey Snow White, I suspect that she's still alive and couch dancing and stripping for the seven little maniacs digging for gold up in the mountains that yield only common coal. Now I know that there was actually a method to *their* fucked-up madness!"

The wicked Queen pondered her alternatives for several days, and her greedy heart gave her mind no rest or requiem. Finally, the old bitch laid-out a viable plan that she regarded as foolproof, even for a major fool in denial such as herself.

'I'll disguise myself as a kind porn' peddler and dye my face purple so that Flakey Snow White doesn't see me green with envy,' the nefarious plotter schemed. And so, carrying a basketful of straight and gay nude illustrations, the Queen, costumed as a typical door-to-door porn peddler, ventured into the wintry forest and eventually arrived at the seven Midgdwarfs' humble domicile.

"Fine wares for sale or rent! I have fine wares for sale or rent with an option to buy!" the old warped-minded conniver hawked from outside the hut's door.

Flakey Snow White was reluctant to answer the outside knock, heeding the Midgdwarfs' sage advice that had been given. But when the dastardly female held-up some other intriguing items and barked, "Porno' magazines of the latest issue; dicks as big as fresh cucumbers! Dildos, spring-operated hand vibrators, ribbed condoms, inflatable big-cocked men to vend!" The fascinated girl could not control her mounting curiosity any longer and decided to unlatch the front door.

The pleasure-starved, royal teenager opened the squeaky front door, not realizing that the saleswoman was the vicious, spiteful Queen, who incidentally could have at her discretion broken any of the hut's windows at her choosing and easily gained entrance into the fragile home. Upon entering, the cunning old hag persuasively addressed the gullible naïve Princess.

"Well, you' innocuous child without any trace of acne or pus-laden whiteheads on your lily-white head or blackheads anywhere on your impeccable countenance," the disguised Queen began her introductory statement. "What a sight you are with that loose bodice and your hard, firm, tantalizing tits hanging out! You appear to be a hedonistic customer that definitely could benefit from using one of my delightful pleasure products!" the Queen solicited. "I even have a tight-fitting black leather outfit that goes along with this free *S and M Manual,* if you elect to procure it? From your general appearance, I believe you'd make an excellent dominatrix, I must say!"

Flakey Snow White suspected no devious threat to her physical, emotional or mental welfare. And so, the quixotic damsel allowed the old woman to dress her in the black, tight-fitting dominatrix outfit with the very small bodice that when fully laced-up, prevented the girl from breathing properly. Soon the maiden, clad in the black leather apparel, sank to the planked-floor and was lying there helplessly without sufficient air passing into her nice set of lungs.

"Now," the wicked Queen meanly uttered, "Flakey Snow White; you aren't the fairest or even the fairie-est lesbian in the whole damned land! I fuckin' am!"

Fortunately, the seven Midgdwarfs had completed their arduous daily labor (finding no precious gold) and were merrily singing and assiduously marching home in a military manner with their pick-axes firmly held against their right shoulders.

"Hi, ho, hi, ho, it's home from work we go,
We'll pay two bits to see your tits,
Hi, ho, hi ho.
Hi, ho, hi, oh, it's us the little runts,
If only we, wee men could find, seven little cunts.
Hi, ho, hi, ho,
We need to find a "hoe",
Where the fuck's Ohio?
Hi, ho, hi, ho, hi, ho!"

When the little men had finally arrived home after detouring and crisscrossing all over the damned seven hills, the dwarfs immediately saw Flakey Snow White lying breathless upon the floor, wearing her black whip-less *S and M* outfit. The seven paranoid idiots lifted her up, plunked her down into a musty chair, forced her body to angle forward and carefully removed her 'black top', which incidentally had no asphalt or tar on it. Flakey Snow White revived after all seven of the little perverts sucked on her firm erect nipples.

"That was no peddler woman that had encumbered and almost cucumbered you, Flakey Snow White!" the first and most gregarious of the Midgdwarfs exclaimed. "That savage bitch was the evil jealous Queen attempting to eliminate your ass from this fucked-up world! Have you been on heavy drugs or drinking moonshine whiskey to not know *that* elementary truth?"

164

"Yes, dear maiden," the seventh and most horny Midgdwarf piped-in. "Don't ever allow that hostile bitch into this house again. Now please put the black top on again. You look much sexier in it than you do stark naked. I suppose my imagination prefers thinking about what you might look like nude rather than what you actually *do* look like nude! So much for the impact of reality, do ya' know what the fuck I'm tryin' to say?"

While Flakey Snow White reentered her normal dull cotton clothing, and while the Midgdwarfs were practicing their traditional voyeurism and squirting semen into each other's faces as if it was champagne being ejected from seven tiny hand-bottles, the malevolent Queen had already returned to the Royal Palace. She rushed-up to the remarkable mirror and addressed the lame-brained object, which like a dumb parrot could only say several simple answers to several simple questions.

> "Mirror, mirror, on the wall,
> Who is the fairest of them all?"

And to the Queen's grief and aggravation, the mirror aptly replied:

> "Thou art not real cool, you silly fool,
> Queen, thou art as fair as an overfull cesspool!
> And since you're a fucked-up nitwit,
> The fairest of the fair wears a black leather outfit!
> And if you want to possess all of the male dicks,
> Become yourself, a black-dressed dominatrix!"

"I promise that I'll think-up an intelligent plan so foolproof and invincible, and my excellent plot will effectively dispose of my smooth-skinned nemesis. And as for you, my illiterate non-loquacious reflecting looking-glass," the petulant Queen angrily predicted, "I'll shatter your existence the next moment after I shatter Flakey Snow White's chaste spirit!"

Now the vile old bitch was quite skilled in the black arts and even had earned a black belt in alchemy. In her cold cellar laboratory, the schemer magically manufactured a golden comb from a honeycomb, and she took the venom from the Queen Bee and from its attendant workers and soldier-bees, and then ingeniously had the poison blended and placed inside the newly-fabricated hair comb, with each tooth having a thin delicate membrane that when punctured, would allow the toxic substance to enter the unwary victim's scalp.

"This poisonous comb will give the little pristine bitch something to *pore* over! Ha, ha, ha, ha!" the maniacal female cackled.

The old witch-bitch again showed-up at the remote forest hut's doorstep and enthusiastically solicited her latest product. "Goods for sale! A free golden comb with each new transaction! Wares for sale! Get your one free golden comb while the supply lasts!"

Flakey Snow White took a glimpse out of the hut's parlor window and beheld the hoary hag hawking her horrendous merchandise. The naïve girl scurried to the locked door and yelled, "I'm not allowed to let anybody in, especially ugly old women with psoriasis like you! Go away and harass and disparage someone else with your fucked-up bullshit propaganda!"

"Okay Sweetie Cheeks, but before I depart," the shrewd old villainess evilly stated, "I also have a free golden scissors to trim your splendid ebony bush and underarm hair that's just a perfect device to accompany the free golden comb. Now," the on-a-mission skanky hag persisted in her rhetoric, "what kind of a bargain-hunter could ignore those two wonderful free prizes?"

The vulnerable girl inside the little hut was so charmed by the notion of receiving her wonderful golden gifts for gratis that she violated the Midgdwarfs' emphatic warning and hurriedly opened the front door. Then Flakey Snow White listened to more of the old hussy's dumb horse crap.

"Look and listen my child, and I'll gladly show you exactly how this golden comb should be worn to achieve the best results from the already horny local male population," the crafty, criminally insane impostor recommended. And then the demented Queen brutally thrust the golden comb into the girl's crown, and the object's sharp teeth penetrated *her* delicate scalp. Soon, innocent and unassuming Flakey Snow White was lying prone on the hut's planked floor.

"You paragon of beauty with your perfect angelic face!" the Queen scoffed in a crazed sort of cackle. "That comb will eventually send you to the 'hereafter', so that I've completely accomplished what I came *here after*! Ha, ha, ha, ha!"

The treacherous, disguised Queen quickly evacuated the premises just as the sun was again sinking into the western horizon behind the very symbolic seventh hill. A few minutes later, the diligent Midgdwarfs came singing and marching home again without locating any gold nuggets in the coal-rich mountains.

166

"Hi ho, hi, ho,
It's back from work we go.
Instead of getting paid,
We wanna' get laid,
Hi ho, hi ho.
By move, by thrust, by shove, by push,
We'll pay four-bits to trim your bush,
Hi ho, hi, ho, ho, ho!"

When the seven Midgdwarfs' eyes perceived Flakey Snow White again lying on the floor, the wee residents immediately discerned that the vindictive Queen had revisited the isolated hut that everybody in the damned kingdom seemed to know about. The little investigators examined the back of the victim's head and alertly determined that the golden comb inserted into her ebony hair had been wholly responsible for the girl's lapsing into an incomprehensible, unconscious state. The very instant that the brave third dwarf gently pulled the shining object out, the bee venom stopped being absorbed into Flakey Snow White's scalp, and moments later, the gorgeous young lady was able to open her eyes and communicate fairly lucidly.

"Flakey Snow White, are you a stupid-assed slow-learner or what?" the fourth Midgdwarf chastised. "Now really, don't you fathom the simple fact that the only damned person visiting this hut and trying to kill you each time she comes is the iniquitous, jealous Queen? As Shakespeare once yelled at King Leary," the fourth Midgdwarf lectured and sermonized, "Get your damned *act* together and don't make a fuckin' scene! Now for the last fuckin' time, don't let anyone in this goddamned house except the seven asshole Midgdwarfs that fuckin' live here!"

When Flakey Snow White was again promising her seven horny virgin roommates not to let anyone inside the mountain hut, the Queen stood inside her castle before her magic mirror and asked her by now familiar refrain.

"Mirror, mirror, on the wall,
Who's the fairest of them all?"

And the bored-to-death mirror yawned and said accordingly:

"Thou are far from fair by lima bean pole,
Instead thou art a royal, giant asshole.
The fairest of the fair has a perfect tush',
And with golden scissors has trimmed her bush!"

The insulted Queen trembled with animosity, and her mouth foamed with fury. "Why the fuck must all certified plastic surgeons live in other more-advanced kingdoms!" the hideous-looking wench screamed at her hideous-looking reflection in the now-reticent mirror. "I must get rid of Flakey Snow White once and for all and become the fairest in the kingdom, or my soul will never rest in this fuckin' life or for that matter, in the next goddamned world!"

The malignant-minded Queen again descended to her subterranean laboratory to concoct another deadly poison, which the female alchemist carefully inserted inside a very appealing shiny apple. "Ha, ha, ha!" the wretched old witch-bitch cackled. "Eve successfully busted Adam's balls with an apple, and I shall duplicate her illustrious feat with Flakey Snow White, ha, ha, ha, ha!" the "Bitch-Witch" hollered in a maniacal state of mind as the rancorous jezebel unscrupulously rubbed her diabolic fingers and hands together while contemplating her next disgusting ruse.

The evil Empress (who had recently poisoned and eliminated the King) placed the beautiful, tainted apple in a basket along with a dozen ordinary-looking ones and then creatively disguised herself as a pleasant nun roaming the countryside delivering good health and good cheer to unwary, lovely teenagers having venereal diseases. The determined roamer surreptitiously crossed the seven hills, adroitly eluding the seven Midgdwarfs' nonchalant and apathetic surveillance. Then the cruel Hag swiftly and confidently knocked on the tiny hut's front door.

"I'm not allowed to let any ruthless strangers inside, even if her name is Ruth," Flakey Snow White automatically mentioned and vociferated. "And the Seven Midgdwarfs have absolutely, positively forbidden me to purchase any goods or merchandise from anyone, especially from baneful hags like you. So old woman, get the hell outa' here, nun or no damned nun!"

"Who says I'm *selling* anything, my dear?" the sleazy scumbag cleverly answered. "I'm giving away good health food here that is guaranteed to make you even more lovely than you already are! These wonderful apples are nutritious and will not cost you anything, not even one lousy copper coin!"

"That's just what I really need to keep my skin bright and rosy," Snow White happily replied through the closed door. "I just can't wait to bite into a *good for nothing* apple!"

Naturally, the callow girl opened the door and selected the most lustrous and largest of the apples, which of course contained the horrible poison. After chewing and swallowing the first mouthful, the easily influenced maiden fainted and her body collapsed to the very clean, wood-planked floor.

"Now let's see those dumbbell Midgdwarfs revive you from *this* devastating dilemma!" the Queen gleefully scoffed and laughed. "Now you, white as winter snow with your blood-red rosy cheeks and your enviable ebony hair, shall eternally rest under my imperial command. Goodbye Flakey Snow White, and good riddance!" the intolerant Queen orated. "Only one remote possibility could break this powerful spell, so sleep well my dear, right into eternity! Ha, ha, ha, ha! Learn to love oblivion!"

And the vile Queen, utilizing her mastery of the black arts, flew home on her gnarled cane because she had neglected to remember to bring along her favorite broomstick to the little men's hut. After she had zoomed into an open palace window, the cantankerous Bitch victoriously stood before her formerly indispensable talking mirror.

> "Mirror, mirror, on the wall,
> Who's the fairest of them all?"

> "At this moment there is no cause to wince,
> For Snow White could only be revived by Prince.
> And until then, the girl will vex you no more,
> So, you can continue being a dirty whore!
> So heartily exercise each and every sex gland,
> Right now, Queenie, you're the fairest, in the land!"

The Queen's normally abusive, covetous heart was finally at peace. But the potential for envy, hatred, jealousy, rage and spitefulness was still there although not quite as evident in the scornful woman's behavior as before.

The seven fickle-but-horny Midgdwarfs again dutifully returned to their humble home from work, only to discover their' Flakey Snow White unconscious and suffering under the influence of another evil spell. It required plenty of fortitude for the now-rueful little cretins to deal with their new-found woe and with their unexpected alarm.

"We must save Flakey Snow White even though there's no banks or savings and loan associations around here to deposit her in!" they all thought and yelled together, which was their singular custom and bad habit. The short-legged gents scurried in a frenzy all over the hut, lit their seven lanterns and carefully laid the near-dead beauty (whose formerly soft flesh now felt like petrified wood) onto a bed.

The scared-shitless Midgdwarfs loosened their lady friend's bodice and fondled her rock-solid tits, but that former solution was rendered ineffectual by the Queen's terrible hex. The rescuers next rubbed her trimmed ebony bush and clit quite strenuously, but to no avail. The seven little men then frantically stroked their beards in meditation, but their peckers remained limp, and they could not stroke their dingles to relieve their tremendous frustration and overwhelming anxiety. And despite the truth that the little men later mourned for three days, Flakey Snow White still appeared alive with rosy red cheeks' as she laid motionless in a deep, deep trance.

"I do believe that the Bitch Witch Queen did this debacle to our poor Flakey Snow White," the sixth dwarf theorized and verbalized, "and if the Old Bag had a set of genuine testicles, I'd repeatedly kick her right in the damned balls!"

"She's as beautiful as ever, but even massaging her breasts and rubbing her trimmed bush has not brought her back to life! Nothing can mitigate this terrible tragedy!" the Midgdwarfs together all sadly sobbed. "And although we cannot resuscitate her by sexual stimulation or by any other intelligent means," the dipshits regretfully reminded each other while shaking their heads in mutual dismay, "we must remain hopeful and vigilant and still keep watch over her brain-dead body!"

The grief-stricken Midgdwarfs went on a wild rampage, breaking every window within a ten-mile radius (except those in their own hut) and then using the broken glass, the seven freaks possessed the wherewithal to melt-down the material and skillfully made a fragile, transparent casket so that the resting rosy-cheeked, ebony-haired maiden could be viewed from every conceivable angle, and on the improvised coffin's opened lid the seven admirers had inscribed in golden letters: "Here Rests Snow White-Our Heavenly Princess."

The stiff, cold girl was gently lowered inside the transparent container, and the Midgdwarfs sorrowfully carried their incapacitated maid off to the highest of the seven hilltops where they solemnly placed the incomparable glass casket near trees and flowers nestled close to a plethora of animal droppings. And only six of the tiny stumpy fellows ventured-out to dig for gold every morning in the highly publicized coal mountain country because one Midgdwarf always remained as a sentinel guarding over Flakey Snow White's "breathless-looking coffin" and also over breathless-looking Flakey Snow White.

Months and years elapsed, and Flakey Snow White still lay in her magnificent, glistening crystal casket and not once opened an eyelid, burped or farted. She remained frozen in a deep, deep sleep on the highest of the seven hills in the deep, deep forest. Squawking birds flew overhead in large numbers, but none of their droppings could ever bombard the opened glass casket no matter how high or low the blackbirds soared or hovered, and no matter how hard the crows and the ravens tried to hit their target with their smelly bird crap.

But then one day a lost Prince looking all over Europe for Sleeping Beauty instead found another sleeping beauty in the form of Flakey Snow White, peacefully resting inside her crystal casket. The curious Midgdwarfs gathered around the royal lost vagabond, who still believed he had found Sleeping Beauty, or maybe even Rapunzel. But then Prince Numnutz of Scrotum checked-out Flakey Snow White's ebony hair and canceled-out her being Rapunzel by the process of elimination, since all myths and folktales described *her* as having golden blonde braids tangled in intricate braidy bunches.

"Is this Sleeping Beauty?" the disoriented Prince Numnutz asked the melancholy Midgdwarfs.

"No Asshole! That's Flakey Snow White lying in there!" the seven nitwits all bellowed in unison. "So, if you're looking for Sleeping Beauty, get your ass into the right goddamned fairy tale!"

"If I could claim Flakey Snow White for my own, I'll give you Seven Midgdwarfs all the gold in my kingdom where we principally mine bauxite, copper, silver, platinum and dirt," Prince Numnutz ignobly offered. "Do we have a deal?"

"Fuck off!" the Seven Midgdwarfs simultaneously yelled as the dumb-shits lifted their pick-axes, feigning instantaneous violence upon the dunce-minded royal traveler. "We would not surrender Flakey Snow White's heavenly body and trimmed bush for all of the gold in the entire universe!"

"Well then junior jerk-offs, please have the decency to give her to me out of the goodness of your lackluster hearts and souls!" the Prince reprimanded. "If you permit me to take her home to another kingdom somewhere else in Europe, the name of which temporarily has escaped my memory or knowledge," the totally lost Prince stammered, "then I'll cherish and guard her as my finest treasure," the clueless idiot finished as the selfsame royal jerk-off put his right hand on his dingle and began vigorously rubbing his crotch.

The kind little Midgdwarfs realized that Flakey Snow White could no longer clean their filthy hut, or couch dance stark naked for them, so the seven runts reluctantly acceded to have the Prince take responsibility for her now-listless but still curvaceous body.

Prince Numnutz called for his lethargic servants, who were preoccupied because some were taking shits in the woods and others were pissing into a fast-flowing stream. The six subordinates arrived on the scene and awkwardly lifted the glimmering casket, placed it upon their shoulders and slowly followed the Prince east, although his kingdom was really geographically to the west. One of the clumsy pallbearers accidentally tripped over an exposed tree root, and the fragile glass casket slipped out of the six servants' hands, crashed to the ground and frightfully fragmented into seven sections.

The severe jolt from the impact dislodged and knocked the poisoned apple chunk from Flakey Snow White's throat, and the piece of fruit swiftly shot-out of the beauty's mouth. The stunned girl then slowly sat-up amidst the remains of her shattered crystal casket, and her bleary eyes scanned her immediate environment in all directions. The awakened Princess was both astonished and perplexed.

The bedazzled Prince extended his hand and assisted the vivacious Princess off of the cold, damp, glassy turf. "Will you marry me?" the eager dunce impetuously asked, not knowing if his choice for a bride had a decent personality or if she were simply a beautiful, mentally challenged retard.

"Yes!" the still naïve maiden impulsively agreed, not knowing if the lost Prince was a flasher, a voyeur, a pedophile, a bisexual or simply a young damsel molester.

Meanwhile, as that particular marriage proposal was transpiring, another interesting event was occurring inside the Queen's elaborate palace. A wedding invitation had mysteriously appeared upon her dressing bureau, so the Old Witch Bitch stepped to her magic talking mirror and then asked a pertinent question.

> "Mirror, mirror, on the wall,
> Who is the fairest of them all?"

And the thoroughly bored looking-glass showed a degree of imagination by answering:

"The fairest of them all will not tarry,
A handsome young Prince, she will marry.
And Snow White is very much alive and well,
Standing near her wedding bell.
And so fair Queen, I bid adieu,
And may every crotch disease known, infect you.
And no more farts shall your anus cut,
For soon you won't be able, to work your butt!"

The emotionally volatile Queen became so pissed-off that she smashed her right fist into the center of the talking mirror, sending shards of glass flying all over the damned bed chamber. One piece had coincidentally lodged itself in her right calf, and as the encumbered sinister scoundrel bent-over to examine her bleeding leg injury, the apple chuck (which had been expelled from Flakey Snow White's throat and had extraordinarily circled the earth seven incredible times) zoomed through the open window of the royal bedchamber and lodged itself up the Queen's asshole as if the airborne fragment was a cork released from a champagne bottle.

And so, the magic mirror's amazing prophesy was righteously fulfilled, and Flakey Snow White, the clueless, lost Prince Numnutz and the Seven Little Midgdwarfs all lived happily ever after in the distant Kingdom of Scrotum, and the nine hapless nutcases remarkably slept together every single night in loony Prince Numnutz's queen-size bed.

About the Author

Jay Dubya is author John Wiessner's initials (J.W.) and also his pen name. John is a retired New Jersey public school English teacher and he has taught the subject for thirty-four years. John lives in southern New Jersey with wife Joanne and the couple has three grown sons.

Jay Dubya has written other adult literature besides Fractured Frazzled Folk Fables and Fairy Farces and FFFF and FF, Part II. Black Leather and Blue Denim, A '50s Novel and its sequel, The Great Teen Fruit War, A 1960' Novel and Frat' Brats, A '60s Novel are adult-oriented literary endeavors constituting a trilogy. Pieces of Eight, Pieces of Eight, Part II, Pieces of Eight Part III and Pieces of Eight, Part IV are' short story/novella collections featuring science fiction, paranormal and humorous plots and themes. Nine New Novellas is the companion book to Nine New Novellas, Part II and Nine New Novellas, Part III. And So Ya' Wanna' Be A Teacher is a satirical autobiography describing the author's thirty-four-year educational career in American public schools.

Ron Coyote, Man of La Mangia is adult humor and the work is an imaginative satire/parody on Miguel Cervantes' Don Quixote, published in 1605. Mauled Maimed Mangled Mutilated Mythology is a work that satires twenty-one famous ancient tales. The Wholly Book of Genesis and The Wholly Book of Exodus are also adult satirical humor. Thirteen Sick Tasteless Classics, Thirteen Sick Tasteless Classics, Part II, Thirteen Sick Tasteless Classics, Part III and Thirteen Sick Tasteless Classics, Part IV are adult satirical rewrites of famous short fiction.

John has also authored a trilogy of young adult fantasy novels, Enchanta, Pot of Gold and Space Bugs, Earth Invasion. The Eighteen' Story Gingerbread House is a new collection of eighteen diverse and creative children's stories.

Jay Dubya likes '50s rock and roll music and he also enjoys pop' songs by the Beach Boys', Fleetwood Mac, the Eagles, the Rolling Stones, ELO, John Mellencamp and by John Fogerty. When not writing or listening to music, Jay Dubya likes watching 76ers basketball and Phillies and Yankees television' baseball games.

Author Biography

Born in Hammonton, NJ in 1942, John Wiessner had attended St. Joseph School up to and including Grade 5. After his family moved from Hammonton to Levittown, Pa in 1954, John attended St. Mark School in Bristol, Pa. for Grade 6, St. Michael the Archangel School in Levittown for Grades 7 and 8 and then Immaculate Conception School, Levittown, Pa. for Grade 9. Bishop Egan High School, Levittown Pa was John's educational base for Grades 10 and 11, and later in 1960, the aspiring author graduated from Edgewood Regional High, Tansboro, NJ. John then next attended Glassboro State College, where he was an announcer for the school's baseball games and also read the nightly news and sports over WGLS, GSC's radio station.

John Wiessner had been primarily an English teacher in the Hammonton Public School System for 34 years, specializing in the instruction of middle school language arts. Mr. Wiessner was quite active in the Hammonton Education Association, serving in the capacities of Vice-President, building representative and finally, teachers' head negotiator for 7 years. During his lengthy teaching career, John had been nominated into "Who's Who Among American Teachers" three times. He also was quite active giving professional workshops at schools around South Jersey on the subjects of creative writing and the use of movie videos to motivate students to organize their classroom theme compositions.

John Wiessner was very active in community service, being a past President of the Hammonton Lions Club, where he also functioned for many years as the club's Tail-Twister, Vice-President and Liontamer. John had been named Hammonton Lion of the Year in 1979 and in 2009 received the prestigious Melvin Jones Fellow Award, the highest honor that a Lion can receive from Lions International.

John also was a successful businessman, starting with being a Philadelphia Bulletin newspaper delivery boy for two years in the late 1950s in Levittown, Pennsylvania. After his family moved back to New Jersey in 1959, John worked at his grandparents and his parents' farm markets, Square Deal Farm (now Ron's Gardens in Hammonton) and Pete's Farm Market in Elm, respectively. He later managed his wife's parents' farm market, White Horse Farms in Elm for three summers.

Also, in a business capacity, for 16 summers starting in 1967 John Wiessner had co-owned Dealers Choice Amusement Arcade on the Ocean City, Maryland boardwalk and also co-owned the New Horizon Tee-Shirt Store for eight summers (1973-'81) on the Rehoboth Beach,

Delaware boardwalk. In addition, "Jay Dubya" was a co-owner of Wheel and Deal Amusement Arcade, Missouri Avenue and Boardwalk, Atlantic City. And then, for 18 summers beginning in 1986, John had been the Field Manager in charge of crew-leaders for Atlantic Blueberry Company (the world's largest cultivated blueberry farm), both the Weymouth and Mays Landing Divisions.

After retiring from teaching in 1999, writing under the pen name Jay Dubya (his initials), John Wiessner became the author of 55 books in the genre Action/Adventure Novels, Sci-Fi/Paranormal Story Collections, Adult Satire, Young Adult Fantasy Novels and Non-Fiction Books. His books exist in hardcover, in paperback and in popular Kindle and Nook e-book formats.

In January of 2022, John Wiessner (Jay Dubya) was nominated into Marquis Who's Who in America, and in April of that same year, was one of nine distinguished Who's Who in America members honored with receiving Lifetime Achievement Awards, all nine sharing a news article of recognition appearing in the Wall Street Journal.

Google: Jay Dubya, books
Google: Walmart, Jay Dubya

www.ingramcontent.com/pod-product-compliance
Lightning Source LLC
Chambersburg PA
CBHW071528120726
47907CB00013B/1252